Future Fiction

Edited by

Francesco Verso

FRANCESCO VERSO

Nexhuman

translation by Sally McCorry

Published by Associazione Future Fiction
Via Valentiniano 40 – 00145 Roma
Tax ID. 15586791004
ISBN: 9788832077827

Title: *Nexhuman*
© 2023 Future Fiction, Rome
I edition June 2023
info@futurefiction.org
ISBN: 9788832077827

*It is the customary fate of new truths to begin as heresies
and to end as superstitions.*
T.H. Huxley

CHAPTER 1
BOREAL SKIES

Kathal Hill is one of the places where I spend my days rummaging through the piles of rubbish. It makes my fingertips so tired I can no longer feel them and I often have to stop and rest. Today I settle into the pilot seat, extract my military binoculars from my overalls, set the zoom to 10x, and watch her.

Alba works behind the window of the travel agency, Boreal Skies, two hundred metres away. She is completely unaware of me watching as she selects sky cruises for indecisive customers or romantic voyages for couples determined to save their relationships.

I increase the zoom to 13x: Her ivory lacquered fingernails flick through brochures so gracefully, it seems impossible that this same paper, suffused with her perfume, could one day end up here, in my muck-covered hands.

I am ashamed to go into Boreal Skies with my crumpled catalogue and show her the trip I would like to go on. With her.

The perfume that she leaves on the paper is not erased so quickly by the kipple.

Someone calls me from below.

"Peter! Get your arse moving or I'm taking you off today's shift."

At the bottom of the hill, the team leader is calling me back. I ignore him—her vivid red hair is tied in a ponytail, adding to the friendly appearance with which she can convince anyone to take a holiday, rather than staying at home in the company of their regrets.

"I told you to move it! If I have to call you again, you can say goodbye to your pay."

I ignore the shout and watch her just a moment longer. One day's pay, one paltry K, isn't much to lose when weighed against the opportunity of seeing Alba in her agency outfit with her silver name tag.

Anyway, I am satisfied with today's yield. In my bag, I have a half-full blister pack of unexpired Mentax pills and some Ecorette tobacco I can sell to the hawkers in Junkland. I can make more money there than in this heap.

Stuffing the binoculars into my bag, I get out of the chair and limp along a muddy path lined with piles of televisions and the shells of computers with smashed monitors and blackened circuit boards. The path leads into a cloud of smoke and ash, lit only by green and amber lights.

The smoke is not the product of a single bonfire. It rises from a fiery belt in the distance, where dozens of hazy figures move and gesticulate in the acrid cloud. We are the Kathal Hill trashformers. Some are raking through the materials with their bare hands, some are sifting through the rubbish, others are stoking and feeding the flames with anything they can't sell. Usually, Rasha looks after our fires, though sometimes Norbert takes his place. The other kids in my team gather up and carry away tangled armfuls of multicoloured wires.

The air bears the stench of the chemicals that will later rain down—if not on us, maybe to the north, on the people in Cali Nova. If the Tuwim decides to blow that way ...

I use my t-shirt to cover my face and walk over to Rasha. He is a kid like me, though slightly less skinny, and he likes the fires. He wears a different turban every day, which he partially unwraps to cover his nose and mouth.

Rasha set our school on fire; we all know he did it. He says it was a mistake; he is adamant about this and I believe him. Rasha produces enough electricity to throw anyone who touches him to the ground. That's why he wears gloves. When he comes to your house to fix something, he doesn't have to turn the electricity off. The touch of a live wire makes him laugh. Anyone else would be electrocuted on the spot, but he only feels a tickle. Once, just for the fun of it, the lads and I decided to measure the voltage his fingertips discharged. We got a reading of eighty thousand volts.

Intent on his fires, hypnotised by the tongues of flame, he stirs the two flaming piles he is tending, then bends and disappears in the whirl of sooty smoke. When I can see him again, he is pulling a roll of copper wire out of a burning tyre. He dips it into a puddle to cool. At the end of his shift, Rasha will take the scrap metal over to the team leader, who will take it to the recycling station. If he is lucky, it will earn him a K. I rest my good hand on his shoulder and he does the same. In our business, it's best not to open your mouth to say hello.

I don't even try to get my pay; instead, I head over to the steep slope towards the exit by the Akeren River. Maybe my brother, Charlie, will have a job for me later. He used to do this job. He said that for a long time, the people of the megalopolis kept their rubbish 'out of sight and out of mind'—but it wasn't like that anymore. Today everyone has the kipple they deserve.

When the council made it illegal to send or sell rubbish on elsewhere, everyone had to do the best they could to recycle and minimise—or live in the middle of it. The monstrous automated bins, the UCUs—short for Urban Cleaning Units—were created to help promote the idea of reconsumerism.

The UCUs move any product that appears to be resaleable in some way to the storage sites. Their noisy alarms are our curfew; their fearful jaws are our competitors. As soon as they move in, we've got to clear the area immediately or face consequences. Over the years, each generation of UCU becomes faster and more efficient.

The price of second, third, fourth-hand-or-more goods is in competition with the residual value of the waste that has been left to rot. In the end, free shopping from the dump is worth a whole day of underpaid work.

Every morning, as I walk along Lucite Street, the road that links my house to Kathal Hill, I stop in front of Boreal Skies. I do my best to get Alba's attention, but in the evenings, filthy from ten hours of digging around in reeking rubbish, I make an equally valiant effort not to be noticed and take a different route to avoid her shop. By the end of the day, the stench of the dump has penetrated my clothes and skin so deeply that I may as well be a junkyard fox. Perhaps Alba would notice me if it weren't for the fact that I reach no higher than her shoulder.

I haven't said anything about this to the lads in my brother's gang, the Dead Bones, in case they take the piss. I haven't told Charlie either; he would only tease me about it. They don't know that when Boreal Skies is empty and I stand, staring at the offers in the window, dreaming of dream destinations, Alba comes outside to say hello to me.

Alba displays a Moore Temple hologram in the window, alongside the all-inclusive package holidays and special discounts. The shop sign radiates a bright message:

Biology is not an end; it is a tendency.
Chips are our real destination.

There is only ever Alba inside. She works alone from daybreak to nightfall, never stopping. She owns Boreal Skies and she does as she likes.

When she is less than a metre from me, Alba bends over and gives me a noisy kiss on the cheek. Then she strokes my head and I don't know whether to smile at her or cry; I can't tell whether this ritual makes me happy or hurts me deep down inside. She makes me feel like a child.

I look up at her. Anyone in my shoes would pray that she doesn't judge by appearances and I am sure she doesn't.

Even when I make anonymous video-calls to her, covering my face with a hood and using a voice modulator, Alba doesn't get angry and she doesn't call my bluff, even though I'm sure she knows it's me.

She is so lovely, I forget who I am.

She is so magnetic, I forget where I am.

It is easier to spend the day rummaging through the dump after a start like this.

I am only fifteen, and she is twenty-three. Of all the cruel tricks fate has played on me, this is the worst. My age leaves me vulnerable to Charlie's pranks. One day, after having seen me lurking around Boreal Skies, he decided to find out why. He wasn't out to hassle me about wasting time, he wasn't looking to amuse himself by crushing my hopes; his only goal is to belittle me in front of Alba.

On that grey morning with clouds heavy on the horizon, while Alba was stroking my head as usual, and I was, as usual, torn between delight and agony, Charlie materialised from behind the shop and took my hand as if I were a child.

"Peter! How many times do I have to tell you not to bother people at work?"

Alba had no doubt that Charlie was showing real consideration; she was too far removed from Charlie's brand of artifice to suspect anything else.

"Don't worry. This young man says hello to me every morning. It's a pleasure to chat with him. There are never any customers around at this time of day..." Alba's soft voice perfectly matches her graceful appearance.

Charlie turns a smile on for her, as false as his earlier words. "You're kind, Miss, but I have to go to work, and he has to be at school soon."

I don't know what my brother is plotting at this point, but he is really trying to show me up. The school has been closed for a year and swallowed by kipple after the—accidental?—fire set by Rasha. The school gates have had 'Evacuated Area' seared into them with a blowtorch. Behind the gratings, the abandoned schoolyard is haunted by an overpowering sensation of death.

Alba leaves us with a splendid smile, smoothing her uniform—Tuesday's rainbow tailleur that always puts me in a good mood—with her usual care. "I won't keep you then. See you tomorrow, Peter."

I gather up all my courage to reply. I don't think she has noticed that I am daydreaming about her. "Bye, Alba. See you tomorrow."

Charlie grabs my arm and yanks me away, and I nearly twist my head off so I can watch Alba slide back in behind her desk and cross her legs. She lifts her hand to wave.

He pushes me until we have turned the corner. Then he puts his hands on my shoulders and shoves me backwards until I am pinned against the wall.

"Forget about *her*. She's..." He sneers, his face close to mine. "Just forget her, all right?"

I don't understand.

Chapter 2
Dead Bones

I've never liked running. Maybe because my prosthetic leg doesn't synchronise well with the rest of my skeleton, or because the muscles covering my bones are stringy, but when it comes to keeping up with the Dead Bones, I manage a speed that's usually beyond me.

At a normal pace my knee creaks, and that wouldn't be a problem except that as I run faster, this creaking becomes a grating noise, a loud squeaking that forces Charlie to reconsider his plans.

"Peter, wait. You can't come."

"Why? You said I could this time..."

"I know, but you make too much noise. You'll get us all caught."

It's the third time this month, and all because they won't choose someone a bit slower to chase.

"Wait for me at home. I won't be long. It's better this way."

Last time, they got a pet robodog; one of the slow, clumsy kind that are popular in the Raon district. Jimmy had it by its front legs by the time I caught up. I'd been left behind, as usual, but I could see him pulling it apart. Jimmy's muscles flexed, and the dog's ribs cracked loudly. The beast lay whining on the ground, broken. Then it dragged itself towards me.

Charlie ordered me to finish it off, putting me to the test on a whim. There are no advantages to being his brother. I put my good foot through its skull.

Tonight, from the neglected end of Oldinvari road, north

of Kathal Hill, I can hear their triumphant shouts. The Dead Bones must have cornered their victim.

Charlie points in the direction of our home, wipes the sweat from his face, then turns and runs to join the chase. He leaves me standing there, alone.

I have hardly started walking back when I hear a pitiful scream and more of the Dead Bones' wild cries. I turn, not daring to disobey Charlie: I am the newest arrival on the lowest rung. I have only just earned my place as a salvager, and only thanks to my prosthetic limbs, which make it possible for me to squeeze into places the other kids can't. The Dead Bones would give me a beating if I dared to disobey the boss's orders—brother or no.

What if they never found out though?

"Help! Please!"

The shout makes me pause, and on the wall in front of me, I notice some bioluminescent graffiti. A Moore artist has glued thousands of radioactive worms to the wall, and as they've decomposed they've left behind a luminescent adage:

What you don't consume becomes kipple

I undo my knee's safety catch, remove the prosthetic leg and stuff it in my backpack. I start hopping along on one leg. It makes for slow progress, but it's quieter.

After a hundred metres, I stop to catch my breath behind a corner before reaching an isolated open area. On the far side, I can see Visconia, a derelict paint and varnish factory, its outer walls now little more than rubble.

I take out my palmtop and scan the area's pop-up info. A night chemist is offering free scans of any suspicious liquid and is selling bottles of SaniBox at half price. The mechanic across the road is looking to get rid of a load of used tyres. 1445 Oldinvari Road, a large block of flats, is waiting for the drains to be repaired.

I switch to thermal vision and see four blotches of orange emanating from the members of the Dead Bones. A metal scan shows me they are carrying shuriken, knives, steel chains, and a hockey stick.

When I close the palmtop, I can see they have their prey surrounded, forced into a corner amidst heaps of scrap and fresh rubbish.

Dumping rubbish in Kathal Hill is a mostly ignored crime—the UCUs rarely come here. Outside the firsthand consumers' perimeter, the mechanical beasts run the risk of being pelted with stones, sprayed with bullets, or torched with homemade Molotovs by those who want to relieve the machines of their load.

Looking for a better vantage point, I strap my leg back on and heave myself up a rusty fire escape. From the third floor, I can see more clearly and my thoughts about the hunt are clearer too: four against one; not very fair. Some forms of fun push the boundaries of the classic gratification, but these extracurricular activities help the Dead Bones finance their other vices.

Charlie takes aim at his victim, shuriken in hand. In a blur, he whips his arm forward and lets it fly. The pointed star cuts through the night air and sinks with a hiss into the victim's shoulder. It penetrates the skin and stops, sticking straight up: a metal object embedded in another sheet of metal.

Eddies of plastic and twisters of paper make it hard to see, but when the victim falls to the ground, caught in the glow of the moon, I can make out that it is a woman. More shining blades cut into her sides, back and thighs. She lifts her head and begs for mercy. "What do you want from me? Stop it, please…"

It is useless to plead with the Dead Bones. They are notorious for their violence and have to get blind drunk to reach the level of senselessness required to carry out their vandalism.

"Charlie, leave this one to me. Look at that arse," says one of them. Jimmy 'the Loins' Lombo has a weakness for womanly attributes that remind him of ripe fruit. A peach like this makes his mouth water.

I know Jimmy; he's an animal. At the last Waxing Moon Festival, I saw him bite off the nose of a Chinook gang member and tear the ear off one of the Beating Beatles, just because they jumped the line in front of him at the drinks stand.

Jimmy goes crazy when the hierarchy established on the field is not respected. The Loins is a product of what is euphemistically called a 'strict upbringing'. When Jimmy had just started to crawl and his mother felt the need to punish him, she would put him in a dog cage behind their house, surrounded by an electric fence. His father, an even brusquer character, continued to refine Jimmy's temperament with a studded leather belt.

When Charlie, wearing finger-touch gloves to enhance his grip, turns to the Loins and shuts him up with one raised digit. He walks around their victim, now defenceless on the ground. She drags her body around; with nowhere left to run, she tries to retreat deeper into the corner.

"Please don't hurt me." She has already guessed how she's going to end up. Some forms of life find it hard to survive even in the best layers of society. Every environment has its own predators and every market its own reconsumers. "I'll give you everything I have."

"Don't talk shit. You're garbage. You have no right to last requests," Charlie says.

Still, she makes one last attempt to escape the inevitable. "I have friends in Rizoma. Believe me, I'm worth more alive."

She is sobbing, and her eyes are overflowing with tears. Mascara streaks her face from her eyes to her chin.

"Alive? You're not *alive*."

Charlie sneers at her as Jimmy the Loins, 'Crispy' Lenny and Mickey 'Mucous' start chanting the Dead Bones' mantra: *Kill the kipple. Kill the kipple. Kill the kipple.*

The sudden shriek of metal scraping across metal makes my hair stand on end. Charlie has grabbed her by the temples and is unscrewing her head.

The young woman screams in terror as my brother continues to twist her neck as if he is turning a crank that clicks at every notch. I cover my eyes with my hands and watch through my fingers.

Charlie doubles over with the effort, bracing himself with his legs wide apart. Some lights have come on nearby, though no one will dare to look out. In the Kathal Hill district, nights are spent behind drawn curtains.

It isn't until this point, when the young woman is writhing unnaturally and Crispy and Mucous are readying their chains, that I recognise her. I take out the military binoculars and zoom to 15x.

Their chant grows louder: *Kill the kipple! Kill the kipple! Kill the kipple!*

They're ripping Alba apart. They're destroying the girl who has made my heart beat faster every day for the past year.

I want to shout at them to stop, but I can't.

I want to run away, to cut short this torture, but my bones won't do my bidding. Whether from fear of reprisal by the Dead Bones or the anguish that is gripping me, I remain silent and immobile.

The gang approaches with chains swinging, covered in rubber to dampen the noise they make, but not the pain they inflict.

"No, wait," Charlie orders. "I want to finish her with my hands."

At the extremity of the rotation, I see his lip curl. Then Alba's eyelids flutter as fast as butterfly wings. They droop and say a last goodbye to the world as her moan is cut short.

Her dying eyes emit a last, slow beam of light that rises into the sky, then flickers out. My brother keeps wrestling with her head until he wrenches it from her neck with a dry pop, like a cork from a bottle.

Tears threaten to choke me as Charlie tests the weight of Alba's head, tossing it from hand to hand. My throat is knotted with sobs, my knees can barely support me, and I have to grab hold of the ledge to stay upright.

The glint in my brother's eyes and the sneering triumph on his face will live inside me forever. My brother is an executioner. And I am livid.

Blood has risen to my face from every part of my body and there's nothing I can do about it. But now I understand Charlie's warning. Alba was not like us.

She migrated into an artificial body to survive biological death, though, in the end, she didn't last very much longer. As if enacting some ancient ritual, Charlie kisses Alba's head on the mouth, places it on the ground, and with the hockey stick retrieved from his pack, takes a long backswing and hits it into the distance, shooting the head over the top of a mound of rubbish opposite. It goes surprisingly far.

"She's all yours. Have fun."

Their chanting becomes a liberating yell. Their excitement, held in check until now, bursts forth in full force.

Kill the kipple! Kill the kipple!

The Dead Bones lunge forward and surround what remains of the headless body, greedy hyenas, guests at a banquet after a week of starvation.

Artery cables as thick as fingers spark as they are ripped apart. The elastic joints stretch impossibly far before yielding with a snap. They rip off shreds of what looks like cartilage and toss it aside. Within three minutes, Alba is in pieces, divided into her component parts.

"Okay, now everyone move out fast. This tart sent an alarm signal to some satellite. We've got to get to Junkland."

Each member of the gang, in accordance with its nefarious hierarchy, takes a piece of the prey as a trophy—Crispy gets the arms, Mucous the torso (breasts included), Jimmy the Loins takes the legs (though he whines that he wants the arse) and Charlie takes the prize piece: the pelvis.

They scatter and I am left watching the empty crime scene. Alba's surrogate blood spreads slowly in a pool of vermillion plasma, marking the scene of a murder. By morning, the ground will have swallowed the evidence.

Twenty-four hours later, I am still thinking about it. I haven't stopped thinking about it all day. I can't stop; I can't forgive myself, and I doubt I will ever be free of this guilt.

Some experiences stick in your gut. In my head, these last twenty-four hours have been going on forever like torture. I wish I could find a way of neutralising the brutality of last night.

Because I did *nothing*.

Because I didn't jump in.

Because I didn't even *try* to stop them. I was too scared of the consequences. I'm a fifteen-year-old coward.

As a salvager, I know that kipple can't be trusted. I know it's filthy and treacherous. I know this because I see it every day as I sift through the endless mounds. The question that's eating me up inside is: was Alba *really* kipple?

She never gave me that sense of decay and rancour I've learned to detect in piles of kipple. I've no doubt about this because I am a kipple *hunter*. I live amidst this waste. I liberate objects from the curse of being useless. That's why I couldn't bear it when Charlie called her kipple, because it was clear to me that he was wrong about Alba.

Her eyes, her movements, were not those of kipple.

Nor was the texture of her skin, or her mouth.

She was nexhuman and destroying her was murder, even though the Government doesn't recognise that yet and turns a blind eye to the problem. Eventually, the murder of an uploaded being will be seen as equivalent to that of a human being. The Dead Bones won't be punished for murder—an indifference that discriminates against nexhumans whose only fault is having chosen to leave their native bodies never to return.

Last month, the scholastic AI messaged me a resolution modifying the *General guidelines concerning the non-discrimination of genetic information*, which prohibited the use of practices investigating the human genome for economic or eugenic reasons to include nexhumans. The nexhuman OS is now protected—just like human DNA.

But this doesn't change the fact that nexhumans are still not recognised as 'living beings', eligible for fundamental personal rights. They remain classed in the same category as PVS (Permanent Vegetative State) patients. As far as the law is concerned, the Dead Bones haven't *murdered* anyone; they have merely pulled the plug on a cadaver held in suspended animation by technology. For me, though, what they did yesterday was unforgivable.

That's why Charlie didn't want me there. Not to protect me because I'm his younger brother, not because of my noisy leg, but so there would be no witnesses.

He used to steal from the hypermarket, or from the Chinook crew, and fight with the Beating Beatles, or kidnap electronic pets from the families in the Genshoij area (where they are all technophiles), but now he has broadened his horizons. The Dead Bones have it in for nexhumans, but I don't.

I have been thinking it over for a night and a day and there is one thing I can't understand: why didn't Alba tell me? Why didn't she let me know she was a nexhuman? If she had, I might have guessed what Charlie was up to. Maybe I could have warned her. Or maybe I could have talked my brother out of his plans. Maybe I could have stopped him.

But who am I trying to kid? You need cojones to do those things, and I would have messed up, as I always do. I would have been crushed.

If I went to the police, they would laugh in my face. My word against Charlie's: all he'd have to say was that I had a crush on the nexhuman and my credibility would be destroyed.

Anyway, there's no body—no evidence—and the police wouldn't go to the trouble of looking for the pieces. And whom would they return them to, if they did find them? Alba was young and should have had some family, but I never saw anyone who looked like a relative. No one waiting for her outside the shop. No one to miss her. Except me.

As it is, the Dead Bones have probably already sold her parts to the men in Junkland, and Junkland would have already sold them on to fuck knows who.

Business never slumps in Junkland, a place where the dregs of the megalopolis meet. It thrives on re-consumerism. People aren't miserly and loath to part with what they obtain through hard work and sacrifice, I can testify to that. There are bits and pieces everywhere, the re-use of objects that have passed through many hands is accelerating exponentially; credit has taken the place of any kind of payment, and even swapping is tolerated so long as stuff keeps circulating.

The upside of this process is Junkland; the downside is kipple.

I bet even Cleo, my mother, would take Charlie's side because of the Ks he brings home after every expedition. He pays the bills. And you don't snitch on your own brother.

In a surge, I realise I'm angry with Alba too. So angry that I'm tempted to leave her to rot in the kipple. Omitting the facts—like being nexhuman—is as bad as lying. It is the same as deliberately giving another person the wrong impression about yourself.

Now I can see why Boreal Skies was open twenty-four seven. Alba must have slept every now and then, two or three hours at a time when she felt like it, but more out of nostalgia than from any real need.

I'm trying to leave it be; I'm scared of poisoning myself with memories, not wanting to suffer for a girl whose body can't even be buried, but the memories of her bright eyes and pale lips knot up my insides... In my mind, I can see her slim thighs obscured by aromatic silk stockings, and if I concentrate hard enough I can almost hear her crisp skirt fluttering in the breeze. I would like to at least be able to say goodbye to her, the way you should with people who have shown you kindness.

Cleo doesn't like it when I go out at night, but as darkness falls, I crawl into my secret passage, the air conduits in the basement which lead from my mother's bedroom to the grating in the pavement outside.

Cleo keeps herself so busy during the day, cleaning and dusting and endlessly re-stacking our belongings, that nothing will wake her once she's finally asleep. I move closer to her bed and she opens her eyes—an unconscious reflex of hers I've seen many times.

I freeze and—as if it were the most natural thing in the world—I close my eyes. It's an old thief's trick that Charlie taught me, that if a sleeping person sees you close your eyes it makes them do the same. I've used it on her countless times and she has never noticed a thing. My mother's eyelids drop and stay shut this time.

I've grown since the last time I got out this way, and I scrape my good hand forcing the external grate open.

I look up at the anaemic sky. There aren't many stars to see; the stars have been missing for a while. For as long as I can remember, even on the clearest nights, I have only ever seen a deformed moon and the weak light of Venus just below it. Instead of the stars, a haze of orange phosphorous cloaks all corners of the sky.

Out of the solid wall of nocturnal mist come the sound of engines and the screech of tyres from cars speeding alongside the Akeren.

I drag myself into the night, so close to the edge of sleep I am almost sleepwalking. Along this bend in the river, there is an enormous installation advertising the latest gamesphere model—the Simbox 8.

You are not alone in the world
even if you are alone at home

I suppose it's strange to play in the sphere with other people who are doing the same thing on their own. I play a lot too.

Following the Akeren, it should take me twenty minutes to get where I'm going. The river is filled not with fish, but with the husks of monitors, the shells of PCs, and electric circuit boards. It mimics my habit of gathering bits of everything as I walk along.

I don't have time to try my luck and I turn into the nearly deserted Lucite Street. There are some stray dogs patrolling in packs of two or three. They howl at each other, paw at discarded plastic bags, gnaw at wrappings, and launch themselves into the bins left open by those who look after them. Anything edible left over from the day won't survive until morning.

When Kathal Hill starts sloping upwards, I begin to look for where Alba's head might have landed. I replay the scene in my head. I quickly estimate that there are about forty metres and a thirty-degree slope between me and the top of the hill. Alba's agonised screams echo inside me, but they solidify my resolve to dare the treacherous terrain at this time of night.

I identify the exact point and note it on my palmtop's map.

The peak of Kathal Hill is an imposing formation, created by the area's flows of kipple, mostly rubbish thrown from the windows of the flats in the surrounding area, or launched from rooftops with homemade trebuchets. The kipple aggregates and forms viscous heaps, becoming ever more difficult to sift through or remove. In the distance, the outline of Visconia doesn't scar the landscape as much as the presence of the rubbish all around me. I climb up the ridge of the hill, sinking ankle-deep into the garbage with every step.

Using my hands and feet, I make my way up a mouldy pyramid of decomposing matter and uncompressed kipple. A painful growling in my stomach warns me of an imminent need for evacuation. The bile in my system can't have done its job properly.

I limp along and part of me is afraid that I'll be absorbed by this amorphous mass of jumbled materials. I speed up, putting more of my weight on my plastic leg, which is stronger and tougher than the one of flesh and bone, causing the metal joints in the knee to rasp loudly under the strain.

When I reach the top—a quivering, spongy plateau—I stop to catch my breath. My eyes range over the view: crumbling ruins, cancerous structures bearing the marks of soot and rubbish, a land where even colour comes to die. I can see the outline of human incrustations, settlements inhabited by beings who are as much the cause as result of this blighted horizon.

During August nights like this, these rotting masses make me think of malevolent volcanos—the peaks sometimes hissing, sometimes billowing, sometimes spewing out puffs of gaseous vapour that reeks of methane. I can always smell it. You would think that I'd be used to it by now. When I'm older, I swear I'll have the receptors in my nose removed in the hope of never having to smell such fetor again.

I scan the surrounding area with my palmtop and a series of promotions jostle onto the display. Live Hair sends me an 'incredible' offer for a cut and style; Krafen, a delicatessen, wants me to try Vermigiano, the latest cheese matured with worms; the post office on Lucite Street informs me that we Paynes—Cleo, Charlie, and me—have accrued a debt of 2030Ks. I flick the data off the screen impatiently.

I look down at the decomposing terrain for the RFID tags that are incorporated into all objects. The tags tell me things: those tetrapacks at my feet are eighty years past their use-by date; the corroded toothbrushes nearby were manufactured by factories in Myanmar; a cluster of disposable razors stopped being effective after the sixth shave; a wad of sanitary towels is stained with oestrogen-free menstrual blood; those nappies will remain in the environment for a thousand years longer than their contents; the majority of pens are still half full; those light bulbs blew after exactly one thousand hours; the Kinea plates are not as biodegradable as their labels claim; some chipped glasses are so old they don't even have tags; and finally a huge amount of iron, brass, ceramic cutlery, plastic and polystyrene packaging that dates back to a period when these objects were the measure of their owners' wealth.

Everything ends up as kipple. Obsolete electrical equipment, soggy mattresses, worn tyres, expired medicines— every variety of object with which people distinguish themselves from everyone else go into the mounds of garbage, leaking with posthumous information.

A stench hits my nose. Beneath me, some unrecognisable matter is expelling its final breaths. Shreds of what must have once been flesh comes away as I move my feet from the surface of the blackened and foul goods and strands of vivid red hair cling to the sole of my boot. I gently peel them off, clutch them tightly in my fist. She must be nearby.

I wonder how many dead bodies are buried under all this rubbish.

Tired from the climb, I look more deeply into the composition of the site, I am a seeker, used to being patient, though the noise coming from my stomach means that if I don't stop soon I will be in danger of messing myself. Like many others, I am forced to drink from the megalopolis broth and frequently fall victim to the bacteria-laden water.

When my strength runs out, I flop down on top of the rubbish. It's a warning sign: I have to discharge my intestines of their daily load of germs. My stump is overheated from chafing against the prosthetic leg.

I let my head rest against the curve of a deflated tyre sticking edgeways out of the rubbish. I make myself comfortable in the hole, lower my trousers to my knees and let go. A spasm in the pit of my stomach readies me for a second round, followed quickly by a third.

Breathe in. Breathe out.

I tidy myself up and move further up the hill. Not long afterwards, I fall asleep with Alba on my mind and strands of her hair in my hand.

I dream. I dream that flower-covered slopes form the silhouette of Alba's body. I dream of a complete emptiness, a space totally odourless and tasteless, where nothing interferes with the present.

I don't know how much time has passed, but when I wake up, night is ending and the sun's rays are just beyond the roofs of the buildings.

My precious find is safe in my fist, and when I stand up, I spot more of Alba's hair nearby amongst the kipple, the red strands illuminated against the filth. No one has sent a droid to mark out the area. No one has made any effort to find the treasure lying under a shallow covering of garbage.

I have to hurry. A nexhuman head, regardless of what Charlie might think, is worth a fortune. To me, it's priceless.

I delve through the rubbish carefully, revealing a pair of eyes—green eyes, still wide open—and then skin, her elegant cheekbones, her small chin and dainty, upturned nose. I lose my balance out of sheer joy. Alba is being reborn under my hands.

It's her ... at least, what's left of her.

I touch her earlobes. My cheeks flush red. I caress an eyebrow with my thumb. Shivers run down my spine. I touch her lips. There's no way she's kipple. She can't be.

In her glassy stare, there's a placid expression without shame, and her slightly open lips hint at a serenity I didn't see in her before. Is it possible that she can feel something even now?

I brush the hair delicately off her face and tilt my head forward. She doesn't say anything; she lets me.

I've never touched a woman's face. I hadn't even tried with anyone before now—the girls I knew at school would have slapped me if I dared to so much as look at them.

Our moment together is interrupted, and I shake away the spell that held us suspended. Something is moving nearby: a furtive seeker, wandering around like me. A swathe of light nearly points directly at us. It wavers from right to left.

Is it another salvager? A night watchman? Or just a curious neighbour?

I lie down and blend in with the kipple; my body vanishes, at one with the rubbish. Warm, welcoming kipple ...

The light advances, and I play dead, imitating kipple against the kipple. I only have one eye slightly open to watch a sliver of the horizon.

Alba's head is cradled to my chest, to hide and protect her, making my heart beat faster. What would anyone finding us think?

Alba's fate is tied up with mine now: one body and two heads to save.

The figure comes closer and appears to be limping. He's probably using a prosthetic leg like mine that does little more than help him keep his balance. He must be a tramp because the air doesn't bring me any clues to his humanity, only the usual smell of those who have been assimilated by these surroundings.

When it's five metres away, the figure stops, bends, and unearths something. As he turns it over, I get a glimpse of the object, blackened by its time in the dump. The man shakes it. Satisfied at the slosh of liquid, he turns and goes back in the direction he came from.

I can relax and exhale. He's found his reward and I'm about to get mine, too. With Alba held tightly against my chest, I count to sixty and hurry back down the hill, tumbling as I go. I end up rolling down in a landslide of rubbish.

We fall to one side, Alba and me, and I take care not to lose my grip on her. Then I lift her to my face—she still smells good despite having spent the night surrounded by filth.

I settle her under my arm and walk triumphantly into the street, head held high like a football player after winning a match.

After a while, the fact that I can't share this adventure with anyone makes me a little sad. The audaciousness of my enterprise deserves recognition from the Dead Bones, or at least the praise of my trashformer mates, Rasha, Norbert,

Duggan, and Pongo, with whom I share every treasure. Then I realise that, when it comes down to it, all I've done is find a head, something that will not be looked on with much enthusiasm. Better to keep my own head down.

Alba's face is drawn and wan, though she shows no sign of fear. That's good—a sign that she will be my girl.

"Hi, Alba. I'm here to save you."

She doesn't answer. She must be a little overwhelmed by the whole situation.

"I'm Peter, do you remember me? Peter Payne, the one who comes to say hello every day. How about if you come with me this time?"

She says nothing and then I realise: she doesn't know where to go, or else she is ashamed of no longer having her own home to go to. A head without a body can't just pick up where it left off.

"I'll take you to my house. It's not much, but it will keep us safe."

She can't have eaten since yesterday. Her bloodless lips, rough with vertical cracks, make her look enchanting.

"I'll find you something to eat later; first, we have to get home."

We are about to turn onto Lucite Street when a grainy torchlight rests on my face. "Who that...? What you doing here?" a rough voice asks.

Shit, it's the tramp... Was he waiting for me, or is this just coincidence?

"Me? Nothing, just walking. I'm going now..." I make a hurried answer, caught by surprise, and walk on. He follows me. A pair of cripples, one after the other; he wobbles from side to side while I drag my dumb leg along the ground.

"You got it, yes? Got it before me?" He looks down at Alba's head.

"Got what?"

"You got the head. I saw it land on the hill."

He doesn't seem violent. His thick beard inspires a certain amount of respect and identifies him as a poor devil concerned only with surviving. Still, I keep Alba hidden in the shadows, just to be sure.

"It's my brother's. He asked me to bring it to him." He nods, but doesn't believe me. Worse, he wants to come with me.

"No one with a sane mind keep a head in a home. Is bad luck."

I breathe in through my nose. Dilating capillaries colour my cheeks. This often happens to me at the worst times. "My brother isn't superstitious. He's the leader of the Dead Bones."

"I see. I see what happened. I bet you not telling truth."

I stop and watch him swaying. Does he want to take her from me? Does he want her for himself?

I blink and moisten my lips. There is nothing I can do.

"I found it first. My brother said I could keep it."

His wrinkled face contorts into a smile, sardonic, but gentle, too. His teeth scare me: four stalactites and four stalagmites, all as ancient as he is.

"Boy, no panic. I not want woman's head. I old, this thing's nothing for me. But I can see? Is nexhuman, yes?"

I clench my left hand into a fist, ready to strike, while with my plastic hand I pull the head out of my shirt. His directness doesn't reassure me; on the other hand, his age makes me think I could deal with him if I needed to.

With the light falling directly on her, Alba looks less innocent than a moment ago. She reminds me of an actress from the gamesphere, Candy Candice or Lorna the Bomb—a bimbo whose lips are always parted just wide enough to draw one into temptation.

These exaggerated features are somehow wrong for her—she must have chosen them herself at rebirth. One of the advantages of being uploaded is that you can live in a better shell, updatable and perfectible. In Alba's case, though, something seems out of place. It is as though the grace and sweetness that I experienced firsthand aren't reflected in the face she selected. Without the makeup or false eyelashes, hairpiece and whitened teeth, she could be my next door neighbour.

The tramp moves closer. "Careful, boy. Difficult to resist dreams. Impossible not to let desires follow."

"What do you mean? She's mine, now. I have her."

He stops, switches off the torch. Behind us, the flickering lilac rays of the sun liquefy the outline of the dump. In the morning light, I recognise the tramp's clothing. He is wearing Reverse overalls, the megalopolis's biggest recycling company, but filthy with kipple stains. Every so often, one of their officers hires us salvagers for an urgent excavation and recovery job.

"Are you from Reverse?"

He stiffens as if I've said something rude. He looks down at the logo on his uniform and sighs. "Is story I don't tell ... I *was* Reverse. Now live here." He didn't need to tell me. The state of him explained enough.

"You found something, too," I say. "What was that black thing?"

"Was filter... have been looking for months. I need for my invention. *AquaSan* prototype."

"A what?"

"Forget I say, please. Useless explaining to you. Go home, boy. Day is nearly here and someone might see head undershirt."

He's right. I must get home before Cleo notices I'm gone.

"My name's Peter," I say.

He extends a dirty hand. "Okay, Peter. My name Ion."

Before I put her away, I look at my girl and she smiles at me. I know this is a day I will remember, a day that compensated for all that came before and all the days that are to come, and I hear Ion's words in my head, "Difficult to resist dreams. Impossible not to let desires follow."

I lie half-awake, imagining the Dead Bones strutting around and boasting about their incredible hunt to the thugs who hang out outside Junkland waiting for tip-offs. I can just imagine Charlie attracting the attention of the gangs by waving about nexhuman parts; Mickey Mucous parading the torso for customers eager for something new, a crooked smile and the usual drip of snot hanging from his nose.

In my head, I can see Crispy Lenny miming obscene acts with the same hands and arms that once stroked my head outside Boreal Skies and Jimmy the Loins singing the praises of a pair of nexhuman thighs– though, in fact, he knows nothing about it. They must have all been ecstatic at Junkland. Someone has probably pulled out their piece to take pot shots at passing flocks of birds or a pack of stray puppies. ReStore, on the other hand, would have had to slash its prices in an attempt to halt the exodus of customers.

It's Alba and me who have paid the highest price for this whole situation.

There is no hope of a good wake-up after just two hours of agitated sleep. I'm consoled by the fact that Alba is warm under the covers. Cleo mustn't find her; she would tell Charlie. She wouldn't tell him out of spite, but because she still thinks he is a good influence on me.

I hide Alba in the wardrobe. The only safe place in our house is the wardrobe in my room, in the far corner, where Cleo's zealous cleaning tends not to reach. Though I can't take it for granted that keeping the key to the wardrobe with me is enough to keep Alba safe from intruders, knowing that

Alba is hidden and secure takes some of the pressure off my chest.

"Peter! Breakfast! C'mon, it's late."

I have to pinch what little flesh I have on my cheeks so I don't fall back to sleep.

"I'm coming. I'm getting dressed."

I wash my face in the basin of water, extracted from the humidity of the night air, and throw on the first thing I find hanging over the chair.

When I appear in the kitchen, Cleo looks at me, and like every other day makes a comment on my appearance.

"That baggy trackie makes you look even skinnier. You're so scrawny I can hardly believe you're my son."

I stuff my hands in my pockets and walk into the living room without answering. Cleo runs after me, plate in hand—two soft eggs surrounded by sausages.

"I'm sorry, I didn't mean ... C'mon, love, please, eat up. I have to go out. I'll see you later, ok?"

I know she loves me, even if she doesn't show it very often.

"All right, then. See ya later."

My mother should worry more about her own health instead of making insinuations about mine. She's not doing so well at the moment. High blood pressure, bad circulation; she's risking a heart attack. I reckon she uses me as a way to rid of *her* tension. In her mind, if she feeds me well, I'll be up to the job of facing the world, I won't feel the need to go looking for adventure, and maybe I won't leave her.

It's different with Charlie; he's *always* in her good books.

I make myself some tea, and just as I start thinking I might be able to have breakfast in peace, I hear my brother's footsteps in the hall. The triumphant sneer of two nights ago turns into an arrogant smile as he slaps me on the back, knocking the teaspoon out of my hand.

"Morning, skinny ribs. Sleep well? You look awful…"

I pick the spoon up from the floor and ignore him. My hatred for him has grown to an almost dangerous level. I make a huge effort not to let him see this hostility—it would only make him want to discover the cause—but I can feel the rage welling up inside and my silence immediately betrays me.

"Oh, you're not still mad about the other night, are you? You're only a skinny kid. You don't need to see that kind of thing. Give it a couple of years and you can quit that stupid trashform job and become a *real* member of the gang."

He laughs. Is there a double meaning in his words? His gang leader talk, his bossy tone, they bother me, but my tendency towards despair often makes me blind to his insinuations.

"I did see what you did the other night," I say, testing how far I can push him.

He glowers at me from across the table.

"Oh, yes? And what did you see the other night?"

Huddling in my chair I don't dare look up. As fearful as a hare, I'm scared he's going to lay into me before I can even articulate my accusation.

"You murdered Alba."

My good leg is tingling. I haven't turned livid; a deathly pale light floods my face and I emanate a different smell. These subtle changes Charlie doesn't bother to analyse.

Instead of answering me, he makes his own accusation. "You disobeyed an order, too. Didn't see *that*, did you?"

I never know when it's Charlie talking to me, or the leader of the Dead Bones. I've never really needed to compete with him and the thought of going head to head with

Charlie terrifies me, now that the challenge is before us. I'm not whining because he killed Alba; I'm not bleating about his cruelty. I am accusing him of a crime and he deflects the attack. By avoiding my question, he is implicitly admitting his guilt.

Then he shoves back his chair and bursts out, "Listen, skinny ribs, do you like what you're eating?"

I fill my mouth with sausage. It's an old question, and one I feel no need to answer again.

"I pay for the food you stuff yourself with. Where do you think the money comes from?"

I remain silent. Ignoring him irritates him, throws him off balance. He walks around the table and flips around a chair, flinging one leg over it with mock bravado.

"I told you to forget about her. Have you forgotten what I said? That thing from the other night wasn't a woman."

I lift my chin to look at him. Where my eyes should be, I have two pits burning with anger, encircled by the bruises of sleeplessness.

"That's not true! She wasn't kipple!"

My terror wins over the insolence of what I've said. I squeeze my eyes shut, ready for the blow I'm sure is about to come. But Charlie surprises me—he seems amused by my unexpected fervour.

"You cheeky little arse, were you listening too?" I don't like his bantering tone, and I curl up a bit more in my chair. He still doesn't hit me and instead starts pacing up and down the kitchen.

"Alright then, skinny ribs. Do you really want to know the way things are? I'm happy to tell you, but don't cry to me after. I've done my best to protect you, but here it is. Ready? I don't care what you saw or what you thought it looked like. I don't care if she was nice to you. She wasn't human. She wasn't alive, so there ain't no sense making a fuss about it."

His fists are clenched as if reliving his part in the episode that has been seared into my brain.

"If you were there spying on us, you must have seen there wasn't any blood to spill. When I took her head off, there were no bones to break. When the Dead Bones divided her up, they cut through cables, not arteries; they broke welds, not muscles. You saw that, right?"

At risk of seeming stupid, I blurt out my innocent truth, "Her spirit was human."

Charlie looks at me aghast.

"Her spirit? Well, listen to all the theories you're full of this morning... You're raving, skinny ribs. That *nexhuman* was like a recording of a woman's voice on a memory stick. If the memory stick breaks, it's no tragedy. You just buy another one. They ain't human."

So this is *his* version of what happened. A recorded voice on a memory stick? I feel an overwhelming urge to cry. Even if Alba were only a recording, she is still a miracle, because just as she had once been fixed in an uploaded version in the past, she can re-emerge again.

My bottom lip quivers. My good hand is shaking as I put the last morsel of sausage into my mouth. I get up quickly and spill tea down my front.

Alba, for me, is like a candle flame: as she burns, she lights up my life. My memory of her is the wax keeping the flame alive. How can you say that something no longer exists if there is someone who still remembers it?

For some people, a person is made up of various parts: a nice pair of legs; a good brain; two heavy hands. For others, a person is an indivisible whole and every detail reflects back on the rest. To me, Alba's head *is* Alba.

With eyes swimming in tears, I hurry to my room, glancing over my shoulder to make sure Charlie isn't following me.

As usual, he has won the argument, and he'll enjoy his usual Luddite gloating. I hope that one day, the megalopolis broth will avenge me. I hope his insides will twist as any biological organism does when attacked by bacteria. I hope he will spend a week, a month, huddled on a toilet, begging the diarrhoea to stop and his haemorrhoids to let him walk upright.

I open the wardrobe to reassure myself that Alba is all right. Hidden in the shadows, her face, overflowing with sweetness, calms me. Then I hear him coming, one step after another. His contemptuous voice spewing paternalistic clichés in the absence of our father.

"C'mon, Peter, don't be a baby. You know we need money. That stuff is worth loads of Ks."

That's the magic word. Ks! For him, Alba is just *technological stuff* worth a handful of credits.

If he finds Alba, I've had it. Keeping a head in your house is worse than breaking a mirror, worse than a pair of scissors falling and sticking into the ground, worse than killing an albatross, worse than a cockerel crowing before midnight.

I shut the wardrobe door just in time, and jump into the gamesphere. He leans in through the doorway, looking like he almost feels bad at having reduced me to this state, a spineless loser who can't stand up for himself against anyone, a kid who is only good for wearing himself out on the rubbish dump and getting himself dismembered by a UCU.

The gamesphere starts to move, swivelling on magnetic joints. My Simbox 2 is a patch job made of parts salvaged from Cali Nova and Worrisham and is the best I have found in the way of pastimes.

I press a button and let the images of another world envelope me. I want to disappear, dissolve in a vortex of pixels.

I set an exciting course through the mists of some generic forest.

Tears are sliding down my face as I accelerate until the places where my prosthetic limbs attach to what is left of my flesh throb painfully. *Tum, tum, tum* ...

I lose myself amongst the immense trees, and run headlong along footpaths to nowhere.

I can't tell if my heart or my leg hurts me more.

Charlie gives up, snorts his disapproval and leaves. There is no way he could understand that Alba is my *only* fortune.

PART TWO
YOUTH – 2045 CE

Better strangle an infant in the cradle than nurse unwanted desires.
William Blake

Chapter 5
Pursuit

Obsessions take a long time to dissipate. This is a certainty: I am suffering from an unfulfilled fixation and have been for five years.

Is it because of my sickness that Alba's presence in the wardrobe fills me with an infinite tenderness? She takes me close to the edge of sanity and makes me suffer many sleepless nights. It is only when I open the closet door that I can feel peace in her mild, slightly condescending gaze, letting me know she knows what I want, but she can't do anything about it. Some people bring disruption to everything around them, others have the opposite effect. It is my Alba whom I've kept safe in the wardrobe for five years. It is my Alba who comforts me and discourages me at the same time. Because she *is* the future; not an extension of me, but a kind of magic that goes beyond the limits of the human race I belong to.

The Kathal Hill gang—Rasha, Norbert, Duggan, and Pongo—gratify themselves three or four times a day in the gamesphere. I don't. It's not that I haven't tried—I have, again and again—but it doesn't work for me. My muscles respond, but the stimuli don't induce the same reaction. I have come to the conclusion that I cannot be physically fulfilled. I'd rather rest with my face pressed against the softness of my new Simbox 4, daydreaming about finding a way out of my situation.

Just now, as I wake up, I am partially disorientated by part of the gamesphere that has been left open. The wardrobe door is ajar. Has Alba moved of her own accord? Impossible; I had put her safely back in the wardrobe after carefully detaching her from the mannequin that substitutes for her body. Did I forget to close it? Has someone been in my room without me knowing?

I hear my mother calling me from downstairs.

"Peter, are you still in bed? Come and have breakfast; it's late!"

Cleo is still alive, despite her deteriorating health, and she still tries to work. A mysterious ailment has left her permanently fatigued, unable to lift anything heavier than her company visor or the pots and pans in the kitchen. She has had to leave her job as cook in the Reverse canteen, but after a training course, the Human Resources department offered her a place on the help desk (the company is too cheap to invest in an automated one). She accepted because she can work from home. Going outside is no longer safe for her health—the fine dust and exhaust fumes exacerbate her condition, putting her life at risk.

"I'm coming..." I hate rude awakenings.

"Hurry up or you'll be late for work."

Over the last five years, I've had to get my life into gear.

I tried the virtual correspondence school, with all those useless experience points, but it turned out to be a waste of time. It was useless for finding a job and even a small amount of credits gave me access to all the wikimirror data I could want, so I went back to doing what I'd always done: living off the junk.

The constant increase in kipple has made business even better for Reverse; it has hired thousands more trashformers—now my official title—to sift through the holding areas and the storage sites. I spent three years eking out a living from the stuff I could salvage or collect from people's homes.

One day, while rummaging through the rubbish, I chanced on something extremely valuable: a mechanical arm with a hand attached. It must have once belonged to a well-heeled nexhuman. It's anybody's guess how it ended up in Cali Nova, but that waterproof Tantalium 4 has changed my life. So has the Podox, the prosthetic leg I obtained through a trade with Ion. Both of these prosthetic limbs are miracles compared to the old pieces of plastic and metal that marred my miserable childhood. Ion grafted them onto me himself. Only Ion and I will ever know how much I suffered through that.

It is a fact that certain areas of the megalopolis are better off than others—it depends on the kipple that feeds them. In districts like Genshoij, Rizoma, or Esperia—where the nexhumans live—you are much more likely to find excellent pieces of discarded technology. In these places, the rubbish hides things that are nearly new, or have never been used, nestling in the original packaging complete with instruction manuals and guarantees. On the other hand, if you hang around places like Vermillion or the slums of Cali Nova, there's nothing for it but to make do with real rubbish, the stuff that people only throw away after an accurate, sometimes heartbreaking evaluation of its residual value.

The UCUs are the things I hate most, after kipple. Now it's easy for me to jump into one of those mobile monsters, and once inside, it's easy to find stuff worth the effort. The problem is getting out again, and I don't want to think about that. I hardly ever do it; the risk is too great.

"Don't make me come in there!" Cleo threatens from just outside my door.

"I'm getting dressed," I shout back.

I stick my head out of the gamesphere just in time to see Cleo's head at my bedroom door. Her brow furrows when she sees that my bed hasn't been slept in, the corner of the duvet trailing from the gamesphere.

"Peter?"

She sticks her head past the door, scanning the room from one end to the other. Then I realise that I am still not dressed *and* there is a nude female mannequin practically on display. She doesn't like me sleeping in the orb as it is, but her eyes pass over me to fix on the nude female mannequin that functions as my clothes-hanger. I slide out of the Simbox and start to get dressed hurriedly. I know how suspicious it looks. I know that this strange passion comes close to folly, but for me, it's the only way of reaching a goal more valuable than anything else: love.

"I told you, I was getting dressed."

"Is that a woman?"

"What?"

"The mannequin... is it a girl's one?"

If I say yes, my mum will think I'm mad, or else, at the very least, a fetishist; on the other hand, denying the evidence would make me seem stranger. I don't have a lot to do with girls—I've never had a girlfriend. The closest I've come is Kiko, a girl I've spent evenings playing multiplayer games with. But I've never actually *met* her.

"Yeah, it's a girl," I say. "So?"

"No, nothing, of course. I was just wondering."

Her smile is a deep sunken line from one cheek to the other. If I could afford an upload, Mum would be the first person I'd give the opportunity of migration.

"Mum, d'you mind?" At twenty, getting dressed in front of your own mother is humiliating.

"Yes, sorry. I'll be in the kitchen."

As soon as the sound of her shuffling feet is at a safe distance, I open my secret door. Rooting around in the pile of clothes I lift out the head and set it on the mannequin. Looking at Alba as if she were standing before me, even in this patchwork incarnation, gives me a stab of joy. There's no point in denying it: I want Alba. Not any other nexhuman, nor even her original master copy, which, as far as I know, could already have been reborn into another body.

When I look at her, I don't see crude, inorganic matter, atoms assembled by who knows what rules of model-making. On the contrary, I enjoy the purity of her energy trapped in this artificial form. I see a creature designed for a better future. I see the suspension of time, the end of all rules, a union between natural and artificial that leaves me troubled and impotent.

"Good morning, Alba. Sorry about Cleo. She's old, you know. There are some things she doesn't understand."

As a trashformer, I have access to eighty-six of Reverse's storage sites, which hold two thirds of all the refuse produced by the megalopolis. Year after year, with patience and devotion, I have salvaged biomechanical parts that had just been thrown away. I've found obsolete limbs, synthetic skin, silicon joints and every other possible material needed to create a body. Not her original body, sold to Junkland by the Dead Bones, but another one, one that I have built with my own hands, guided by my memories of her.

"Last night we were on holiday, you and me. You chose our itinerary, a boat trip around the islands off Belize City, but the ad hoc excursions were *my* department."

I don't often laugh this much. I open the gamesphere, and go inside with Alba next to me.

"I thought we could go to the Barton Creek cave..." The rustling forest sounds, the smell of exotic fruit and the velvety light of a high-resolution paradise on our skin.

"Impromptu excursions are the best way of getting to

know a place," I say. "You should avoid the most-visited areas, the tourist traps, the destinations in the guide books. This is the only way to travel. That's the theory you taught me, remember?"

We are surrounded by blue. The waves chase each other into the distant horizon, then seem to continue upwards, becoming thin layers of cloud.

"One day, we will put all of this into practice. For real."

Then my guts clench. It's not the realisation of how unattainable our dream is, but the insistent call of the toilet.

I hurry out of the gamesphere, closing Alba inside before running into the next room. I get there just in time, and I've hardly sat down when the shit comes, spraying the sides of the bowl. It feels like a surprise every time. I try to control my intestines but am unable to prevent another discharge. A third spurt drains my abs of any strength they might have had left.

I flush straight away, so I don't stink the place out more than I already have. I am so embarrassed, I puff a little *Phoenix* into the air. It is Cleo's favourite deodorant but the smell reminds me of insect repellent.

At last, my stomach is settled enough for me to leave the house, though I'm not exactly leaping with joy at the prospect of my shift in Cali Nova.

I go back to my room, take Alba's head off the dummy, and put it back in its hiding place.

When I am in the kitchen, I make my announcement.

"I'm not going to work today."

Cleo's ashen face is doubly surprised.

"Why? Don't you feel well? Shall I call the doctor?"

I put on my raincoat and pull the hood up.

"I'm fine, but today I feel like taking the day off. Charlie'll understand."

Cleo doesn't even pretend to sympathise.

"Your brother works like mad every month to send us Ks, and you want to take a day off just like that, without any reason?"

Over the course of five years, this argument has become tired. I answer by rote.

"You're right. I'll send him a message if that makes you feel better."

"Don't do it for me, do it for the job. Charlie is above you at work; you owe him respect."

There is little point in arguing, and even less in trying to explain what is disturbing me. I say goodbye at the door, cutting her off.

"Okay, then, I won't tell him at all. See you later."

Sooner or later, I will track down whoever has the pieces of Alba. The only clues I have are a series of serial codes that I derived from the chip embedded in her head. Everything, as soon as it is created, is given a manufacturer's chip and a tag to interact with its surroundings, so I have reason to hope.

Yesterday evening, during my shift in Cali Nova, I caught a signal over the RFID visor, beeping as I came close to it. The Tuwin blew at my back, bringing breath from outside the megalopolis, hard gusts that can blow fortune my way or take it away.

Today it brought me this: 8–952–395–78–08–02.

Every day at work, thousands of items of data flit past me, a cloud of info-marketing and promo-vapour that overlays every aspect of reality: dates and places of manufacture, distribution channels, purpose, expiry dates, disposal instructions, and all those elements involved in the general process of goods-info valorisation.

This is why I don't class myself as a simple trashformer,

but as a *salvager* of materials. With my kit, I can prolong the expected life of anything, without, of course, expecting to be able to bring things back from the dead. Reverse issues all trashformers with two devices: a visor for salvaging and a low heat dispersion incinerator for redeeming.

Salvaging and recycling is my mission: I revive materials on behalf of Reverse.

Honing in on the beeps, I start to dig. My Tantalium 4 keeps me high on the list of the best trashformers in the western part of the megalopolis. My mechanical limb means I don't have to fear acid corrosion or a bullet exploding at close quarters.

My hands were beginning to uncover an antique clock in a wooden case, the small pendulum swinging as I lifted it out as if it were still intent on measuring out time.

As I was bent over my work, the RFID recognition icon appeared on my visor. It was no coincidence that the code had managed to get through the network of filters I set up. I'd picked it out for recognition a long time ago. The numbers revolved like the lurid hearts, cherries, and diamonds of an old-fashioned slot machine.

Buried under six metres of sedimentary rubbish, those digital numbers represented a much-longed-for find: after five years, I had intercepted the code of one of Alba's original parts moving somewhere nearby. Without a second thought, I abandoned the clock and starting chasing after the flashing code on my visor. I ran after it on foot until I got to the junction with Venison Street, and then went south across Lazar and beyond. It was a block away and advancing every second.

While working at Reverse, I have learned to seek, evaluate, and choose every single piece of rubbish before it degrades into kipple. The final '2' of the code 8–952–395–78–

08–02 tells me I have caught a signal from Alba's torso—the part Mickey Mucous took. The other numbers denote the names of goods, their manufacturers, commercial category, and so on.

The direction of the signal took me southeast at about twenty-seven kilometers per hour, what I consider my safety speed. The signal got closer, then further away, as if continually stopping and starting. Maybe it was in a car or a van?

I ran without giving a moment's thought to fatigue. Adrenaline coursed through my veins and my limbs answered. Up and over a bank of earth, pulling myself up with my Tantalium and pushing hard with the Podox—if I had had these beauties when the Dead Bones were still together, they would not have excluded me from their missions—I might have saved Alba in the first place.

I bounded up a stairway and flew past a gate lying alongside the wall. I dove, somersaulted and landed on my feet on a balcony that overlooked the street from where the signal was emanating.

Then I saw it. My target was squat and compact, a four-wheeled van with grimy windows and old rubber tyres. She, or rather her torso, had to be inside. I was trembling at the thought of being able to touch her at last.

I threw myself down the ten-metre drop, softening the landing with both of my enhanced limbs, only eighty metres from my goal. It was a straight stretch, but even at my fastest, I couldn't close the gap.

My only hope was the next set of lights. I had to trust the megalopolis and its traps.

The van accelerated, determined to make the light. I gave chase, but after four kilometers, the toll felt on my muscles became too much. In 150 metres, another treacherous set of lights shone green, and at that moment I hated the megalopolis with every atom of my body. To my left, a private coach overtook me, and with the strength of desperation, I grabbed hold of it to catch a lift. The Tantalium's grip on the rusty bumper was strong and I huddled up against the back of the vehicle.

I was making up ground; I was nearly there.

I could see the roof of the van, but not the number plate. Visors only receive signals if they're pointing directly at a tag. Some tags have a limited range; others have batteries that run down quite quickly.

I let go of the bumper, but mistimed my drop, rolling to the ground and straight into the path of two oncoming vehicles. I slipped to one side of the first, then jumped straight upwards to avoid being hit by the second, landing first on its bonnet, then vaulted up and over its roof, landing on its boot and bouncing off onto the ground as it raced on.

As I was performing these acrobatics, my target took the ramp down into an underpass: the awful tunnel that joins Lazar and Raon. The megalopolis hated me today. I reciprocated with all the fury in my body.

On and on I ran with no breath left in me, knee-deep in the putrid water that fills the tunnel every time it rains. The sign in front of me pointed in two directions: Kudzu Gardens to the left, and Visconia to the right. The van was nowhere in sight.

I came to a halt and doubled over to catch my breath, defeated.

Chapter 6
Derelict Visconia

Today I'm going to Visconia, looking for better luck. Giving up gets you nowhere.

When I first started my quest, I asked around Junkland, naïvely, if anyone had come across nexhuman parts. I even sent Rasha, Duggan, Norbert, and Pongo to sniff out information among the losers who hang around there. I presumed the Dead Bones had offloaded the parts in exchange for a memorable week-long drinking session, so I expected someone to know something. I hoarded valuable chips and electronic hardware, enough to entice anyone into trading for information, but I got nowhere. No one ever came back to me with a tag or a clue for me to follow. No one knew anything about Alba.

Boreal Skies was dismantled a week after Alba disappeared. Everything inside was taken away; the brochures, the exotic holograms, even the furniture, removed to make room for a recycling franchise identical to hundreds of others scattered around the metropolis.

Unwholesome vapours rise from the derelict suburb around me. The gate to the factory has been ripped off and wedged horizontally to half-bar the entryway. Along the outer walls, covered with symbols and glaring graffiti, there are rough cracks and lumps of lurid kipple.

I wait for my visor to adapt to the weak light filtering through the filth-encrusted skylights above. The noise of the old machinery has been supplanted by the eerie hum of wind blowing through the support columns and rusted roof struts.

Nothing more than a devastated spectral skeleton remains of this building where solvents, paints and industrial varnishes were once produced. The floor is covered by a delta of dried effluent from fake-snow spray cans and a blend of paint.

Pieces of discarded flexopaper litter the floor, perhaps left behind by Moore acolytes after clandestine meetings where they plotted attaining the nexhuman condition, despite lacking the essential requirements. I pick one up. The ink is almost completely faded; the text is difficult to read:

The immaterial soul does not exist
The body is a prosthetic, the first but not the last to be used

I stick the pamphlet in my pocket and penetrate deeper into the dim expanse. In an effort to avoid the deeper, and likely more toxic, puddles, I jump from one dry spot to another until I reach the northern corner of the warehouse. In the distance, I can just see a gleam of light, bouncing off an accidental pond surrounded by squat plants, their curled leaves grotesque in the half-light. Bunches of swaying fruit hang like cysts. Suddenly, one of them explodes. The bang is followed by the squelch of fruit hitting the floor.

I crouch in the shadows and watch.

A quick scan reassures me that there are no weapons nearby.

With surprise, I realise that two kids are using the fruit for target practice. They are shooting at them with rudimentary blowpipes in a bid to impress two giggling girls. When the burst the pods release spurts of black, oily juice, the girls scrape it off the ground and apply it to their skin like eyeliner.

Their activities are illuminated by a glass jar filled with long, luminescent worms emitting a light that makes the air seem blurred.

I inch forward carefully, in time to see them discover some kind of animal. They pounce and tie it up by its tail. It is a curvilinear little beast, an amphibian with patches of light blue on orange skin. Its colouring must have mutated to adapt to the derelict Visconia.

"Quick—put on your gloves," one of them urges.

"Why? It doesn't even have teeth."

"Not for its bite, you idiot. These little nippers have spit that burns like mad."

"How do you know that?"

"Guess. It'll burn your skin if you touch it." The cleverer boy sticks out an incomplete tongue.

"That's disgusting. You licked one?"

"The bastards tricked me. They said it was a trip…"

These two boys could have been me and Charlie ten years ago. They immobilise the animal with a pair of tongs and then, wearing latex gloves, the 'smart one' chops off the salamander's tail with a splintered end of wood. An innocent bit of amputation that I cut short with a full-throated yell.

I can't stomach this kind of behaviour. Not anymore.

"What the fuck do you think you are doing?!"

I stamp the Podox on a sheet of metal and all four kids jump in fear. They look at each other for a moment in surprise, assuming I am a mad tramp, then wisely opt for running away.

I move closer to the lumpy mass; it is still writhing on the floor. The mutated salamander's tail has been cut off completely, and while its body writhes in agony, the disembodied tail continues to wriggle convulsively beside it. Then something incredible happens.

Its body's desire to get the missing appendage back is so great that it starts growing another one. Clicking its tongue as if in the grip of delirium, the salamander performs a miracle.

Within a few minutes, the old tail, now a withered stump, stops moving, and the salamander has a vibrating new one.

The sight leaves me speechless. If only I had this power! If only I could grow back what was taken from me as a child! Such a simple idea, yet so absurd: tissue regeneration.

The salamander hisses with joy and scuttles off to hide under some fallen beams, leaving me standing pensively by the side of the pond. The Tuwin outside is now lashing the building with howling gusts, making me shiver.

I feel cold, and at the same time feverish, with inspiration. I get up and hurry away, all but skipping out of the factory.

What would happen if the process I have just witnessed were applied to Alba? Could it possibly work for her? Desire has never before been this audacious.

I know who can help me.

Just then my bladder hits me, and as I let go against the side of the building, I see a couple of pushbikes leaning against a side exit. The kids must have left them behind in their rush to get away from me. As I piss, I snigger at the thought of adding a little acid to the already-toxic of the terrain. I'll never get even.

Blackened signs warn that the area is protected by video surveillance, but they are of as much use as scarecrows. Thousands of electronic eyes watch everyone, on the lookout for illegal activities. They work together like a pack of starving bloodhounds.

I check the positions of the various webcams, making sure that I stay in their blindspots. The bikes are chained together, but there are no alarms or wireless protections. It is easy to lift them and drag them into an isolated corner. Then I choose a link of the metal chain and twist back and forth until it grows hot and then cracks open. The Tantalium proves its worth again.

I get on one of the bikes and set off down Oldinvari Road at speed, guiding the other bike with one hand. The Tuwin blows in my favour and I grin in triumph, thanking the wind for its help.

I have remained good friends with old Ion. Since we traded the Podox he had found for the 3D plans of the Reverse buildings I'd acquired, he has treated me like a son.

I have no idea what he wanted the plans for, but the advantages of the Podox were more than worth the risks involved in downloading a file from the company's database.

Doing favours can be worth your while.

Riding my 'new' bike and wheeling the second one beside me, I face the distance from the Visconia to Kathal Hill with a light heart.

I can tell from the steely colour of the Oldinvari Road smoke—the burning of the sulphurous kipple—that tomorrow will bring acid rain. The sky, a compact surface reverberating with electrostatic rumbles, is a splendid sight. Slim aeroplanes and space shuttles criss-cross freely like the crows and gulls that swoop undaunted over Kathal Hill.

My determination raises its head. Dismounting from the bike, I set off along the path beaten out by trashformers. Two bikes are an attractive proposition, so it's only sensible to launch a protective scan.

Someone shouts from the other side of the first hill.

"Identify yourself! What are you carrying?"

A pair of tracking beams plays across the surface of my raincoat. I lift the Tantalium and the bikes in a gesture of peace. As I move forward, gangs of dump dwellers wave at me from the gulches and barricades. I zoom in amongst the lopsided axles and hulks of the gutted cars and I see two figures, Babababa the Stammerer and Naasim the Smiler, Rasha's uncle. He is always the first to spot me.

He nods in my direction. It's as warm a welcome as I'll get.

I carry on walking, and when I reach Ion's cabin, I find him sitting in his favourite deluxe reclining swivel chair, studying the holograph of the Reverse building plans projected on his camp table: barred windows, mechanical arms, conveyor belts, electric switchboards, and all the other devices that have contributed to today's endemic over-production of objects, the need to recycle them and the subsequent agony of kipple.

Ion has a fixation with kipple—everybody does because kipple affects us all. But Ion is not like me; he analyses kipple as if it were a mathematical problem that might actually have an answer, as though he were trying to reverse the laws of chaos.

Even Charlie's life revolves around kipple. After he left his Dead Bones rebel period behind, what he once hunted with the aim of cleansing his neighbourhood became his daily bread. Still, as team leader, my brother is not interested in the ontology of the phenomenon, but rather in how to make as much out of it as he can. He's after a position, status, and I'd be willing to bet that he'll find a way to kiss arse until he has climbed all the way up the slippery rungs of Reverse's hierarchy.

Then there's me. Compared to Ion and Charlie's, my attitude is more hostile. Since the attack five years ago, my personal relationship with kipple has changed. Perhaps, though, it is being surrounded by garbage, working in the midst it for twelve hours a day, that has changed my perception of reality.

Where Charlie sees opportunity in kipple, and Ion an emerging phenomenon, I see it as a nightmare. As a trashformer, I hunt kipple. At the end of every shift in the dump, I have to compile a report recording the objects I have found—not just for me, but for the whole community.

Mr Stinky, Ion's pet pig, is in his nearby pen, scratching at the ground with two cloven trotters. He has unearthed a maggot-infested growth and doesn't think twice about gulping it down.

Ion is so lost in thought, he doesn't even notice me.

I lean the bikes against the 4x4 prefab cubicle. 'Hi, Ion, look what I've brought you.'

He looks up for the first time.

"For me? A bicycle? Thank you, Peter."

"No problem. I found two lying around at Visconia. Well, not exactly lying around, but whatever... you can have this one."

"Let me have closer look at this beauty."

He gets up to inspect the bike. He runs his hand over the tyres, the rubber smooth from use. He checks the brakes, straddles it to try the softness of the saddle and the springiness of the suspension, scrutinises the tension and running of the chain. He strokes the frame with the same tenderness he'd show a wounded animal.

"What do you think?"

"Very good. Surprises not often so nice. Thank you, Peter. I have no ridden bike twenty years. Very good for moving."

"I'm pleased, because I have a proposition for you. Are you up to taking a look around Kudzu Gardens? If you can keep up with me."

"Kudzu? I saw born ... Kudzu grow fast. Kudzu change everything."

"Let's go, then. How long is it since you last came away from here?"

"I don't know, Peter... I'd like to. Only must work. My time end soon."

Ion's hands are swollen and distended like all the damned of the dump. I only have one hand, and in a few years it, too, will look like his.

"What are you working on?"

"Old plan, a dream maybe I can't make true. Bastards at Reverse throw me in trash when they don't need me anymore."

I know what he means; he's explained it before. Ion was once an engineer of 'molecular positioning technology,' until one day a group of inspectors inserted a plate into his temporal lobes, extracted the contents of his memory, and fired him on the spot. The official report cited mental health problems, though he says it was a set-up.

"I had nearly got it ... I was close to result."

The discouragement in his eyes borders on depression. I know how he feels, living with shattered dreams, the shards of an awareness that those dreams will never come true. He and I are sailing in the same direction, on opposite sides of the same river.

"All right, no Kudzu. Is there anything else I can do for you?"

"One thing there is, Peter... risky, though. You must enter protected place. You might be right person."

"Fire away. With the Tantalium and the Podox, I can even steal from a UCU."

In reality, this has only happened twice. The first time was a long time ago when the UCUs weren't as advanced. I don't want to talk about it; I don't even like thinking about it. The second time, I got into a fight with a unit over a solar jacket bearing the red and yellow logo of NASA on its breast.

Ion knows the pieces of threaded metal that protrude from my flesh to join me to my prosthetic limbs well. It was he who grafted them onto my stumps, one halfway along my forearm, between the wrist and elbow, the other just above my knee.

Lifting his eyes, Ion reads the time in the darkness of the sky and opens a tin of gelatinous meat and beans. He tips the pre-cooked contents onto two indifferently clean tin plates.

"I'm sure Reverse kept designs. Good of them to let me remember *me* at least..."

"Are you asking me to snoop around in your section's archives?"

"Yes, easy for you. But be careful; controlled area. Really controlled."

He passes me a fork to try the mess on the plate. As he chews, his jaw clicks in and out of place: *uck, uck, uck.*

My thoughts go to Ion's library, buried in an underground bunker, where he hides himself away when the weather turns vengeful. When the weather is at its worst, he sometimes disappears for days on end. He studies and reads, reads and studies, trying to catch up with himself.

"I can go to Charlie's office is in the central tower. If I can invent a reason to go see him."

I'm hesitant to swallow the mess on my plate. The thought of eating tinned food without even enjoying it, just to expel it hours later, obliterates my meagre appetite. My organism is not just dehydrated due to the difficulty in finding drinkable water; it is frequently further dried out by visiting bacteria.

See Staphylococcus aureus.

See also Escherichia coli.

See also Vibrio cholerae.

See also Entamoeba histolytica, Rotavirus, Adenovirus, and Shigella, just to mention the ones Ion has told me about.

Ion claims biology is turning against humanity. My intestines agree with him—it's not simply a notion of his deranged imagination.

I fork up a lump and swallow it quickly.

"It's disgusting, I know. Look well at food, look at rubbery pasta flavour worms plus aroma, read instructions how it's made. For me, it all comes from big industry, or factories, all the same. Food sent along underground tubes to restaurants, bars, and supermarkets, only have to turn on a tap, pull a lever. Food on tap. There's no other way. It's all disgusting."

He laughs with his mouth open. His huge Adam's apple goes up and down every time he swallows.

"I've got something to ask you, too. It's a little embarrassing," I say.

Under the skin of my cheeks, hundreds of blood vessels dilate in mortification, turning my face bright red. My temperature goes up a couple of degrees.

"All right, but wait. I have to go before..."

He doesn't have time to finish his sentence before he runs to the cubicle where he has installed a chemical toilet.

I count to five and hear the effort of overcoming constipation, then an awful noise, only bearable because this time it is not being made by my body. While I wait for him to finish, I study the holograph, marked with dots forming a path through rooms, corridors and emergency exits.

Ion has worked out my route through the Reverse complex.

For a moment, I think that Charlie might know a way of sneaking me into Ion's old section, but then I remember that, when there's nothing in it for him, Charlie's attitude towards helping me falls somewhere between indifference and irritation.

We rarely see each other except at shift changeover, or when there are problems at work—if you don't count the times he has 'invited' me to lunch with the other team leaders. I'm not concerned about spending a lot of time with Charlie.

Every now and then, he shows up and visits Cleo and me, when festivities compel him to fulfil his filial obligations. He detests this so much that he spends more of his time in the basement than with us. I'm happy he's not around all the time, but it's hard on Cleo.

When he comes back from the can, Ion flashes his best grin, apologising for the interruption. I lay my request for help before him.

"Listen, do you remember that head from all those years ago? The one I was carrying when we met here at the dump?"

"The head? Yes, it was nexhuman."

"Exactly. The Dead Bones murdered her and then sold the parts to Junkland."

I abandon the meat on the plate to its own fate.

"Bad story. Don't tell me, your brother, he keep head in house all this time."

"Well, really, it wasn't him..."

If he had been my father, I expect Ion would have looked on this with more severity and disappointment. Ion, though, shows a certain amount of understanding as he swallows another forkload, spilling some down his shirt.

"You in love, yes?"

"Her name's Alba, and I want to rebuild her. I wanted to know... if I find all the pieces, can you put them back together?"

He looks at me, surprise at the absurdity of my request written on his face. With his fork suspended mid-way to his mouth, he looks wrong-footed. An uncomfortable silence descends on us.

I know that life is a dark experience we spend our lives trying to give meaning to, a puzzle without instructions we have to solve as fast as possible. It's not so different from love—but, at twenty, what do I know about love? I have been in love with a dead head for the last five years.

Ion fishes a dried lemon rind out of a pocket and starts chewing on it, jaw clicking.

"I was engineer before... erasure. I can help. Once, when I was young man, colleague convinced me to cut off monkey head... put on another body. Twenty operations to connect veins and nerves. Then, when electricity applied, monkey lived for a moment, just time to bite my nose before it die."

I swallow drily as Ion taps his temple with a gelatine-smeared finger.

"Memories still in here. In time, with books in bunker, I get it back; but I guarantee nothing... might take years."

The prospect gives me a scrap of hope that—for the moment—is enough. After so much time, Alba's original parts could be impossible to find; they might even have been destroyed.

"It's important to me. Yesterday, I found one of her pieces. It was in a van on its way from Lazar to Raon. I lost it in the tunnel."

"Peter, my task, difficult—yours: pure folly. After so long, you still think about that head?"

I lower my eyes and fall into silence. Is there an expiry date for love? Is there a deadline beyond which sentiments are no longer worth anything? How long does it take for love to become a secondhand emotion? Three years? Five? Ten?

There is something about Alba, an indefinable strength that draws me to her. Perhaps because she is never in a hurry, or because I can tell her about anything, it doesn't really matter. She accepts me just the way I am.

I pick up my fork again, fiddle with some of the meat on my plate, piling it into abstract mounds.

Ion must understand what is driving me. He, too, has been forced to grab hold of a lifeline, however bizarre, to avoid ending up as kipple himself.

"It really make you happy?"

My eyes light up. It is the first time that anyone has ever asked me a question like that, a question that assumes that I am capable of happiness.

"Ever since I was fifteen, Alba has been the only person to make me count the minutes until I could see her again. Every day for two years, I walked passed Boreal Skies. For an hour a day, I spied on her from Kathal Hill. Even now, when I talk to her in secret, I keep her hidden in my wardrobe and keep her existence hidden from everyone else. If I look at her for too long, I lose my sense of time. When I talk to her, I feel better. I'm not sick, Ion, I swear I'm not."

He spits out a piece of gristle and it lands on the tin plate. He nods as if what I'm saying is nothing new.

"I believe you, Peter. From how you talk, though, this Alba seems more cure for unhappiness than way to happiness. How much time and energy have you thrown into feeling less bad, to feel less miserable? But, if anyone is good at recognising value, it is he who has none. This is definite."

When Ion talks like this, I can't follow him. It's my fault, too, though I can't expect to throw the pieces of my absurd story at him as though all of this were normal.

"I hear your words, they are sincere. I remember at school when I was innocent. Passions burned without fire... Like temporal jump, when you are so immersed in one thing, so obsessed with an idea, that a moment or an eternity might have passed, and you couldn't say which. When you click back, everything different, time has happened and you were there, wherever *there* is. I understand it can be a shock... Philosophers call it *eudaimonia*."

"Ion, what has school got to do with it? I'm talking about love, not science fiction or philosophy."

"It has everything to do with it. When you are in *eudemonia* time stands still and you feel whole. Consciousness stops and you run in time with interior music."

Sometimes, it feels like Ion mistakes me for his own personal information dump. I understand how hard it is for him to put his thoughts in the right context, and fuck knows how much brain the company's invasion left him with. Still, his stories have the power to impress with the power of transforming information left lying around into useful data.

Though I am not sure I have grasped the concept, I carry on listening. In the midst of the stench of Kathal Hill, his pale lips start chronicling nostalgia.

"I warn you, Peter, you're not in true *eudaimonia*. For the ancient Greeks, there are three types of happiness and you have experienced only the lowliest: happiness of pleasure and repetition. There are lots of things like this: drink, sex, luxury and other exterior facets. This you feel for Alba."

Ion is wrong, though. That might have been what I felt five years ago. The whole thing is more complex, now. I don't know how to explain it.

"Second happiness is called 'good life.' Not crude sentiments or arousal. Good life is putting down roots for growing, learning types of strength and use in life, in love, work, friendship, and family. For philosophers, he who uses principles is visited by demon—good demon—who donates happiness and satisfaction."

The pain and solemnity in Ion's catarrh-thickened voice inflame me.

"What? Are you saying that if I manage to rebuild Alba, a demon will appear and make me happy?"

Ion finishes eating and throws the few remaining pieces of meat to Mr Stinky, who grunts in gratitude. Then he takes a brush from a side table and moves over to his pet, to give its wiry coat a good grooming. The animal wriggles all over, snorting with piggish pleasure.

"Yes, more or less. Demon-like force, judging actions done in his name and weighing up sacrificial offerings. This is why only passive happiness comes from senses. Bring Alba back to life is gesture of love and Demon is child of Absence, because it does not have what it wants, and through Wit, uses whatever method it takes to get close to what it loves."

This I thought, I understood: owning was not as good as desiring; desiring to bring something to completion. Excitement surges in my stomach.

The world I live in is made this way, suspended between the unreality of the gamesphere, the necrosis of the dump, and the sinister air of the wardrobe, where Alba lies. I bite my nails and rip the cuticle, making it bleed. Ion brings me back to earth.

"Third kind of happiness is quest for meaning, being part of something bigger and more important than ourselves. Biggest experience you part of, most happiness you will ever have. Raising children, planning the future for humanity are meaningful things, saving whales, same thing; also kamikaze, dying for greater end, or firemen saving lives are meaningful things."

I don't know these kinds of happiness: I've never seen a whale, except in the gamesphere, I don't feel ready for self-sacrifice, and above all—something I am almost sure about—Alba will never give me children.

"Have you ever wondered how happiness is measured, Peter?"

I blink. Measuring happiness sounds like a contradiction to me, but hiding somewhere in his memory, Ion must have come across an amazing concept for him to make such a claim.

"Not really, no. I'm twenty; you're always forgetting that."

"Age doesn't mean you can't ask questions. Quantity of gratitude is combined with levels of happiness. The less gratitude you express, the more happiness you feel. Interesting concept, yes?"

I agree and look around. Mr Stinky is still rooting about nearby. He tests the air with his grubby snout. The chain that keeps him a pet pulls tight, allowing him to reach a puddle of tarry water.

Quite often in the afternoon, the horizon lightens a little, but then it darkens the puddles scattered across the ground. The darkness above us is, after so many illuminating words, has become clear, almost limpid. I don't want to exaggerate the sense of what I have taken in, I need to think about it.

"You've given me a lot to think about Ion. I won't get bored cycling home."

He gets up and disappears inside his hut. When he reappears, he's holding a buff envelope. He hands it to me and I look inside to see a disc and a page covered in handwriting. I see *AquaSan, Atmospheric pollen*, and *Heliotropic tree*.

"Take this, look at plans before acting. Tell me if you need more."

I reseal the envelope, say goodbye to Ion, and heaving the bike over my shoulder, head back down Kathal Hill.

I can't keep my news to myself. I am safe in my room. Cleo is sleeping. Charlie has been living with Jo, a girl from Durenico, for the past two years. He met her during one of the Dead Bones' out-of-neighbourhood excursions.

Only the wardrobe door separates me from Alba. If you don't aim high with your desires, they are easier to fulfil.

I pull her out of her hideaway and place her on top of the mannequin. Alba is so pale that the freckles stand out on her cheeks. Her face has the fraught look of a sacrificial virgin, but her flaming hair still lights a storm of hope within me.

I wonder if seeing how I live first-hand has disturbed her a little.

"I've got wonderful news for you."

Her milky paleness is the same as on her last night alive. Her eyes are as bright and intact as ever.

"Ion and I are going to rebuild you. First, I have to find all your pieces and then he will put you back together. Then we can go on holiday, on one of the tours you used to sell, like Guangxi, Belize or Cappadocia. We will fly to the ends of the earth; we will rest in the flickering shadows cast by an African bonfire; we will watch as twilight falls over the Mongolian Steppe; we will have the excitement of a destination, the joy of arriving, and the vapour trails in the sky will show us the way."

I blush. I can't dissipate my internal heat when she is in front of me. Even the contrast between the beauty before my eyes and the horror that Alba has had to bear isn't so intrusive as to scare me. Will we be able to continue like this? Will the horror surface, blinding me to what I know I have to do? It hasn't, yet; I wonder whether it will in the future.

I take her face in my hands.

"The past isn't dead. For me, it's not even in the past. I just wanted you to know that."

The gamesphere's LED blinks on. The memo-agent on my visor is reminding me I have an appointment:

Incoming match request

Kiko wants to carry on with our adventure, where we left off last time.

"Wait a minute, Alba. I'll tell her I'm busy—I'll be right back."

Kiko and I are engaged—just not in real life. We have been in a simulated relationship since I was eighteen and she was seventeen; multiplayer games are more intricate than single-player ones. Non-individual choices create suspense, they generate expectations, and the trust you place in your game companion to complete a mission is an unending source of disappointment and betrayal—and also unexpected successes—all within the space of a game.

In DREAMED LIVES, we were two singers who hated each other at first sight and then fell in love and became a steady couple. We broke the box office records of half the (virtual) planet with our tear-jerking duets.

In LIVE AND LET LIVE, we had to defend our love against thousands of dangers: powerful parents who were set against our union, jealous ex-lovers, envious friends, threats of being fired, attacks by the press, retaliation, spurious lies, and all sorts of other provocations.

We finished the game in two weeks without ever shutting an eye.

I slip into the vortex of the dataverse, keeping one eye on

my surroundings in the real world. The transparent layers of data gently dissolve.

I open Kiko's channel and see her avatar waiting, visibly annoyed.

"What's the matter, today? Did you oversleep?"

"No, but I don't have time now. How about tomorrow?"

"Maybe *I* won't have time tomorrow."

When she's this persistent, she makes me want to change teams, but Kiko is very good at making quick decisions and that's a valuable gift when you find yourself fighting hundreds of enemies, unravelling enigmas, and working out how to get your arse out of an ambush. Even now, her cutting retorts hustle me along, giving me no time for thought.

"Another time."

"When, Peter?"

"When we both have time."

"We have to finish the mission in Bolivia, or have you forgotten?"

In EXTREME JOURNEYS, we were on an expedition to recover some archaeological artefacts stolen from the Tiahuanaco tomb in Bolivia, but a moustachioed man wearing the *Guardia Civil* uniform at the border station between Peru and Bolivia 'forgot' to stamp our passports, and then on our way out, the same official suddenly claimed we'd entered the country illegally. It's a common trick used by small-time officials to bully travellers and pad out their salaries.

When we last paused the game, we were stuck in the middle of nowhere, in a place where they don't accept Ks, with the *bureau de change* about to close and an interminable queue of peasants and lorry drivers snaking down the street.

It seems the local guide, a *chico* with a little *Uros* blood, might help us, though he has made it clear he's going to want payment too. Kiko and I don't have any money. So, because of my gullibility, we now find ourselves at the mercy of a load of jackals.

I had paused the game because I'd been overtaken by panic.

"Who could forget the border? But I haven't come up with anything."

"I have."

"Okay, but... I can't right now, Kiko."

Her avatar grimaces, knowing that the team's reliability ranking is of fundamental importance. In the dump, the odds of being double-crossed are high, but in the gamesphere, where relationships are based on reciprocal trust and the associated credibility ratings, it isn't the same. If our ranking falls, we risk compromising our team's unity and becoming easy prey for the enemy.

"Are you sure you don't have an open channel with someone else?"

"What an imagination you have, Kiko. I'm not plotting anything behind your back."

My avatar pretends not to get it. I feel a rush of gratitude for this nearly obsolete third-hand software that can't transmit some of the more subtle emotions as clearly as it should.

"I won't forget this. Next time *you* need me..."

Kiko snaps the connection closed, leaving me looking at a sphere of pixels that gurgles and trills before disappearing.

If we lived in the same block of flats, she would already be pounding on my door with a knife between her teeth. I know that grimace: it's the same she wore when she slit the throat of the lorry driver in Iraq, who wanted to steal our documents. The same one she had on her face when she threatened the boatman in Mekong to make him take us back to shore after he tried to extort money from us by pretending to have broken down.

I hear a commotion in the hallway. It can't be Cleo—she usually sleeps ten hours straight with the help of sedatives. A few moments later, my worst suspicions come true. The front door is five metres from the door of my room. Those heavy footsteps can only belong to Charlie; my brother is paying me a surprise visit. The clink of glass bottles announces his appearance at my door.

Why *now*? Why *me*?

He pokes his head into my room and grins stupidly from ear to ear, holding a pair of beers.

"Eh, Skinnyribs, fancy a drink?"

I poke my head out of the gamesphere. We're a metre apart, both of us stretching our necks, facing each other, but Charlie's eyes are not on me.

He is immobile, frozen. He and Alba haven't seen each other for years, and that last meeting was no pleasure at all.

I curse Kiko.

I curse Charlie.

Then I curse myself.

"What the *fuck* is that head doing in my house?"

I don't know what story to feed him. Every angle I think of is full of pitfalls. Every excuse is transparent crap. My face is flushing, but I try to feign confidence in my words, even though I know I'm a terrible liar.

"You mean in *our* house. You don't live here anymore, big brother..."

I force myself to smile.

"...and you only come when you feel like surprising us. Like now."

His forehead is furrowed in confusion.

"It doesn't matter where I live. I asked you a question."

If Kiko were online, she'd know how to get out of this. It only took me thirty seconds to get myself in trouble.

She's right; I am a prick.

Still, in real life, it's worth remembering that Kiko might not even exist. That little round face with oriental eyes might be a front for an Artificial Intelligence, or a fat boy with a fixation, or maybe a bored housewife, fed up with cleaning and cooking, looking for adventure.

Whatever—my brother wants an answer. And so do I.

Sweat is dripping off me. Damp patches are spreading under my armpits. I don't know where to look. I suspect the flush of my initial surprise will soon be replaced by a dull, ashen pallor.

It's not embarrassment, but panic, an alarm bell.

"I get it... You went back to find the head. This explains a lot."

Good. I have no intention of adding anything else. Charlie takes a step into the room, moving closer to Alba. He scrutinises her more closely, then spits out his verdict.

"I told you this stuff brings bad luck. You can't keep a head in the house. And you ... you've been lying to me and Cleo all this time."

Charlie's place in the sentence is deliberate. He is convinced that as the eldest son, it is his job to take on the role of our shared, but absent, parent.

"Cleo can't work or leave the house. She's stuck in here like a hostage... I've been expecting a promotion for months... I won't get any of what I'm entitled to and this is why. It's all that head's fault!"

If my mother wakes up, the whole situation will degenerate fast. The thought of talking about this in a full family meeting terrifies me.

"That's not true; Mum's illness has nothing to do with this head. What an idea... and I *do* look after her. We've even recorded some memories for when she isn't here anymore.

We've recorded lots of things from the past. All you do is send us Ks that in the end, we don't even need..."

"Ah, you don't need it? Are you sure about that? Shall we ask her?"

Not much has changed in all these years. Charlie's intelligence hasn't been improved by bureaucratic cultivation. At twenty-four, he still reasons like the leader of a teenage gang.

"There's no need to wake her. Let her sleep."

I will him to drop the argument, but he won't let it go.

"You've got to throw it away, Peter. You can't mess about with these things. Don't you remember Todd?"

Todd 'Scum' Morkan, leader of the Beating Beetles, was Charlie's biggest enemy during his adolescence—until the day he disappeared.

"He did this, too. He liked keeping heads in his front room as hunting trophies. He began to attract lightning. During thunderstorms, you wouldn't want to stand within ten metres of him. His house became the focal point of a vortex of electrical discharges, and when the idiot went up on the roof to put up a lightning rod, as you can imagine, his arse got hit by a streak of lightning, he slipped, fell off the roof and broke his neck. After that, he got rid of the heads in his front room, but he's stuck in a wheelchair and watches the weather from behind a window. That's why Todd left the band and Yerson took over. He told me all about it a few years ago."

"Am I supposed to believe that?"

"Shit, man. Listen to *this* then. You know Rafail Ciconi, who works in Junkland? Well, one time they left him a head in a box in the storeroom. Whether it was a joke or an accident, no one knows. Whatever—when he got home, his son Chip was in hospital because he had gouged his eye out knocking into a fence, his daughter Laura was admitted to hospital with food poisoning, and that same evening, his wife tripped at home, fell and fractured her kneecap in three places. She'll never walk properly again. The people who left the box didn't get off as lightly as Rafail. Like I said, you mustn't underestimate certain forces."

I try hard to turn the situation around.

"So the leader of the Dead Bones is scared of a head?"

"Careful. Don't piss me off, Skinnyribs. That's not just a head; that's a head that has been *dead* for five years. It's a fucking skull in the closet. A decrepit piece of kipple you hid away like a thief. A dead rat would be better... So, stop spouting shit and get rid of it."

His attitude fills me with anguish. The words 'get rid of it' evokes an end I had not considered, an end that is tantamount to putting a noose around my own neck.

"Or do I have to deal with it?" he asks.

Put like that... my choice is clear.

"No. No, I'll do it."

I walk over to the mannequin and start taking Alba's head off its neck.

Our raised voices have woken my mother from her slumber.

"What's the matter, boys? You're not arguing, are you?" Her voice is sleepy.

Charlie reverts to the role of mature, responsible elder brother. He lowers his voice and turns on the sugary charm.

"No, Mum, everything's fine. Go on back to sleep."

I put Alba back in the wardrobe and lock the door.

"I won't tell her anything, but only because I don't want to break her heart. You might think you're looking after her, but you've no fucking idea..."

His hypocrisy is more disgusting than an attack of diarrhoea. Charlie clinks the bottles together and then threatens me.

"I'll come and check up on you when you're least expecting me. Don't think you're going to get off the hook with that pathetic excuse for a promise."

With that, he goes into the kitchen and drains both beers himself, while Cleo, oblivious to the whole episode, falls back into her deep narcotic sleep. Quiet returns, but the quiet after the storm is never authentic.

A warning like this makes it of pressing importance for me to re-examine the security measures protecting Alba. If Charlie could be appeased by just knowing she is no longer in the house, all I would need to do is take her somewhere else; but if he wants proof of her destruction, then I'll have to come up with something to convince him of my word.

Could I find another head like Alba's?

Dare I show my brother a burned lump and pretend it's her?

How much time do I have to disinfest the house and liberate it of this jinx?

The next morning, I put Alba in a holdall and I set off for Kathal Hill, determined to find an answer to my problem.

On Lucite Street, I bump into Rasha, begging. He has invented a pitiful trick for extracting a few Ks from passers-by. He motions me to wait to one side and not interrupt him. I watch him as, sweaty-faced and appearing upset, he works on the sympathy of a seemingly well-to-do old lady.

"Excuse me, do you know where the nearest chemist is?"

"Just a moment, son, let me think, there should be..."

Rasha plunges in, unfolding his drama.

"Quickly, ma'am, please, I have to find some medicine for my sick little brother."

"Well... It's that way, after the Earthsalvage sign."

"He's been so ill for three days, he keeps vomiting and cries, he cries without ever stopping."

"I'm so sorry, what about your parents?"

"They're not here anymore. I mean, my mum is but I don't know where. My dad, on the other hand, ran away from us. The medicine is expensive, ma'am, it costs two Ks."

The old lady falls for it and fishes something out of her bag.

"Listen, dear, I've only got this with me, but take a K. I hope your little brother gets better soon."

"Thank you so much, ma'am. I can tell him there are still some good people left in Kathal Hill."

Then Rasha runs for it and pulls me by my arm to the corner of Lucite Street.

All day long, I can feel Charlie breathing down my neck; it's more irritating than kipple in your trousers. I live in terror of some kind of retaliation and just concentrate on my work.

I find a bottle with seed oil inside, a nearly-new tyre for my bike (it's a bit small and will need enlarging), and an old vinyl record in its cardboard sleeve. The picture on the front cover is of a prism refracting a beam of white light into all the colours of the rainbow.

Then my fingertips brush against a human skull. I consult the net: a comparison with some photos and the data in a number of tables tell me that over the last twenty thousand years that skull has not changed much; it's remarkably similar to that of the Neanderthal.

I toss it up in the air and catch it on the way down, testing its weight. The same skull, unaltered for such a long time... The development of human intelligence has reached a plateau, while artificial intelligence, flowing through circuits and processors, is growing exponentially, constantly. I drop the skull and it tumbles down the slope.

Rasha, Norbert, Duggan, and Pongo all call to me at the same time. Gesticulating, they let me know they want to show me something they have found under a pile of newspapers, something wrapped in rags.

"Hold your nose."

The smell forces us to put on our masks. The police logo has almost completely faded from the body bag containing a dead bag lady. One of those who didn't make it through winter.

Rasha wants to burn it instantly.

"It's not that I *want* to burn it... You know I can keep myself under control with fire. It's just there are diseases waiting to jump out from under there."

On top of that, his Hindu origins require him to cremate the body, so that the five elements it is composed of can return where they came from: air, water, earth, and fire to the earthly world, and ether to the spiritual world.

"Maybe you're right," I mutter.

Having seen the body, and smelled the beginnings of putrefaction, I concur with Rasha.

"It must have been here for a while... Those maggots are at least an inch long."

Clouds of unstoppable flies buzz around above it.

"At least let's cover it with something."

Duggan pulls a tarpaulin out of his pack and throws it in front of us, scaring away the swarm. This will stop the insects—always on the prowl for fluids to feed on and holes to lay their eggs in—from flying into our eyes, nostrils, ears, and mouths.

Today's team leader, a scab with a holographic clipboard, calls an ambulance. It takes twenty minutes to get to us, during which time the corpse is relieved of its now-worthless belongings. Once they get up the hill, the paramedics kick up a fuss because, without valid insurance, they are not obliged to take the body away. The old woman doesn't even have documents, let alone health or burial insurance.

The team leader pulls Ks out of his own pocket to get it off the site and us back to work.

He closes the episode with a laugh.

"I'll get this back on expenses from Reverse."

No one else laughs with him. Nobody else can claim 'expenses'.

From the way they load the body into the ambulance, I'm almost tempted to follow them to steal the head. I'm pretty sure they'll toss it back in the dump as soon as they are around the first corner. Then I have a better idea. If you die in hospital, your body is taken to the morgue—a place where no one gives a shit and no one wants to know what happens; a place where dead bodies stay until they are identified and undergo autopsies, before ending up cremated or buried in mass graves in Mundur Cemetery.

At the end of my shift, I get on my bike and pedal over to the local morgue—the one on Venison Avenue—to look for a substitute for Alba's head.

I'm not afraid of seeing dead bodies, nor am I scared of the morgue. The building is clean and surrounded by slim trees, a species that I have never seen before.

A defective flashing arrow is pointing the way to the basement. A shadowy ramp leads down to an anonymous entrance, no sign. I push open the door and find myself looking down a seemingly endless corridor. My first instinct is to use my visor to check the map; establish where the emergency exits are. In the booth, the porter raises his bored gaze from a crossword puzzle.

"What are you here for?"

His first question has me stumped. I prevaricate, unable to tell him the truth. I look around the corridor, hunting for an excuse, and spot some flyers on the wall proclaiming the benefits of cremation, advertising grief support groups, offering discounted coffins and the services of professionals who will serve death notices and contact people connected to the dead.

"It's a private matter. Could I speak to the psychologist?"

He laughed awkwardly. This can't happen to him often.

"The psychologist? There are only dead people here. You have to bring your own psychologist."

At this, I decide to pretend I am here for a legitimate reason.

"I have to identify a body."

His expression changes and he blurts out a rehearsed response.

"At the end of the corridor, turn right and go through the plastic curtains. Then ask the orderlies."

Before starting off down the tunnel, which must be more than a kilometre long, I put the holdall with Alba's head in it in a locker and turn the key in the lock.

The barren atmosphere of the basement makes an icy contrast to the outside of the building, with its fancy windows and repainted colours. The signs that appear on the walls as I walk along the corridor mark mortician chambers, cold storage cells, and autopsy rooms.

At the end of the corridor, I push aside a waxed curtain with black stripes and enter a room that oozes with death. On the shelves, orderly rows of jars contain embalmed internal organs. There are a number of cement beds, and just beyond I can see some zinc-lined coffins, still unsealed.

There are two undertakers, one dozing with a baseball cap pulled down over his eyes, the other on duty at a neat desk. It's hands-in-pockets cold and my breath is condensing in little grey clouds.

"The porter said to come to you."

This time, I'm leading the conversation or at least that scrap of story I've come up with so far. The undertaker has a horsey face with two dangling strips of flesh for ears and the absent look of someone who is desperate to escape from his present.

My tongue cleaves to the roof of my mouth.

"I'm looking for my sister... She disappeared a week ago and I wanted to ask if... Has she turned up here?"

"Have you looked in the hospital? You have to go there first when you're looking for someone." He blows through his nose and doesn't bother to hide his annoyance at having to talk to me.

"My sister was in a bad way. She was living on the streets. She didn't have insurance."

There's a disturbing smell of methanol in the air. He shakes his head.

"She's not the only one... Name and surname?"

This is where the problems begin.

"Tara Lowandowski, but I don't think she wanted people to know. She hasn't had ID for years."

Irritated, Horse Face pushes away the register. There's no malice in this, just indolence.

"Listen, lad, what do you want from me? I can't exactly give you a guided tour of the morgue."

I should be so lucky; that's more or less the service I need. I try to keep my nerves steady.

"Of course, but how many girls under twenty-five with dark hair and green eyes have you got lying around here?"

He throws himself back in his chair and turns to his colleague.

"Eh, Mickey, listen to this guy... He says he's *lost his sister*. Can you help him? My shift's nearly finished."

The other bloke lifts his visor and I nearly jump out of my skin.

"His 'sister', eh?"

First, he glowers at me and then inhales, pondering. If he wanted to, he could give me away. Instead, he walks over to me. He puts an arm around my shoulders and takes me behind the desk.

I can't believe it. It's Mickey the 'Mucous' from my brother's old gang. Named for the abundance of his secretions and his awful habit of cleaning his nose on anything that came to hand. I can't believe it. His attitude is ambiguous; he is behaving like my accomplice. Does he even remember me?

"Of course, I can. Leave it to me, Georgie Boy."

Georgie Boy nods and tidies his desk before leaving. Mickey turns me around and leads me into the cold room.

"All right, then, what do you want this sister to be like?" the Mucous asked.

It occurs to me that he might, in fact, have figured me out and is being ironic on purpose. We walk a little and he shows me a few bodies lifted from their coffins.

"The ones on the tables are almost *warm*," he says, lifting the sheet off the nearest one. "Fresh in yesterday afternoon. We only put them in the liquid for a little bit, just enough to stop them shrivelling too soon. They're a bit swollen, but what can you do, we have keep them *in shape*. Look, there's not the least sign of rigor mortis. I'm the one who cuts their tendons. I tie up every member and block the other orifices to keep things clean. With suicides like this one, I'm careful about sewing up their wrists; it's a delicate job. They taught me at the cemetery."

I am astonished. After the Dead Bones days, Mickey found a specialisation.

"They teach you this kind of stuff at the cemetery?"

"Well, obviously not in Mundur, but in the old one in North Lobony, at Koyn Dva. It's more to make them presentable for their relatives than anything else. Burial and all that. Only for those that can afford it though. Believe me, no one manages *not* to look at the departed, even the hard men and those who think they can be indifferent."

Mickey pushes his fringe out of his eyes. He hasn't changed at all: the same pointed teeth and predatory hands. Only his fringe is a little greyer, his posture a little slacker.

"Sorry about the eyes. I don't usually remove them. Lots of us like them better than those metal ones; they're really disgusting. I leave their mouths open so you can do what you like. I just ask that you replace the plug when you've finished. It's a precaution, to keep the tissues elastic. Believe me, these are all *tried* and *tested*."

He sniggers and then lifts another sheet to show me a man of about fifty, greying, thick hair on his chest, his stomach cut open from side to side. Next to him, under another sheet, lies a little girl with red hair. She has been put back together clumsily and her small arms have been folded in an unnatural position over her chest. Her pathetic body is covered with so many grazes and bruises that she looks like a trampled lawn.

I force myself not to vomit.

"Thanks, Mickey, but I'm looking for a girl of about twenty-three, with dark hair and green eyes."

"There was one a bit like that, she was almost thirty, but we moved her over to Lobony. They only stay with us for as long as it takes to find someone to cremate them. Four or five days at most. It's what I used to do, but I've been promoted. You can't imagine how cold it is down there, when you slip into one of those dead bodies..."

We stroll on down the corridor. The smell of formaldehyde hits my nostrils.

"The meat in here is warmer."

While Mickey lifts the lids off other coffins, I feel an overwhelming need to breathe, to take a break from this desperation of swollen, burned, rotten, sawed, gnawed, mummified and dismembered bodies. There are so many bodies that they're not removed as quickly as they should be. It looks like some will never leave this place. A few, mostly elderly, are skeletal, reduced to piles of bones, fleshless and bare.

Flesh vanishes during putrefaction, erasing wounds, but the bones remain and, even if they heal, they never forget: on a battered skull, I can see the marks of a childhood fall; cracked ribs from a bar fight; another shorter body's femurs bear lots of tiny fractures left by a car accident.

Bones capture these moments. They map out pain.

"Sorry, Mickey, is there a bathroom? Y'know, the water plays bad tricks..."

"There, on the right. Then we'll carry on with our tour."

I have to calm myself down. In the mirror my eyes are dripping with disgust. The smell of decomposing flesh is as unbearable as a dagger thrust up my nostrils. It sits so heavily in the air that I'm not sure I can continue.

Compared to this place, the dump emanates perfume.

Bent over the edge of the toilet, I reckon that in this state, comatose with flashes of pitiful lucidity, it would be easier for me to tell Mickey what my intentions are, but I have no idea how to reveal myself to him.

I leave the bathroom after drying my eyes and find Mickey with his fingers in his ears. He rolls up the wax he has dug out and leaves it to harden on the cold tiles. Mickey Mucous hasn't lost that revolting habit either.

"You know, *Peter*, I've been thinking. Last week, a blonde with those characteristics was brought in. If you're not too picky, she could do for you. What do you say?"

This is the first time he has used my name and I am frozen, ready to empty myself again. After this, I'll be able to put another notch on my own personal wall of the horrific.

"Let me take a look."

From a wall full of numbered cells, Mickey pulls out a metal drawer and opens it up. The contents are pretty, but nothing special compared to Alba. However, the girl, or rather her head, is an excellent candidate for fooling Charlie.

"Pretty, right? Pity about the tits, a B-cup at most—too small for my taste."

I agree with Mickey on this; a bosom should be abundant.

Mickey puts on a pair of sterile gloves, and then another pair before washing the body. He dips some balls of cotton wool in insecticide, stuffs them in the girl's ears and nose to stop any insects laying eggs, and wipes wax over her lips to stop them cracking. I bet it's not real wax, but I quickly banish the thought. He rolls her over and dilates her anus with his fingers to let out the trapped gasses.

"Mickey, do you think hair dye will work on her?"

He looks perplexed, as if the question is absurd. He looks at me more carefully to make sure that I am me, the same kid he knew five years ago.

"Well listen to you? I'm offering a piece of still-warm totty and you complain about the colour of her hair?"

"Sorry, I'm... I'm just particular about certain details."

He whips his hand across his forehead.

"I don't know. We could ask Georgie Boy, he's been here for twenty years. He must have come across something like it."

Twenty years. Enough time to screw an entire generation of corpses. How many people have they violated after death? A bit like kipple with rubbish: where energy gives up, kipple reaches out.

"Never mind, I was just wondering. I'd like her to remind me of a person I once knew."

That was a mistake. Mickey was *there* that night; he took away Alba's torso.

"Who would that be, then? When you were in the Bones, I never noticed you had the hots for anyone."

I look down and swallow. I might not be anything special, but compared to Mickey, I'm a genius.

"Exactly. You don't know her; I met her later."

Now comes the hard part. Even if he leaves me alone with the corpse, how am I going to cut off the head and take it away without anyone knowing?

"Look, sorry about my ignorance but how do you usually..."

At least, this time, being Charlie's brother has some use. Mickey is indulging me. I'm the relative of a friend, after all.

"I'll take the body into the autopsy room. If there aren't any special requests, the visit with the *lost sister* lasts for thirty minutes. Seeing as it's you, I can let you have an extra fifteen minutes."

He winks at me and I suddenly realise that, back in the reception room, I accidentally stumbled on the secret code words of a band of necrophiles: I was looking for my lost sister. Suddenly another question starts buzzing around in my head.

"While we're here, I wanted to ask you another thing... There's this bloke in Kathal Hill with a weird fixation. Do you ever get nexhumans in here? Even old ones?"

"Nexhumans? Nah, they get taken to Junkland. Those smooth types can get a tidy pile of Ks." Mickey raises his eyebrows and stops. He's just realised something. "You're not telling me everything, are you, Peter? First you describe a girl, then you ask about nexhumans. I reckon I've got your number: you're looking for that one from Boreal Skies. Am I right?"

Here it comes. The blood drains from my face and I turn the colour that seems most popular around here. I've just run the risk of ruining everything that I've managed to get out of him.

He wipes his nose on the corner of the sheet, blowing out a long, wet, and clearly satisfying trail of snot. "I remember her, all right. That nexy was so hot we didn't sell her."

The news hits me like a sledgehammer. I have to lean against the trolley to stay upright. I blink rapidly, my pulse beating hard in my temples. Talk, Mickey; please don't stop now.

"What, d'you mean you didn't go and get drunk? Charlie told me you used it to get blasted..."

Mickey is the kind of bloke who needs only a little encouragement to willingly spill his guts. With an openness that Mickey mistakes for innocence, I persuade him to tell me what I didn't see that night.

"That's what usually happened, but not that time. We were close to the shop when Loins threw a fit—you know what he was like. He insisted that he had to screw, right then, right there. If he knew where I work now, he'd never leave me alone, he'd be around all the time..."

Mickey sneezes once, twice, three times. I protect my face with my arm.

"As I was saying, Jimmy was being really heavy. He wanted us to find him a hole at any cost—a whore, a bitch— anything he could screw. Your brother said to him that if he really couldn't wait he could give himself a foot-job with the nexhuman's feet. Jimmy whined that he wanted the backside, but Charlie was immovable. Then, seeing as we were there too, we all decided to have quick ride with each of our own spoils. A kind of gangbang y'know? Each with their own nexhuman parts. I had the tits, Lenny the arms, the Loins was set for a foot-job, and Charlie, well, he had that fabulous derriere, didn't he?"

I think of Alba's torso, 8-952-395-78-08-02, the part that went past me by Kathal Hill. How was that possible?

"And then? What happened next, Mickey?"

A wolf-like grin spreads across his face. The memory of that night is a pleasure to him, but listening to this does nothing for me but open wounds that have never stopped weeping unhappiness.

"What happened was that none of us wanted to get rid of her. That nexy had a smoking body. Perfect hands and feet, thighs and tits to die for, and a peach of an arse. None of us wanted to give up the pieces. None of us."

My brother the executioner.

My brother the great pretender.

My brother, who accused me of having sought out Alba's head, while all this time he had kept her pelvis.

I am appalled by the truth, but I still have to smile to string Mickey along.

"No way. I don't believe you. You all took a part of her home? Like trophies?"

It wasn't an empty question.

"I don't know about the others, but I did. I keep mine in the van for when I get the urge."

Bullseye. A demon rises high above my shoulders. This time, my smile is genuine. I laugh, shedding the same tears that were tormenting me a moment ago. Mickey laughs with me; he hasn't the slightest inkling I'm about to get one over on him.

"Isn't she a bit old? The tits must be wrinkled and dro-opy."

He stretches his fingers and slides them under the sheets to give the blonde's yellowing nipple a squeeze.

"Yeah, well, they are a bit worn, after all that rubbing. But a new pair would cost an arm and a leg. Get it?"

I pat him on the back and go on to illustrate my offer, to ensure his eternal gratitude. Sincerity can be so misleading. "Not for you, Mickey. You're helping me out here, let me help you. I'm a *trashformer*; I can find you a new pair of tits. Not first hand, obviously, but better than what you have now."

"Really? Fuck me, that'd be fantastic," Mickey says, drops of spittle flying from his mouth. "And you can have a go here whenever you want and tell Charlie to come visit."

"Thanks, but I don't see Charlie often. He doesn't call much either. He doesn't live in Kathal Hill anymore. I just wanted to say, though, for the almost-new breasts, there's a condition."

"Shoot, mate." An impossibly long snake of mucous is hanging out of his left nostril, but before it drips onto his shirt, he snorts it back up with extraordinary force.

"I'll have to take the old ones, though. You know, company policy. One in, one out. You know the rules."

His leer tells me I've been successful.

"In-out, in-out. Of course. We all know the rules, we use that rule here too!"

He cackles at his own wit. Dear old Mickey, who used to sneak into restaurant kitchens and spread scabies mites in the pantries, who used to hide in Kudzu Gardens and slip red ants into the Genshoij girls' fancy bags for fun.

The demon has spread his wings over me and his shadow is a prodigious blessing. It might be true that generally, faced with the disappointments of life, people become more cynical and cowardly. For me, it works the opposite way around.

Mickey's enthusiasm is so great, I even dare ask him the absurd.

"I only need this one's head. No point carrying the whole thing. That okay?"

"No problem. No one wants this one anymore, anyway. Do you want to know who it is?"

Looking at the scars zigzagging on her scalp, visible but almost closed fissures, I decide she must have been between thirty and forty.

"No, not really."

"All right, then, give me five minutes and I'll gift wrap it for you."

The old flame I used to see in the Dead Bones days shines in his eyes. He opens a locker door and pulls out a handsaw. He sets it at the base of her neck and starts to cut the skin, flesh, and bone. The saw makes the same sound as a blade cutting through polystyrene. I look the other way while Mickey holds up the head to let the blood and other liquids drain, then puts a folded towel underneath it. When the head stops dripping he puts it in a bag and hands it to me.

"It'll dry soon."

Pleased with the deal he's made, Mickey accompanies me to the exit. We walk back the way we came to the booth where the porter is still rocking his chair back and forth on its hind legs, engrossed in his crossword puzzle. I remove the holdall containing Alba's head from the locker, taking care not to let Mickey see her, and add the unknown woman's head to my bag.

We leave the basement and go to the parking area where in the back of the morgue's van, the RFID appears on my visor. There, wrapped in plastic, is Alba's torso. Mickey hands me this second package, oblivious to what it means to me. My heart is bursting with a flow of silent explosions.

We take leave of each other with a load of back-slapping and the promise that I'll be back with a large pair of tits as soon as I can. When Mickey already has one foot on the ramp I try one last thing.

"I don't suppose you know where the others ended up? What happened to Lenny and Jimmy?"

He lets out an explosive breath, making me happy I'm standing so far away.

"Shit, Peter... Did you have to ruin my day? It's not good. Not good at all. Lenny lost it and went crazy. They committed him to Villa Blaga. You remember the place we used to go to shoot at animals? It's been turned into a care facility. Poor bastard, he's in a bad way. He doesn't remember anything or anyone, just mutters nonsense. Bad story."

He gazes into the distance for a moment before continuing.

"I lost track of Jimmy. The last time I saw him was near Junkland: he was driving along Piccalorda Street in a flashy car. We stopped at some lights and I looked in through his window; he almost didn't recognise me. He said he'd opened a shoe shop in town. He must have developed an obsession with feet... Whatever, it looked like he'd made a pile of Ks. I left him my number, but he never got in touch. Whatever."

I lift my hand in farewell.

In a single attempt, I have solved three problems: I have a head to substitute for Alba's, and I've recovered a second part—maybe even a third.

Under the Lazar night, I can see the red gleam of hundreds of fires. Towards the north, in the dark sky of Cali Nova, the winds of change are blowing. Flashes of lightning descend from the sky like immense spiders, illuminating the panorama almost as light as day.

I get back on my bike and pedal home, more determined than ever before.

Chapter 10
The Blaga Residence

Norbert and I are heading northeast to the barren fields of Colchide, their edges merging with great expanses of kipple. Here, I find it hard to tell the difference between a log and a fallen roof beam, a stream from a toxic leak and a patch of violets bursting from polluted earth, but I have no problem identifying the slopes belonging to the villa once owned by Mordecai Blaga.

There are places people think of as evil, and so they avoid them. The mere fact that 'the Madman's Villa' has escaped the onslaught of kipple makes the building exude an air of unease.

The roads beyond the Durenico dump and beyond the Selam River are reduced to tracks traced out by the tyres of the few cars that venture this way. Norbert was the only one of the Kathal Hill gang who was willing to bring me here and wait to take me back—even though I offered two Ks for the favour. As I get out of his wreck of a car, I remember the rumours we used to hear about the Villa as kids.

They say that Mordecai Blaga was a distinguished gentleman, a doctor who devoted his entire life to looking after others. He was a psychiatrist, and after an illness took away the use of his legs, he received patients in the family house. He fell in love with one of his patients—a woman suffering from a serious form of psychosis induced by years of humiliation, often sexual, meted out to her by her husband. The woman was torn in two: she claimed to be happy satisfying her husband's desires, yet she was slowly starving herself to death.

People say that Doctor Blaga went mad trying to save her.

One day, he invented an excuse for his patient and her husband to come to his studio. He calmly explained the cause of the woman's illness to her husband and concluded that he believed the cure was simple. Then he shot the man full in the face, burned his body, and scattered the ashes in the Villa's garden.

The woman stayed with the doctor until the police came to Villa Blaga's gates. He had been barricaded inside for weeks, a precaution against this very eventuality. According to the news, he managed to hold out for five hours.

When the police finally forced their way in, they found him sitting down at the table, eating withered meat. The doctor's face bore a self-satisfied, utterly harrowing look. Apparently his last words were, 'She's mine. She is part of me now.'

Mordecai Blaga was executed by lethal injection three years later. Rumour has it that his ashes were scattered in the gardens of the Villa Blaga, so as not to defile Lobony cemetery. Since that day, people began to call the nettles that grow there, 'the flowers of evil.' On the wall next to the gate, someone painted a mural of the thorny plants with these words underneath:

We are nettles born of rubbish

All of this is only a story, hearsay, passed on over and over. This much is true: Villa Blaga was confiscated by the state, after years of standing vacant, and turned into a mental health facility.

With these horrors inside my head, I say goodbye to the bushy mass hiding Norbert's face and begin the ascent along a path snaking around the outskirts of the ruined garden.

As twilight descends, the uneven ground fills with shadows. The stinging nettle leaves seem like just the right prelude to the pain I can sense seeping out through the windows.

On the first floor, I can see a figure rocking back and forth. The man next to him is banging his head sideways against the wall. A bony hand waves at me from the second floor, and on a third-floor balcony, a lone woman howls a nocturnal warning.

'Devil's work! Dance for me, baby.
'Devil's work! Demons out!'

I don't have a plan, but I figure Lenny will be on one of the upper floors, where the more dangerous patients are kept, sectioned off for their own safety as well as for that of others.

If Jimmy was the randy goat of the Dead Bones, and Mickey the hook-beaked vulture, then Lenny was the cold-blooded reptile. When Jimmy was ambivalent over whether to carry on laying into the adversary, and Mickey had stopped to catch his breath, Lenny was the one Charlie chose to finish the job.

In the Villa's waiting room, there's an open book with an up-to-date list of patients. I flick through it idly, just to see if I know any of the names. I notice that the doctors have written why each patient was committed.

In the space for 'reason for internment,' there are sentences like: hallucinations of an imperative or destructive nature; orphan; poverty; bellicose temperament; damaged nervous system; systemic lupus erythematosus; mythomania; uraemia and porphyria; Wilson's thyroid syndrome; Huntingdon's disease; lesions of the temporal and parietal lobes; epilepsy; drug abuse; dementia; schizophrenia; reactive; cyclic and puerperal psychosis; and paranoid delirium.

I approach the front desk, where a bored-looking nurse is flipping through a magazine.

"Hello, I'm here to see Lenny Ratzko."

The nurse, whose name badge reads Sheela, asks me to sign the visitors' book. The last visitor to Blaga Villa came over ten months ago. The one before that, two years earlier.

Sheela consults her notes and informs me that at this time of day, *Leonard* usually has a rest.

"But you can go up, anyway; he might still be awake. He's just had his medication. Room 313."

"Thanks."

I wonder what cocktail of drugs they are giving Lenny. It can't be easy to sedate someone like him. I remember him being as lithe as a cobra and as ferocious as a crocodile—animals I have seen in the gamesphere with Kiko, on National Geographic when we're preparing for next adventure. Only you couldn't turn Lenny off or even put him on pause. He would carry on until his victim's eyes rolled backwards in their death throes, a mass of agonised whimpering. Afterwards, we had to put him in quarantine or he would be unapproachable and bad-tempered for a week. Charlie was convinced he needed to run his batteries down completely and let the acid he held within him out. My brother knew his boys well.

Turning into a badly lit corridor, I glimpse a small garden at the back of the Villa, through an open window. Below the containment walls, there are a number of pens holding a range of birds. I have to consult my visor, which tells me they're peacocks, ostriches, and emus—species close to extinction. This must be where the inmates are allowed to raise animals, those suitable for an enclosed space.

Nothing gets out of here. Not beasts or lunatics. Everything is under lock and key, fenced in, electrified, and the only way out is the way I came in. Outside the walls, and for two kilometres in every direction, kipple runs rife. The land is devoid of life, traversed only by the clouds that skim overhead.

The lunatic business is growing. I don't know whether it's the kipple or the megalopolis, but places like this are proliferating, and you have to be really mad to be committed. Even prison would be a better place to end up.

I turn and see a display announcing dinner with a melodic jingle.

18.30: dinner time. Chronic ward, everybody line up.

Within the space of five seconds, the hall is filled with shuffling people dressed in colourful clothes; pyjamas jostling, sport suits rubbing against dressing gowns. Each armed with a plastic plate, a white bowl and a packet of non-lethal plastic cutlery, the inmates gather together. There are scattered tables and chairs for them to sit at, and as they settle down, the low murmur of voices is soon replaced by the sound of plastic knives and forks clattering against the plates. It looks more like a kindergarten dinner hall than a madhouse.

I leave them to it and call the lift. An old man comes to stand beside me, his hair soft white and his skin dark and tortoise-like, the unbuckled straps of a straitjacket dangling from his arms.

"It was a frame-up," he says to me.

I don't answer him, not wanting to encourage him.

"That bitch of a journalist... the jury only believed her because she was famous."

I nod.

"How can you turn a jokey allusion into an accusation of sexual harassment?"

His teeth are all black, broken, or made of metal. The mad are terrifying close up, but he politely steps aside to let me into the lift first.

"Where do you need to go, sir? I used to be a lift boy; I have a certain amount of experience in the sector."

I swallow drily at the idea of being alone with a man in an unbuckled straitjacket.

"Top floor. I'm here to visit Lenny Ratzko."

Despite his hands being confined in the long sleeves, the old man performs the necessary manoeuvres on the lift's control panel with the affected movements of an employee in a grand hotel.

"Oh, yes, young Lenny. He doesn't come down for dinner. They feed him in his room."

Nervousness compels me to make small talk.

"You have lots of animals in the back yard, but I thought this place was full of cats."

He strikes a pose, arms folded over the hospital shirt.

"It used to be because this place used to be overrun by rats. Now there are mosquitoes."

"What's that?"

"They put mosquitoes with malaria in boxes, with lots of holes so that their stingers poke out. When the fever comes on, they go into a coma. Every day, into a coma and then wake up again: wake up, coma, repeat. But it keeps them under control and they don't cause trouble."

I nod, as though this makes perfect sense. His face has been ruined by his time spent in the Villa: skin ravaged by experimental treatments and cuts—self-inflicted? Attempts to escape his body before his time?

I don't ask any more questions. I just bob my head in acknowledgement to the old man waiting for me to step out. When the doors close, I begin looking for room 313.

I hope Lenny remembers his former life.

I hope he can remember me.

Chapter 11
Lenny and Nancy

Lenny Ratzko's body is strapped down to a convulsor, a restraint bed fitted with straps and surrounded by rings and bars, more like a cage on wheels than a bed. My imagination is getting away from me, picturing him overpowered by convulsions, tearing his own muscles. I can almost hear him yelling against the hold of the nurses.

I shiver at the thought of what might have happened to him here. Who knows how much he wishes he could return to his Dead Bones days, drinking with the lads and getting so wasted we wondered whether there were more alcohol molecules in his blood than cells in his brain.

Lenny is either surprised to see me, or his reaction is another kind of reflex. His jaw drops slowly to his chest. A branching vein on his right temple throbs, confirming that he is still in the world of the living, although close to the point of being classified as a vegetable. I move closer to the bed and he stares at me with eyes that seem possessed. His pupils are as small as pinheads, but they haven't managed to sedate his glare. The patient in the bed next to his looks like he's been skinned; his head has been shaved and he has no nose.

"Hi, Lenny, can you hear me? I won't ask you how you are. Just let me know if you can speak."

His tendons have been weakened. He can only wobble his head in an approximation of assent.

"You are... not... *them.*"

I want to be sincere with Lenny. No stories.

"No, I'm Peter, Charlie's brother. The Dead Bones. Do you remember?"

His mouth curls into a hard expression that vanishes as quickly as it came.

"Hunt the kipple... hunt the... kipple."

"Good man, Lenny, that's right. Talking about kipple, do you remember the arms of that nexhuman woman?"

He drops into an abyss, his nostrils flare and horror overcomes him.

"Kipple is evil. Kipple is waiting for us. We must make sacrifices. To kipple! Ion foretold it. Ion knows everything."

Why is Lenny muttering about Ion? Does he mean *my* Ion?

"Who do you mean, Lenny?"

His is a strange form of catalepsy. He is in a permanent daze without respite. Now Lenny pants, huffs, and bends his neck "They say he can beat the kipple. Ion knows how."

"How do you know Ion?' I ask, but Lenny flips his head from side to side. 'Was Ion here?"

"...here. Yes," Lenny squeezes out through his clenched teeth. "Before me... but... they remember him."

Lenny's face darkens and he shudders. I don't know whether this is due to his medication or the ebb and flow of his consciousness. He's completely incapable of moving a muscle except in a spasm.

I take a tray from the bedside table and show him a spoon.

"Was Ion here? Where did he go?"

With his chin, Lenny points to the right, the bed next to his. Empty. Then the window.

"He escaped? Did he jump out? Do you mean he leaped out?"

"They say he flew... against the kipple. He will never be... kipple."

"Did he take the arms with him? Tell me, Lenny, where are the nexhuman's arms?"

"They're kipple. All of them. Everything is kipple."

At the entrance to the room, a woman with grey hair hanging limply onto her shoulders peeps through the door.

"If you want to know, I took those arms of Lenny's, sir. Only borrowing, of course. He's always saying 'everything's kipple, everything's kipple,' so I thought he didn't want them anymore."

She seems like quite a nice old lady. It shouldn't be hard to convince her to give me the arms.

"I'm not a sir; my name is Peter Payne. So, you know where they are?"

She smiles mischievously.

"Yes, Mr Peter Pan, but you'll have to come to my room. I don't have them with me."

Lenny's raw neighbour lifts himself on his elbows and screams.

"Leave him alone! What's he ever done to you? If I could only get out of this bed... you old witch."

The old lady winks at me.

"Don't listen to him. He's just a madman eaten up by envy."

With that, she vanishes. Lenny has dropped off to sleep, exhausted from our conversation and unable to fight the medication any longer, so I leave him and follow her down the corridor. She is shuffling quite fast, almost skating with her slippers. Every so often, she turns and beckons me with her hand. I hope she's not going to take me for a tour of the Villa with my throat being cut as the grand finale. She stops by the doorjamb and strikes a pose.

"Here we are. This is my room. Please, come in, sir."

"I'm not a sir."

"Of course, of course." She smiles.

This wing of the Villa is reserved for female guests. Simple rooms, furnished with dignity.

"I keep them under the bed. They didn't fit in the wardrobe."

She bends over and moves to the left, her arse in the air until she is rubbing up against my trousers.

"They're right here. Just a moment..."

She hauls out a large suitcase and heaves it onto the bed, sitting down next to it. She is silent as if expecting something.

Above the head of the bed hang some faded photos of a young woman pole-dancing. On the floor, I notice a pair of shiny boots, another pair of platform shoes.

"May I see them?"

"Straight away? No foreplay? Just how I like it..."

She unbuttons her blouse and underneath I see a black bodice and suspenders holding back two large breasts, at least double-Ds or Es.

"It's been a long time since anyone made me an offer like that. I'm flattered."

"Wait a moment. That's not what I meant. I just want the arms, the ones Lenny..."

She is clearly not listening to me. She opens the case and takes out a rubber phallus. It is black and longer than a hand span. Among the other objects inside—whips, handcuffs, and steel balls—there lie a pair of arms attached to Alba's elegant hands.

"I used to be beautiful, you know? A dancer. Then they said I was stealing from the till. It had nothing to do with me, it was that monster, my mother—she was the thief. She was always envious." She takes my hands. She pulls me to her.

She might not be kipple yet, but she may as well be for the way she feels. Neglected flesh; dead meat. I feel sorry for those who start to fade before they're ready. I wonder briefly if Alba was this age when she uploaded.

"I'm sorry, but I don't... I've never done this before. Someone might see us."

She pulls a key out of her blouse pocket, smiling craftily.

"We girls have the right to our privacy. Don't worry about the other thing. Sweet Nancy will look after you."

Who knows what this 'Sweet Nancy' is capable of? Who knows what she is in here for? Better to grit my teeth and comply. If I push her away, she might scream or attack me, bringing nurses and other inmates to help her. I fix my mind on Alba's arms, on the fact that this is the only way of getting them back.

"You can close your eyes if you want. I'll take care of everything."

It's part of my work, I tell myself. It's my mission. I am a salvager of matter. I give back hope to things that have none left. I blow a breath of life into organic degeneration.

I open my arms wide and she unzips my fly. She moistens her dry lips with her tongue. With her eyes, she is already imagining the tenderness of flesh from which to suck out a small amount of warmth to make her feel alive again. When Nancy opens her legs, the sight of her wrinkled skin makes me hesitate. But once I'm between those flaccid folds, it's as if I have plugged her in. Nancy writhes beneath me as if hit by a flood of hormones.

"Good lad! Young, fresh, like Peter Pan!"

I think of Alba. Only of Alba.

I understand those who aspire to become nexhuman.

I understand that the risk of losing the life we know is worth escaping this life, as a prisoner of a body that doesn't bear the weight of your desires or help the yearning to last.

"Yes, like that..."

If humanity needs this to feel alive, what do nexhumans need? They have inorganic apparatus, but with this, they satisfy the same requisites as living beings. So they can fuck, they can make love. Do they do it for all eternity?

My concentration wanders from the present. I imagine a future with Alba. I feel like I am floating; as if I can launch myself into the sky like the light that came from her dying eyes.

After just three minutes of adrenaline for her and meditation for me, I am still hard. Being twenty is worth something after all, where erections are concerned.

"You're skinny, but you have a good muscle. C'mon, be a good boy, give me some more."

I nod with my eyes closed. This is not what I expected to hear from an inmate of the Villa. I ask myself if Alba and I will enjoy this kind of corporal pleasure, or if our contact will be mechanical, electrical, magnetic, or quantum.

Another twenty seconds are enough for me to dive from thought to action and shoot my sperm into her arid body. She blows me a kiss as if I have given her the most precious thing in the world: a few minutes in the past, a temporal leap to another dimension.

I pull out of Nancy and step back.

"Can you give me the arms now?"

As I start to get dressed, she gives me the same smile as earlier. Her wrinkles look less deep.

"Let's do it again. I'll teach you something that'll drive you *crazy*."

I don't like the idea of going crazy.

I mount her again and she pulls my bony hips against her almost hard enough to hurt herself. Nancy is blinded by passion. Her expression is so desperate, it excites me. Even her perfume distracts me just enough to keep going.

I'm no longer thinking about Alba and this repels me. I do my best not to touch her, to avoid every inch of that parchment-like skin. I lose my rhythm, and opening my eyes, see the handcuffs dangling from the headboard. Nancy is raving, lost in the monologue of a porn film, egging herself on.

"Yes, stick it in me. Fill me with flesh. I want your cock!"

I lean over the bedside table and lock the first bracelet to the headboard. Her eyes sprint open. She sees what I'm doing and wriggles with excitement.

"Oh, yes! Handcuff me! I'll be your prisoner..."

She doesn't guess my plan until the second cuff is clipped around her wrist and I pull out of her.

"What are you doing? Where are you going? Please, just one more time!"

When she realises the fun has come to an end, she starts cursing.

"I did what you asked,' I say. 'I have to go home. Thank you for the arms and for... the rest."

I grab Alba's arms and stuff them in my bag. As I leave the room, I hear Nancy sobbing. Secure in the knowledge that she can't follow me, I head back to Lenny's room to say goodbye. He hasn't moved a muscle in all this time. His brain has been turned to mush, unable to un-mix things that might be true, from hallucinatory fantasies.

"Even if you can't understand me, I just want to say I'm sorry. Not all kipple is negative, not everything is kipple. I know someone called Ion, too, who can't sleep at night for thinking about kipple."

Lenny groans and I make out, "Re... verse."

It seems we *are* talking about the same person. Was Ion here, in the Villa, too? Did he escape? Ion has never told me about his past, partly because he can't remember it—or maybe because he doesn't want to. Maybe he needs to avoid thinking about it, in order to be able to *function* outside the Villa.

A dribble of bright blue spit falls onto Lenny's bib.

"They were... *mine*. Not theirs... not *yours*."

He leans his head back, letting his eyes close until they are only open a slit, beaten. Lenny the Reptile is more defenceless than a toad.

I hurry to the lift. Sweet Nancy's laments echo off the walls of the corridor. I have given away my virginity to get Alba's arms. I have made another notch on my wall of horror. Perhaps, somehow, I am a better man for doing this terrible thing. When she calms down and the anger has faded, she'll be left with a sweet memory with which to face the rest of her days.

My elevator friend welcomes me back into the lift, takes me back to the ground floor and bows as I leave. I sign the exit register and make my way back down the crest of the hill.

When I get home, I can try to attach Alba's head and arms to her torso. She may not be alive yet, but she is taking shape—her shape. Who knows what I'm going to be forced to do, to get the legs from Jimmy or the pelvis from Charlie. I can feel my demon standing over me. It keeps appearing as I get closer to my goal.

Norbert's dilapidated car is waiting outside the gates; Norbert leaning against it, having a cigarette. A pile of butts on the ground next to him testifies to how long my interlude with Nancy prolonged my visit. Even though we can't see the moon clearly, blurred as it is by a blanket of clouds, its light drips down from above.

When we reach the end of the garden, where the last of the nettles disappear into cement, a howl rips through the thick air, 'Peter Paaan! Come back! Take me with you!'

Did she really think I was Peter Pan?

CHAPTER 12
REVERSE

A few days later, I learn a lot about Ion Wharton.

All I had to do was pass myself off as an apprentice and they sent me to re-sort Reverse's archives. I modified my profile on the server, printed a fake name badge, and I was set. With a little imagination, even the most secure doors can be thrown wide open.

I learn a lot about people by spending time up to my elbows in their rubbish. Dustbins are like safe deposit boxes: they contain secrets that people had thought would disappear. By counting how many condoms they throw away, you can tell *if* and *how often* a couple makes love to each other; a girl's empty perfume bottles will tell what to send to her as a gift; discarded tickets from venues and shows tell you where to take them on a date; if you make a note of all the creams someone uses, you'll find out just where their insecurities lie.

Tell me what you throw away and I'll tell you what you are.

Match the right product to the right person and you earn the right to a favour. If this person, in addition to sifting through rubbish by my side in the dump, also happens to work in Reverse's data collection centre because he is as bright as Duggan the Geek, all I need to do is call in a personal favour, which I will return on my next shift at Kathal Hill.

It's a favour, not corruption. This is legitimate restitution, not theft. All he had to do was issue a temporary transfer from Kathal Hill to the archive in Durenico to re-order recycling data. And all I have done is to go through the data from the year in which Ion was kicked out. I save all of his missing memories onto a memory crystal.

Since everyone else in Reverse has had access to the file, I don't see why he should be denied the right. Information, like matter, wants to be free, I know this; I am the means.

Reverse is a cathedral dedicated to rubbish. It collects the trash of half a million bins. More than three thousand UCUs scattered across the six dumps of the megalopolis execute nine thousand collections a day, every single day.

In its entirety, Reverse represents the laziness of the citizenry, forever dumping their waste, leaving the trashformers to sift through the expanses of kipple.

It is out of professional habit that I rummage through waste bins in the corridors, take a look at what is in the rubbish bags in the bathrooms, and peak into the external skips.

Ion's plans show every single place worth stopping at. The staff tolerate me sifting through plastic, tins, packaging, and containers. Deep down, they are only too happy to have someone else deal with what they don't need anymore.

When I have finished searching every single area, I allow myself a cup of coffee from the rest area vending machine; something so everyday to others, but for us, trashformers remains a rare luxury. Coffee is something we normally collect in tepid dribbles from discarded plastic cups.

While I am luxuriating in this moment, I cast my thoughts back to Ion. Perhaps he is acting in good faith. Perhaps Reverse is, too. Was his confinement to the Villa really a 'precautionary measure' like it said in his personal file?

Ion's fixation with kipple had become an obsession, a direction that was as dangerous for his laboratory colleagues as for him. The notes in his profile say that he badgered the other staff with his unsettling visions of kipple domination and insisted that the company should take action to counter the proliferation of rubbish. He was so insistent that he flew off the handle every time anyone dared contradict his theories.

It's no surprise that all the inventions registered under his name are geared towards combating the same phenomenon: an orbital lift with which to send kipple thirty-six thousand kilometres to a geostationary deposit anchored in space; anti-ozone spores, composed of micro solar panels; a nano-molecular unit that could be shot into the stratosphere, to collect chlorine compounds—the idea was that, once separated, it would recombine as sodium chloride, salt. When the sodium runs out, the spore implodes and falls back to the ground. In the end, all that would be left were innocuous grains of salt, a completely biodegradable waste product, and a cleaner stratosphere.

Then I find something that interests me. An AquaSan water flask, capable of cleaning even the dirtiest water. The best purifier on the market only filters down to two hundred nanometres, even though the smallest bacteria are about half that size, and microscopic viruses slip right through. The pores of the AquaSan filter, with a diameter of fifteen nanometres, would make it possible to extract water suitable for drinking from even the most polluted sources.

I must ask Ion if he ever finished one. A bottle like that would save me from many stops at inopportune moments.

Perhaps this mission to destroy kipple really did drive Ion mad. It's possible they erased his memory to save him from himself. Perhaps, like many others, he had become enamoured of his own madness, lucid and illuminating, without realising the risks he was running.

Now, though, he just wants to get back what was taken from him. How could I, in my condition, not understand him and his pain, not want to help him and humour him?

I remember his words of so many years ago: "Difficult to resist dreams. Impossible not to let desires follow."

I wonder if it's because of our desires that we get scared. But how can you be happy without desiring something?

I throw away the plastic cup and vanish from the Reverse headquarters as unnoticed as I entered.

It is unusual to find the sun shining down on the megalopolis. It's very pleasant, so I pedal slowly. Realising that it will happen again and again, that the sun will give a little joy and a little warmth to everyone, from nexhumans to the lowest tramp in Kathal Hill, almost makes me cry.

Pedalling along Rotterquay Street, I come to the Green Towers building site, an immense, open excavation that in a few months will be a huge residential structure. The holographs in the area display a collection of hanging gardens, solar walls, mobile shelters, flying docks and all the new gadgetry of the most advanced home automation systems.

It's time to give Ion the good news. He's expecting me to call him the moment I can.

"Peter! How did it go? Did you manage?"

"Yes, all your memories are in my bag. I'm on my way back to Kathal Hill. I'm going to call in at home and then I'm all yours."

I turn into Piccalorda Street and zoom past thousands of shop windows filled with the 3D faces of actors inviting the public to try the merchandise and images of twirling plates dressed up as presents.

"Excellent news. I am out right now, but I'll be back."

The line drops—my distance communications depend on the scraps of credit left over in the disposable visors I find in the dump.

The carousel of cars, motor scooters, megabuses, levitating vehicles, and aeroplanes create a stupefying effect. I fade out the panorama, leaving only the backlit animation produced by the chippery and recycling info. I endure the

Earth-salvage price-lists, the various ReStore catalogues, the kitschy Oriental offers, and above all, the Babailon menu, the bite-and-run restaurant out of whose trash I savour the delicacies of the world. It's my favourite dustbin.

What comes out of Rizoma and Esperia is first relocated to Genshoij and then Raon. Then the Laws of Value come into play, where the price of a reusable object corresponds to the difference between the Stock Value (SV) of the material to be removed that the seller receives and the cost of the Removal Service (RS) which goes to the trashformers.

$$SV - RS = V$$

This is a generic formula. More often, a flat rate is applied, where intuition prevails over an objective evaluation of an object's condition. Following this reasoning, anything, given a certain amount of time, can end up being mine.

After twenty minutes of offer after offer, discount after discount, I finally reach Junkland. Here, and only here, the value of anything works like a backwards auction; an item's price goes down over time until someone agrees to buy it. I'm not stopping to barter today; there's nothing I need. I head straight past to Kudzu Gardens, and from there to Ion's cubicle.

When I arrive, Ion's nowhere to be seen.

I scan the area. Every hiccup of life seems to have been stilled. Even the boar is missing. I catch nothing but the odd tag, sporadic flashes of recent codes that respond to the constant call emitted by the RFID tracker in total reception mode. The rest of the material is silent, kipple. To prove this, you only have to measure the MIPS (Million Instructions Per Second) per milligram: if it doesn't think, it doesn't really work or live, it's only rubbish clumped together in crumbling piles.

"Ion! Where are you hiding?!"

I shout as loudly as I can. On the ground next to me lies my bag of desires: four pieces of Alba that he will attempt to put together as his part of the bargain.

I sit down on an old crate and wait. When I spot him, he is coming down the hill in the distance, bent under the weight of something he is carrying on his shoulders.

Zooming in with my visor, I can see that Ion's hair is greasy, as dark as iron ore; his mouth is crooked with the strain of his burden. For a few moments, I worry that my good friend Ion might actually be an escaped madman, a lunatic with a kipple obsession—a lunatic I need. He catches sight of me, and suddenly happy, waves me over to help him. I run to hold up one end of the pole he is carrying, an almost four-metre-long rod that is bouncing dangerously as he walks.

"What do you need that thing for?"

I grab one end of the pole and the strength of the Tantalium makes Ion sigh in relief. He straightens up, looks at me uncertainly.

"I don't at all know. Something tells me good for something."

Ion and his juddery memory. Ion and his scrambled grammar. Once I give him the file, he will finally be restored to his former self, or be more himself than he is now, at any rate.

Even without his memories, Ion isn't so dull as to give objects a value they don't deserve. There must be some secret connected to this pole.

"Everything all right, then?" Ion asks me.

I can hear Mr Stinky rooting around, scoffing nauseating titbits found amongst the rubbish.

"Yes; I've got it all here. I brought the pieces of Alba too."

We drop the pole when we near Ion's shack. He abruptly falls to his knees and I can see his socks, bunched up around his bony ankles. He is wearing someone else's worn-out shoes.

"Give it to me, Peter. I must know now."

I hand him the crystal and he gets up, hurrying into the tunnel. I walk the last part of the way alone. On the verge of downloading the contents of the crystal, Ion's worn fingers hesitate. He scratches his head and mutters to himself. "Bastards, kipple is everywhere. And you don't do nothing."

He reminds me of Lenny and their shared passion, but this is not the right moment to approach the subject of his imprisonment. I sit down. I want to see if Ion will manage to swallow his medicine, that part of himself he has wanted back for so long.

Ion stalls, playing for time by putting the kettle on the camp stove to boil.

"Boy, thank you for this. I don't how long it will take. When the water is ready, make tea, please. Bag in, on the shelf."

I nod and in the meantime open my bag and take out the parts, arranging them on the ground in front of the cubicle: the head at the top, the torso below, and the arms at the sides.

Ion is sitting as though he is about to perform a magic ritual, only he, the medicine man, can't remember exactly who he is, or what to do. If this goes well, all his lost memories will come flooding back in a stunning brainwave. If it doesn't, I'll have to coax them out of him with careful questions.

"C'mon, Ion, download the crystal."

Ion is trembling, but I'm buzzing with anticipation. My future depends on him. The visor display gurgles in fast forward mode. Then Ion descends into his past and I see no signs of him coming back up until his head bangs against the table and the boar grunts loudly.

The tea has been ready for a while. Now Ion and I know the same things about him, but only he knows how to use the formulas and the equations in his head. To me, they just look like mysterious patterns and doodles.

His hands are clutching his head at the temples as though he is trying to contain a mass of data and memories that are threatening to explode his brain.

"Not tea. I need a drink!" Ion stands up and grabs a phial. He opens it and pours at least half of its contents down his throat.

"Better... Peter, I'm sure now, our identities don't reside in a specific part of our bodies. That lot at Reverse are experimenting with uploading, but they haven't got it right yet. D'you see? It works both ways, even from an external source to a human body!"

His loose lips tighten into a broad smile.

"Listen to you talk!" I exclaim, but Ion's less interested in his linguistic improvement than in rediscovering himself.

"How many parts of the body do you think we can get rid of and still be ourselves?"

If Ion was hard to follow before, he's now beyond reach. He's talking more to himself than to me.

"Does installing a mind in a stronger, longer-lasting container allow us to carry on being ourselves?"

This is a question he should ask Alba. A question she must have answered with a 'yes' when she chose to transmigrate her spirit.

"Listen to this story. It says that the ship that Theseus, an ancient Greek hero, travelled on was preserved over the years and that as the various parts deteriorated, they were replaced by new bits. When all the parts of the original ship had been replaced, people realised that it was, in fact, a new ship, even though it looked the same as before. The question is, then: was it or was it not still Theseus' ship? In other words: if the substance of an identity is modified without changing its shape, is it still the same thing? Or is it only similar? Now, try applying this paradox to the man who, over the course of time, changes but still looks like he is the same person."

"I really hope that's how it is."

I hand him the head that is so dear to me. I can't suppress my fear as I do so. Ion's grimy fingers leave greasy marks on Alba's smooth skin.

"I can try putting her back together. But bringing her back to life is another matter. First of all, I need her other bits. Then, I have to find out if there is a way of rebooting her, always assuming she will be the same as before."

"What do you mean?"

From under his stool, Ion removes a rusty toolbox. Moving like a forensic pathologist, he analyses severed cables, ragged seams and the frayed edges of Alba's joints.

I know she is not in pain. Still, the scraping sound of her head being turned about, as Charlie prised it away from her body, comes back to haunt me. Ion leaves me no time to indulge in self-pity.

"In fact, the upload process created *two* Alba's: a master and a copy. I don't know which of the two you met, but if we manage to wake her up, she will at best be the Alba of five years ago, the Alba that *crashed* five years ago."

After soldering the connections, reconnecting the joints using improvised spacers, he attaches first one and then the other arm to her torso. The curled scars on her shoulders have the appearance of a ruched blouse.

"You mean this won't be the real Alba?"

My eyes glitter with a light stronger than any in our surroundings.

"Yes and no. This could be the *real* Alba, a perfect copy of the original, but it might not be, and in that case, the new Alba should be considered another person. There is also a third theory: Alba might be an exact copy of the master, who moves gradually *away* from the original Alba as time passes."

A crowd of gulls rise from the rolling hills of rubbish. Their skeletal wings make them look like bats; only their trajectories, united and compact, show the difference. My insides roil and I don't know whether to blame this on a bad premonition or a sudden need to discharge.

"Peter, listen to me, the third theory is based on fuzzy logic, an extension of Boolean logic. According to this theory, the truth is only *partially* true or false. When Alba was duplicated, the original Alba and her copy, Alba-A, were the same person. But as time passes, the copy becomes less and less like the Alba of the past. This decrease in similitude varies in the same way in which you and I become different to our *younger* selves. Alba and Alba-A are the same at first because they share the same past up to the day of duplication. From that moment onwards, their histories take different paths—they go on to become different people."

"So, they were only the same because they had the same experiences?"

"Exactly; it depends on time, not on the person. In this, animals, human beings, nexhumans, and AIs are the same."

"So then, why do so many people see nexhumans as kipple?"

The wires in Alba's neck, her nerve endings, are about to be joined to the head, where the connexions become emotions. Something vibrates when Ion touches two cables together, making them spark.

"For them, nexhumans aren't biological beings. They think they can establish whether a thing is good or bad based on whether or not it is natural. They are wrong! I have seen very bad natural things –intestinal parasites, famine, polio—and I have seen equally bad artificial things: car accidents, bombs... kipple."

When Alba's head is reconnected to her neck, a great roll of thunder announces the imminent arrival of bad weather, worse than it has been in a long time. The shuffling of Mr Stinky scratching at the ground makes me fear the worst.

"If nexhumans aren't copies, what are they?"

Ion lifts his eyes to the crumpled horizon of detritus and wrecks. The cubicle, exposed to the angry weather, is easy prey.

"Think about reproduction. Conception doesn't transfer us into another person but creates another being growing from its parents' genes. In the same way, an upload creates a new being, except for the first time in the course of evolution, it also produces a detachment from organic matter. Life is not only organic. It might be indigestible for many, but it is true in the same way as intelligence does not belong to man alone. It is a prejudice that is bound to undergo a tremendous shake-up as soon as the number of nexhumans overtakes that of humans. In addition to Homo Sapiens, there will be Homo *Nexus*. When that day comes, no one will doubt the nature of humanity. When that day comes, it won't matter anymore whether a nexhuman is or isn't the perfect continuation of the original person."

I hug Alba's torso to my chest. True happiness isn't what you live through; it's what you are able to imagine. Alba exudes beauty and is now emanating a taste of eternity. I can feel my demon laugh in satisfaction as my colour rises.

"How does transmigration work?"

He hurries to replace his tools in their box.

"It's not my field, even though molecular physics is a branch of nano-engineering. I seem to recall something about the substitution of neurons."

I help Ion put his bits and pieces back in the cubicle. If the storm hits this part of Kathal Hill, who knows where his living quarters will end up?

"Millions of nanobots enter the brain and install themselves next to the neurons. Each one records its neuron's activity until it is capable of understanding how it works and how to forecast its responses. Then the nanobot crashes the neuron, taking its place. After a while, the whole brain runs on artificial neurons that transmit data to an external computer. This makes a copy that can be installed—like any other software—in a different vessel."

Ion tightens the bolts along the edges of the structure, to make sure it will weather the force of a hurricane. Then he does the same with the makeshift windows, openings cut into the sides of the structure with a blowtorch.

"Somewhere out there, Alba's original software still exists?"

"So? That is an Alba you have never even met. What would you want with her?"

My bag is too small for the reassembled Alba.

"Do you have a bigger bag, Ion?"

He turns his face to the sky. His refuge is too fragile to compete with the force of the elements. Every now and then, the water pooled in nearby ditches ripples when the thunder rolls.

"Take the trolley while I go down into the bunker. But bring it back straightaway—I need it. I have to come back to the surface as soon as the storm ends. The vultures and jackals will already be preparing for the hunt."

"I'll fly like the wind. I'll leave you my bike."

We release Mr Stinky from his chain, put Alba in the shopping trolley, and cover her with a shiny tarpaulin.

Time is running on. The sky is covered with threatening clouds above, and moaning winds closer to the ground, as the storm approaches. I feel like kipple about to be flooded by rain, defenceless before the threat of the storm. Kipple and I, each exposed to greater forces and our reactions take strange paths.

Ion pedals down into the tunnel with the boar running beside him as I start pushing the trolley down the hill. Outside Kathal Hill, everybody is looking for somewhere to shelter. The beggars and street traders on Lucite Street disappear like rats into cracks and crevices.

North, towards Worrisham, I see a terrifying spectacle as powerful lightning bolts flash against the smoke of the evening fires. Tornadoes rise up, towering over the horizon, creating black twisters of kipple. The first barrage of wind hits us, announcing the imminent end of the world.

Ion's trolley allows me to gain precious minutes. Every now and then, I look over my shoulder to recalculate the position of the storm.

I fasten the trolley to a grate and slip into the house with my bundle over my shoulder. Cleo is busy in the kitchen and talking to Charlie—he's on his weekly courtesy visit. I can't get past without them noticing what I'm carrying. I retreat before they hear me and head somewhere nobody goes very often, a place where people leave objects they haven't the courage to relinquish to the kipple.

We Paynes live below the ground floor of a block of flats, a sub-level that has been taken over by people who make a living by collecting recyclables. No one here pays rent; all the shelters are illegal, with utilities siphoned off from those who can pay. We draw our electricity off a splitter Charlie attached to the power lines when we were kids. The centralised boiler doesn't run on gas or coal but is fed by rice chaff we buy from a food-processing factory in Lazar. Light makes its way in through a complicated arrangement of skylights and mirrors installed by the locals. Down here, nothing has changed for years.

Below us is the basement, a second underground floor held up by pillars that rise up out of filthy water, an urban lagoon filled with the detritus of the city.

The place reminds me of an excursion I went on with Kiko in the U Minh forest on the Mekong delta, only that time there were modified mangroves, not a building project of concentrated squalor. When we were children, Charlie and I would skip stones across the surface of this water. He had unerring aim; I always got it wrong. If he used a pointed stone, he could usually catch what used to swim around in the murk.

Each squatting family has claimed an area between the pillars down here. Small cubicles rise from the water, packing palettes for foundations, their walls made of found planks hammered together. Jumping from brick to brick, laid out like a stepping-stone path, I reach a door with 'Payne' chalked on it.

The key creaks in the lock. Inside, the space is packed to the brim. Over the course of years, Cleo, Charlie and I have cumulatively stuffed all manner of things in here. It is full of mementoes and memories: the Payne family archive.

I look around for a place to hide Alba. I shift boxes, old record players, antique radios, a couple of cathode tube TVs and the pushchair in which first Charlie, and then I, explored the neighbourhood.

Looking up, my gaze encounters my collection: nine boxes containing thousands of shells. I don't know how these made their way to Kathal Hill but I liked them and was always picking them up. Next to them are my glass snow globes, gathered from goodness knows where, and bags full of fortune cookie notes. I open a box and pull out a slip of paper.

Reason and love are sworn enemies.

I frown; I want a different one. I rummage around again until I feel sure, and then read.

When you are closer to your goal, you will receive a helping hand.

That's better. I put it in my pocket and rest Alba on the floor. I uncover her head. The scattering of freckles on her cheeks moves me. She deserves an explanation for what I am doing.

"It's only temporary. As soon as I can, I'll take you upstairs. I just have to convince Charlie I've scrapped you."

Her fixed gaze is so attractive. I am tempted to kiss her, but the thought of the encroaching storm hurries me along. I cover her again and put everything back in its place, turning off the light as I leave.

If I hurry, I'll be back in time to enjoy the spectacle of the storm on one of the gamesphere's video cameras. It took me fifteen minutes to get here with a load of twenty-three kilos; now it should take me only half that time.

I run along the banks of the Akeren, the sound of my Podox joined by the noisy trolley wheels rattling over every bump. Next to me, the river is running recklessly, carrying waves of detritus, broken branches, and tyres. A few distressed RFID signals reach my visor. Their call from the floating slurry distracts me as I jog. It's not easy to suppress of my obsession with residual value, and in my distraction, I almost trip up. I hadn't counted on the difficulty of handling the empty trolley accurately.

I can hear Kathal Hill's sirens, and in the distance, those of the neighbouring areas: the megalopolis is bunkering down to defend itself, alerting its inhabitants to the imminent danger.

I am running in the midst of the fury of the elements and I have to pretend I haven't noticed those warnings. Funnel-shaped swirls of wind dance in the skies over Esperia and head towards the Green Towers at speed, swooping past the geodesic dome protecting Rizoma. I don't remember ever seeing so many atmospheric enemies hurl themselves at the megalopolis at the same time.

I push harder and my healthy leg struggles to match the speed of the Podox. My gait has developed into a caricature of running.

I turn towards Kathal Hill and some hooded passers-by motion, urging me not to go on. I ignore them, increasing the Tantalium's grip on the trolley, steering it into the wind. At the entrance to the bunker, twenty metres into a gorge, I kick at the door and Ion opens it a crack. Behind him, I catch a glimpse of the tunnel's metal throat with grey sludge filtering through from above. The acidity of the megalopolis drips right down into the ground.

Swapping Ion's trolley for my bicycle, I pivot and throw myself down the hill on my bike at full speed. Now the wind is behind me, blowing as though it wants to lift me up and carry me away.

I manage to keep ahead of the storm for two kilometres, rushing between cars that have got stuck and the occasional, anguished pedestrian.

It seems like a sign from my demon, another warning alarm. As I turn into Lucite Street, a flash of lightning bleaches the air around me. A deafening rumble follows and I don't notice that the Zenith jeans billboard is on fire until the top half of it, bearing a model's scorched face, crashes down just ahead of me, forcing me to swerve sharply to keep from colliding with it.

I can't keep going—the rushing water is too powerful for my bike's light frame. Horizontal rain is rent by enormous, forked lightning. Rolls of thunder rumble to the west. Dripping and panting, I rush to take cover in the bus shelter just outside our building.

The storm is beginning to turn and is now whipping Genshoij, on its way to lash Raon. Instinctively, I grab hold of the metal bars over the semi-circular windows of the shelter. The wind makes the structure creak as it whips down the road. The plastic shrieks in complaint, but holds.

I tighten my grip and the Tantalium anchors me to the

metal grill. Lowering my gaze to protect my eyes, I see I am standing on a skylight. A weak glow emanates from far below. I look more closely ... and see Charlie kneeling next to Cleo, who is lying on the floor. Somehow, I've landed up directly above our basement storeroom—the same room I left only minutes before. Next to them lies Alba's top half, hidden by me only minutes before.

A lightning flash behind me casts my distorted shadow over them. Moving my arm shifts my shadow below, and I see my mum is holding a memory crystal in her hand. My eyes widen and my head is whirling with wild suppositions. Could it be that, if it hadn't been for this downpour, I'd never have been found out? Could it be that if this dark sky hadn't induced such melancholy in Cleo, she wouldn't have felt the need to pull out old family films to cheer herself up and find the strength that enabled her to give a shape, however uncertain, to our family? At her side lies another object it takes me a moment to recognise. My brother hurries to cover it up with a sheet again, but I have seen its smooth, rounded contours and know that this was Alba's pelvis, the piece that Charlie took that night in Kathal Hill.

Understanding hits me like a flash from the sky. My brother kept Alba's pelvis in the basement, so he could stick his prick in it every time he came to visit.

The surprise must have been a great shock to Cleo. I can almost see her horror on coming face to face with what Charlie kept hidden there all these years. I can almost hear the cry that escapes her when she realises why her eldest son came down into the basement so often.

How did my visor never pick up anything near home, even when I visited the storage room? Did Charlie bring the pelvis with him from home every time?

All that time I spent with Mickey to get hold of a head to fool Charlie was a waste, as was all the hard work to get my hands on a pair of fake breasts to send him like I promised.

There's no two ways about it, this is my brother all over. He prefers to *take* a pleasure rather than make it happen. This is different, though. He's not just screwing just anyone. He has been nailing Alba behind my back for five years.

I search my memory and suddenly realise that I've heard his panting coming up through the outside grate before. I must have peered down at least a couple of times, but in the absence of a signal, I had no reason to suspect that this was what he was doing. When he was younger, he bullied, committed crimes, even murdered to placate his demons. Now thirty, he hasn't changed; he's merely found a new way to let off steam.

He must have figured out my plan to collect Alba's pieces years ago. He must, somehow, have managed to remove the tag, to make it impossible for me to complete my mission. Perhaps he only needed some tinfoil to obstruct the RFID signal, the same method I used to hide her head in the wardrobe.

My brother, the swindler.

My brother, the pervert.

My brother, the bastard.

If I could only hear what they are saying, my brain would stop whirling. Charlie would surely try to convince Cleo that the pieces are all *mine*, that the pervert is *me*, and only me, that I disobeyed him and kept the head and the pelvis to satisfy *my* depravity.

My mother's lips move; it looks as though she's trying to speak. I want to go down to her, reassure her that everything will be all right, defend myself from Charlie's accusations.

Then Charlie raises his voice, loud enough for me to hear him, 'Mum, answer me! I'm going to call an ambulance.'

She sags back, unconscious, and Charlie lifts her and carries her out of the basement.

If the ambulance paramedics behave as they usually do with people without insurance, I'd better come up with Plan B. Perhaps I can sell them some of my blood, to convince them to take her to the hospital as fast as possible.

First, though, I have to help Alba: as soon as I'm sure Charlie and Cleo are back upstairs, I creep down into the basement. Quickly, I gather Alba's top half with the Tantalium, grabbing hold of her pelvis with my other hand. Then I see the crystal: I must know what's on it. It activates as I touch it and I see the truth that hit my mother so hard.

Charlie has filmed a holograph of himself fucking a piece of plastic. It's my brother all over. He wants to play both the leading role and be a spectator.

The audio is one long moan of pleasure during which he pulls out his member, takes it in his hands and plays around before using it. He is so aroused, he looks like he's about to faint before he even penetrates Alba, or rather her synthetic vagina.

I don't watch the rest, but stuff the crystal in my pocket for a day it might prove useful as evidence, or as a trade. I run, leaving the light on as I found it.

Let Charlie wrack his brains trying to work out what has happened. Let him stew, wondering who made off with his stuff.

My euphoria lasts only as long as it takes me to reach the top of the stairs.

"Peter! Where the fuck do you think *you're* going?"

If I hadn't wasted time looking into the crystal, I wouldn't now be standing in the rain, Charlie blocking my way on the landing.

He's had the same splendid idea of getting rid of the pieces of Alba in the cellar, and without thinking twice, has left Cleo alone inside. I can hear a siren in the distance coming this way.

We are facing each other as he comes down the stairs and I force myself to stand my ground. Face to face, we both know the secret that unites us: we know it is Alba dividing us.

In this position, dark and pained, tight lips and hooded eyes, no one would ever imagine that, for the first time in my life, I am enjoying this. The Tantalium gripping a piece of Alba gives me courage: now only her legs are missing. Not even Charlie can take her from me without pulling my arm off. All of Charlie's happiness rests in the illusion of getting what his wife won't give him, whereas my happiness derives from reliving what I lost by his hand so many years ago.

Charlie moves closer and I begin to change colour. A flash of lightning blinds me, surrounding us in a cage of electricity. There is no more rain and no time to do anything except by instinct. A whimper rises from inside me and threatens to become a tempest of pain.

I call on my demon, but this time, it doesn't answer.

It is no longer just bitterness—the resentment I have harboured for years has decomposed and its festering has tied a hard knot in my throat, a nodule of rot that turns Charlie's presence into a block of irritation.

Motionless, I find myself full of acid that not even this rain can dilute.

The temperature drops and goosebumps spread across my skin.

With water dripping from his eyebrows, nose, and ears, Charlie appears spectral. Drops of rain are bouncing off his shaven skull and shoulders, surrounding him in a fine fuzzy mist as though he were wearing armour. He is tense but doesn't dare make the first move without knowing exactly what I saw in the basement.

My guilt is clear, and hanging from my hands: half of a body that I have always believed belongs to me and a pelvis I have only just rediscovered.

"Is that the *spirit* that you miss so much?"

Charlie's wet shirt is clinging to him, outlining the contours of his muscles.

"Yes, what *you* hid in the cellar." I want to add: "The bit you've been screwing for years. The bit that shocked Mum into being ill." But I hold back, testing the ground as I go.

"You disobeyed me again..."

I let the accusation go.

"How is Cleo?"

"I put her to bed. I thought you would be more concerned about her than these old pieces of nexy. I see I was wrong."

"And I thought that you came to visit us... but instead, you were visiting *this*." I lift up the pelvis. 8–952–395–78–08–01 is the head, 02 at the end is the torso, 03 the arms, 05 should be the legs. I'm still not receiving the tag 04 that Charlie has removed from the pelvis.

A violent gust of wind makes Alba sway in my hands. I interpret this as yet another sign. Alba is reminding me that Charlie is her assassin, her abuser, both before *and* after her death. Alba is asking for the loan of my hands, not having the use of her own.

I need to unbalance him or he will walk all over me like he always does. I have to seem so weak and so pathetic that I'm not worth attacking. It is hard to appear in his thrall now when I don't feel at all inferior to him.

"What are you going to do to me?"

"Let go of the nexhuman. This whole mess is its fault. I'll deal with it, seeing as *you* can't manage even that."

Here it comes. My skin is flushing with colour. The Podox quivers. Flight or fight?

"Yeah, right, and are you going to deal with the rest of it like you dealt with the pelvis?"

Charlie exhales sharply, blowing rain off the end of his nose. He breathes in deeply, nostrils flaring, and leaps forward to attack me. I step backwards and he misses by a hair's breadth.

We face each other again.

"You've gotten fast, Skinnyribs."

My heart has got stuck in my throat. The sense of constipation worsens. A clap of thunder behind Charlie seems to make his threats more terrible.

"Mum would hate to know you're just leaving her there to die. C'mon, drop the nexy. It's over."

He is still trying to make me feel like an ungrateful kid,

small and miserable, but this isn't the end of it—it hasn't even begun.

"You're the one who reduced her to this. She saw what *you* did, so don't try pinning it on me."

He stops in his tracks, realising that I *know*. I have seen what is on the crystal.

"You're just the same old peeping Tom, aren't you? You haven't got the balls to do anything yourself, so you spy on those who do."

He lunges forward and grabs me by the neck. Charlie pushes me backwards and I am on the floor, gasping every time Charlie hits my face. I lift my knee up underneath him and charge the Podox, then trigger it hard against his chest to throw him off. He lands two metres away, whimpering from the pain of the impact.

My inner temperature is so high that when I exhale my breath condenses in front of me in angry clouds. I spit out rainwater that tastes of chrome, chlorine, and mercury. The sound of the siren is irritating, only a few streets away now.

"Don't make me angry, little brother, I'm thinking about you, too." He likes to play the part of the father, to wield the power to decide for others and *about* others.

"At least I didn't screw a piece of plastic."

"No. You fell in love with it, which is so much worse. You can only use that *piece of plastic* if you know what you're doing. And you have no idea. C'mon, you must see that it's madness."

In love with a piece of plastic. This is what I am to him: a madman with an obsession. Like Ion, to be sectioned off for our own good. Like Lenny, driven out of his mind by kipple. Do these neuroses make us heroes, saints, or simply madmen?

"Alba *exists*, she just can't communicate with me."

When we were little, Charlie taught me how to defend myself. Everyone bullied me because I was so skinny. At school, when they stole my lunch, I would go hungry rather than fight over it. I never told Charlie because he would have beaten up everyone and I would have looked like a weasel who ran crying to his big brother.

I used to just swallow my pride, like now. Time absorbs everything. I remember the phrase Charlie used to berate me with: 'If you want them to leave you alone, you have to show them what you're made of. You have to hit back twice as hard as they hit you.'

I let Alba's pieces roll out of my grasp and get back up. My mouth has no saliva left in it, but my bladder is still holding. My visor alerts me to my haywire biometrics, but I feel alive, ready for action. Adrenaline floods my whole body.

"Well done, Peter. You know I'm right. Let's just go back inside and see how Mum is."

I let him come closer to pick up Alba. Charlie has made me more angry than scared. Some people know how to take advantage of anger in a fight. I don't know if I can, but when he turns away from me, I make a fist with the Tantalium and lunge. The Podox powers my run-up, and as I leap forward, I thud four steel knuckles into his neck. I can feel his spine crack as I hit, metal winning over flesh.

Charlie's neck bends at an unnatural angle and he falls to the ground. I lean down and turn him over. I am almost crying. He is laughing.

"Idiot, you'll never be free of that fucking scrap heap."

I shiver as though he's put a curse on me, and then I feel more heat rising within me. Against him, against me, against the absurdity of this situation.

"Fuck you, Charlie."

He faints.

I pick up Alba and run inside with her. I have just enough time to drop her in my room before the water I have swallowed begins to take its revenge—one should never stay out too long in the megalopolis rain. My guts twist, but there's no time; a light flashes and the siren falls silent, so I rush outside.

The paramedics run over to Charlie with a stretcher.

"Not him," I shout. "She's down in the bedroom!"

I lean over the unconscious Charlie and I can't hold my guts any longer. I crap my trousers and vomit gastric liquid, a worm wallowing in its own liquids.

After a minute of painful cramps, the two nurses come back upstairs, noses held against the stench.

"I'm sorry. The lady has had a heart attack. It was fatal."

These aren't trained nurses, but they are the nurses we get. If we were in Rizoma or Esperia, they would have put my mother into suspended animation by substituting her blood with a freezing saline solution and arresting her cerebral activity. Then they would take her to Papillon hospital, where she could be treated properly after pumping new blood back into her veins.

One of them is trying to load Cleo into the ambulance.

"Can't you do anything for her?"

The other is checking Charlie's condition.

"Nothing. Can you sign these papers, please?"

I don't care anymore. Not about them, not about me.

One of the two ambulance men asks me to help him load the two bodies, one dead, one alive, into the vehicle. I refuse. He keeps at me, then calls for backup. Only he doesn't call more paramedics; he calls the police.

PART THREE
ADULTHOOD – 2055 CE

Everything that we manage to see in the finite universe appears to us incomprehensible and disharmonious if we don't see it as part of a bigger infinite picture. The fact that this infinite picture is mainly unknown does not mean that we should deny its existence.

'Even Science Needs to Dream' Ennio De Giorgi

The squeaking of the washing machine wakes me up at six in the morning. It must have been programmed to start at this time to annoy me. There's no more annoying way to wash away your dreams than with a rinse and spin cycle.

I code-lock myself in the bathroom. From a drawer with a false bottom, I pull out my tobacco and cigarette papers. This is the only place I can lean back and enjoy this pleasure between my metal fingers. I inhale the smoke of freedom, exhale as I let my thoughts wander, and let the cigarette burn down until the heat reaches the sensors in my synthoskin.

I look at myself in the mirror. My eyes are dark and dull, like the cigarette butt I stuff in my pocket. The mirror tells me that, in thirty seconds, the ventilator will have finished changing the air and then I can leave the bathroom without worrying about being caught in the act.

From my secret nook, I remove a ten-millilitre phial of clean urine and pour it into the toilet. I set it aside last night, during my pre–drinking-session piss, to trick the bathroom's sensors.

My other new nemeses await me in the kitchen, where the fridge starts admonishing me as soon as I open the door.

"No more sweet things. You are on a diet," it commands with a peremptory squeak.

"Listen, I'm not in the mood to argue."

"Until you lose weight and your cholesterol goes down, you cannot have any more high-calorie food."

"Fuck you," I reply.

"It is no use insulting me. This is for your own good."

The eggs are locked away in a compartment that only opens at the sound of Kiko's voice. There's nothing for me but the cocoa-less and sugarless chocolate bar that is left on my shelf.

I lie down on the sofa in the living room. A sip of lactose-free milk helps soften the hangover. Kiko's bionic crows pretend to respect my privacy and caw to themselves, but I'm pretty sure they're recording my every movement.

They were a gift from my mother-in-law, Eiko, to her daughter. Ostensibly, they are there to increase the coverage of our home surveillance; in actuality, this includes spying on me.

"Peter, if you're up, could you make me some coffee please?"

Kiko's awake. The calendar, which I consult each morning, shows that today is the 31st of October, 2055. It's been a long seven years of living side by side.

I enter the instructions for the coffee machine: half a cup of coffee plus a quarter cup of milk with lactose. No sugar.

"Yes, Kiko. I'm on it."

Kiko means well. It's 'for my own benefit.' I'm grateful to her for having paid the fine that allowed me out of prison after nine months, instead of twenty-four. The fight with Charlie saw me charged with premeditated assault against my brother. Charlie was sent to hospital with a fractured spine, a concussion, and a gash along his neck. He was discharged long before I was let out and he took all of Alba's pieces. Just as Kiko did in the gamesphere, when the border officer insisted on a bribe to let us out of Bolivian territory, she got me out of a jam in real life too.

Her generosity and perseverance held me in her thrall for a while. Gratitude and a sense of indebtedness compelled me to start seeing Kiko outside of the gamesphere. She replaced Cleo as the only flesh-and-blood female I spent any time with.

Without a K to her name, after the bail she had paid for me, Kiko insisted we live together and have a real relationship. She insisted she didn't want to be just a virtual partner anymore, that immaterial entity I had been so captivated by in my adolescence.

A chair moves in the bedroom, then the door of the wardrobe creaks and her bag of old socks is pushed aside. A brush smoothes her hair and the zip of her short, white jeans chatters as it goes up. I recognise her every sound.

"Peter, did you remember to book? I got our bags ready last night. Why don't you take them downstairs while I get dressed?"

Kiko and I have lived through everything together. We've travelled around the world in all kinds of vehicles, from dilapidated wrecks to luxurious limos, but despite how all-encompassing it seemed, in the gamesphere, we never smelled each other, held hands, or looked each other in the eye. We never tasted each other's sweat or felt each other's warmth.

"Coffee's ready when you are."

"Thanks, I'm just looking for something... be with you in a minute."

The first time I saw Kiko in real life was from behind bars in Lobony jail, a sad place set up in a section of the northern sewer network, abandoned until someone had the bright idea of adapting it for penal use. From human refuse to human refuse.

My cell was a mouldy cave, the bed a pile of cardboard and packaging materials. In my incurable naivety, I had let myself believe I was a prisoner in an adventure like *Live and Let Live—Part II.*

When Kiko came into the visitors' grotto, I noticed that she looked exactly the same as her avatar. At the time, this had seemed like a good omen, even though reality, like an avatar, can hide unpleasant surprises. But I didn't know anyone else who would be able to get together the four hundred K for my bail. And I needed to get out.

It was immediately obvious that she was sour. It became clear later that she was also sly.

There was a limit to what virtual agents could tell me about her. My right to watch her over the webcams in no way revealed the mystery behind her mild eyes and absent gaze, and it took me a long time to scratch the surface of the secrets hiding behind her facade.

I knew Kiko hadn't had two parents: her mother, Eiko, had wanted to become a mother, with or without a husband. Wavering between a procedure to remove the Mongolian set of her eyes and having a child, Eiko decided to have an egg implanted with her own DNA. Then she sold her house and moved from rich Genshoij to middle-class Raon. With the money, she wanted to give herself some hope of motherhood.

Kiko's flattened face, framed by raven black hair, gave her a regal appearance marred only by the scars of juvenile acne. These signs of her adolescence should have raised some doubts; instead, her milky pallor, almost reminiscent of a sacrificial virgin, moved something inside me.

The patience she showed in dealing with my idiocy seemed, to me, to be an indication of the value she gave to our relationship. I was deceiving myself, or rather we were deceiving each other.

"Peter, I can't find the beach towels. Do you know where they are?"

With an effort, I get up from the sofa and grab her monogrammed bags from where she left them in the hallway.

"I don't know; you deal with all that stuff. Have you run a search?"

"Yes, but they aren't answering."

I know what she is about to ask me to do, so I go back into the kitchen and slip a slice of bread in the toaster.

Destroyed by my brother, exhausted by the loss of Alba, and without Cleo's support, all my ambitions have gradually vanished over the years. Cleo's death made me feel vulnerable, but it also gave me an excellent excuse to do something that, under normal circumstances, I would have considered hasty, if not downright reckless.

That's how I let myself be hoodwinked.

Kiko, for her part, had always known what she wanted and found me up for sale: a man with nowhere else to turn. I wonder if, when saving me from internment, she wasn't already harbouring hopes of gaining the fiancé she'd been waiting for.

I once knew what I wanted, too, but in my case, fate—or rather Charlie—gave and then immediately took back everything I had ever desired.

"I certainly didn't throw them away; they were only third-hand. Perhaps they're in the basement."

I knew she was going to say that.

I still live in the same house by the Akeren, but since Cleo's death, I've only been down to the basement once, and that was when I first got out of prison. It hurts too much looking around down there; it is full of anguish and junk. Kiko knows this, but for some reason, she likes to see how far she can push me.

Cleo is resting in Mundur Cemetery, where Charlie has rented her a multimedia grave. It's only thanks to my mother's posthumous mediation that Charlie and I still speak occasionally when we leave flowers on her grave.

My silence reveals my anxiety to Kiko. Perhaps she is also watching me through the eyeball cameras of her crows and is contemplating her next move.

"So, are you going downstairs? We need those beach towels... You're not planning to use the bath towels, are you?"

At the start of our physical relationship, I thought it was normal for someone to look after me. I felt like I didn't know anyone of the equation's elements and wondered if anyone knew the true formula of love.

When we had sex, I heard sounds that weren't in my language, Chinese invocations that sounded like magic spells, and it was only when I set the translator app on the visor to run in real time that I understood her climactic exhortations.

The endorphins used to put me—put us—in a good mood. Seduced by chemistry, neither of us could believe that all our love was there and only there, in that hormonal spasm.

"Listen, I'm having breakfast, can't you go?"

I grab my toast; it has my initials burned on it because Kiko likes everything to be traceable. Kiko likes making sure nothing is left to chance or uncertainty.

"Me? I have to finish doing my makeup. Have you booked our places? Come on, Peter; what's your problem?"

When I was younger, I was accused of loving an inanimate object. Now I'm not even sure I care about the people I'm meant to care about.

The bad thing about this situation is that, without even realising it, we have both fallen into two parallel universes that never meet, not even in bed.

I allow myself sporadic bouts of nocturnal self-abuse. Goodness knows what titillation she resorts to. Our relationship started with complicity and has continued as a minimalist conversation.

Kiko calls me again, and I obey, but I take my time. Instead of going downstairs, I go out on the landing, where there are two metal display racks of colourful clothing. Our neighbours, three Vietnamese women, run a textiles workshop from their flat, sewing without rest to produce dressing gowns and kimonos for the shop windows of Genshoij.

I lurk around the building's front entrance, stalling.

If Kiko wants me to go down into the basement, she'll have to give me the time I need to prepare. Just as she is amusing herself with the wikimirror, where she can spend hours sharing her picture with her girlfriends.

From the doorway, I gaze at the decaying horizon, a layer of adipose kipple. Every day, the rich part of the megalopolis produces four kilos of refuse per person. Kipple grows and attacks everything from inside, from the overflowing bins, from the sewers and rubbish dumps creeping ever closer to the buildings.

It's not unusual to make friends at the dump like Ion and I did. You get to know and recognise people by what they throw away and what they collect. What tins did you throw away today? What clothes did you pick out of the heap? What holidays would you choose from that mouldy old brochure?

No one is ashamed any more, not like when Cleo was young. On the contrary, this behaviour is part of the 'logic of sharing'. Sharing is our preferred survival tool and information barter about kipple is nothing less than commerce. This happens when you realise that you are part of a phenomenon affecting everyone—everybody except the nexhumans.

This is the Earth's new fat: a layer of energy covered with industrial molecules, a heap of consumerism concentrated in unnatural excess.

I wonder if it is because Kiko is so skinny and short that this greasy panorama makes me feel better.

I wonder if it is because Kiko adores aerosol perfumes and wet-wipes that I have reached the point where I can't stand pictures of flowers or those awful, distilled odours that irritate my nose.

Turning on my visor, I put the dataverse back online. The pop-up windows start informing me of the state of reality. Alarming news bulletins mix with the latest ratings of every imaginable commodity and statistics of the most brutal crimes. I ignore it all. There is nothing that deserves even the slightest attention.

I open a link to book two beach loungers with umbrellas at Waterworld.

It is Halloween, the day of our anniversary, and Kiko wants to celebrate with a swim in the pool, even though the real-time videos make it look more like a bowl with sand dumped around the edges.

I can't stand water and the heat makes me sweaty. It might have something to do with the fear I've carried with me since childhood, of unexpectedly shitting myself in awkward situations. On the other hand, it would be so good to pollute the chemically purified water with just as chemically defiled dirt.

I pull my heavy robe tighter around me. The Nubrea, the autumn wind, is creeping up my legs, numbing as it blows. In the distance, a wavering glow bathes the offshoots of Vermillion. The morning mists are nearly impenetrable and I'm forced to use the zoom function in an attempt to make out details.

Years ago, the rubbish from the centre of the megalopolis used to be removed to the suburbs of Cali Nova in the north, Colchide in the west, and Vermillion in the south. This 'liposuction procedure' was supposed to protect Esperia and Rizoma from the consequences of their own consumerism.

This process, first born of a natural desire to be beautiful, was turned into an unnatural one and became a hypertrophic, almost malignant ritual of the megalopolis. It became worse without anyone caring too much about it and in the end, the kipple began attacking from the skies with toxic substances and metals that burned like incinerators. The ground boiled with poisonous blisters, and below it seeped murky effluent. It follows the path of least resistance in its proliferation. We are surrounded by it. Kipple never stops.

In this midst of this state of siege, all Kiko cares about is allowing herself the luxury of a swim. When I turn around, she is standing in the lobby.

"Are you still here? It doesn't take much to find two beach towels. Get a move on and I'll get some food ready."

It's just an excuse. It's just to underline that food is the reason why she torments me with this exhausting diet. In seven years, I have gained five inches in girth. I've gone from being no more than skin and bone to becoming a fat pig.

"I'll go downstairs now. Just wanted to get some fresh air."

Kiko shuffles back inside. It's bizarre that, after excluding me from all household decisions, she's so eager to consult me on such crucial matters as beach towels. It must be because it is the anniversary of our engagement.

I no longer get any pleasure from looking at her or touching her.

As she reaches the door, Kiko calls, 'Hurry up. We don't have all day.' Her voice rising like she's taken a lungful of helium.

When I reach the cellar, I find it difficult to get past the door, and I bump into every corner of every object and box that is filling the space. I wonder if my mother felt like this when she came down here to remember our past. Everything that is stuffed in here holds meaning for one of our family.

Now the space is also packed with Kiko's stuff, and I must root furtively among memories that mean nothing to me. The order she has imposed on this pile of souvenirs makes it difficult for me to organise my thoughts, focus my ideas. Nowhere else depresses me quite as much as this cellar does.

I fight through a barrier of packaging that reveals its contents to me in the corners of my visor. New things fight for my attention, flashing cursors marking their existence, the older things stay to one side.

Layers of dust cover years of dirt that has become a living skin over the laminated surfaces. I tighten my fists and take a deep breath to placate my anger. I hate kipple disguised as mould.

Kiko used all her savings to give me back my liberty, and now shamelessly lords it over the domestic appliances. Sometimes I feel like I am just another of her many trinkets.

Instead of hunting down the beach towels, I start looking for anything without a tag. The silent bags, the mute boxes, all those objects that have to be unwrapped and touched to wake up and communicate. Just like when we were children; when learning by discovery was the only way to experience something, to satisfy our curiosity.

My collection of bottles still sits atop a set of shelves, flasks filled with nothing but air. For some reason, this reminds me of Alba. It was something I did every year on my birthday. Twenty-five years in single file. From 2028 to about 2053. I stopped some years ago.

Opposite me, an entire wooden wardrobe sits hulking, silent. It is a relic of carpentry with three doors and, if memory serves, Charlie and I brought it down here before the walls between the pillars of the cellar were even put up. Inside, from the chrome rail, hangs a row of jackets I know nothing about. The small size and classic style assure me they don't belong to Charlie—he hates retro fashion. They can't be Cleo's either; their style is too masculine.

"Peter! Hurry up! Don't make me come down there!" Kiko yells.

Her shouting seems to activate an automatic procedure in me.

"Here I am, I'm coming... I'm putting in the search settings."

I put in the RFID data 'bags+beach towels' and feed it to the visor to process. The codes start to flash almost immediately from a gold bag in a corner. I grab it and leave, locking the door behind me.

It's a relief to get out of there, but facing the stairs, I am still filled with dismay. Could those jackets once have belonged to my father? The thought leaves me feeling a little disorientated. Why would my mother have kept them? Is this the real reason she came down to the cellar that awful day?

As inattentive as a sleepwalker, I throw the bag to Kiko who glares at me in surprise.

"Aren't you dressed yet? I'm ready."

I put on my best expression for lying. "Listen, I think I've caught a virus. I wouldn't like to risk losing control ... y'know, in the swimming pool."

Kiko bursts out laughing. When she does this, she lets out a kind of howl, her mouth opens and her nose wrinkles up, her eyes become slits and she raises her shoulders as she rocks her torso back and forth clutching her stomach.

"Peter, you crack me up..."

"No, really. You go, I've already booked the places. Call a friend and give her a present for Halloween."

Kiko's face falls at this. She tries to give our relationship an acceptable shape, but sadly, the foundations are missing.

I can hardly blame her for the look of pure disdain she shoots at me, and I also can't blame her that, when she rests her cold lips on mine, she no longer dares slide her tongue in where she can't see it.

At the end of my next shift, I decide to visit my mother.

On the way to the tube, while collecting flowers for Cleo—they grow through the kipple of Kathal Hill—I find a strange plant. It's rare to find free-growing vegetation around here, so I bend closer and scan it. On the net, I discover that it's called rue. It takes all of my Tantalium's strength to uproot it.

I don't have green fingers but I think it'll be a nice present for Rasha's mum, who'll almost certainly be able to do something with it.

The L1 leaves me in Rizoma, where I switch to the L3, which takes to Varmaq station in the south.

In the carriage, I sit down near the door and lift my visor. I suddenly realise I am the only person to have done so. The world we are living in has been redesigned by frequencies, radio waves, and laser beams. We assess every point of light in a forty-metre radius through net crosschecks and data. We measure everyone in as much detail as is permitted by our processing power and the privacy limits set by each individual.

When my gaze meets those of another passengers, what I'm really doing is identifying the brand and model of their purchases, the public personalities they display, the avatars they use in social interactions.

The reflections fluttering off the train windows force me to drop the visor back in place.

Outside Varmaq station, the air is still humid. Beyond the Sangamon Highway lies the stationary slab of Lake Mongo, an artificial body of water reduced to the appearance of a large gob of spit.

The only life form left in it is a kind of purple stinging algae that thrives on the lake bottom. For a radius of metres around Lake Mongo, the Earth has withdrawn and dried up. It reminds me I need to top up my water supply. I still on occasion succumb to my old problem, even though Ion's AquaSan has been like a miracle. It gives me at least four hours of freedom without fearing not being near my home and its toilet.

The stench of decomposing matter, like a kind of glue, spreads over the lake and permeates the air so strongly that, even though I am starving, it makes me lose my appetite.

I head over to a puddle and collect half a bottle of a liquid I would hardly dare to define as water and slowly pump it through the filter. Five or six vigorous pushes and I remove the central tube from which I drink a jet of clear, purified water. I clean out the outer compartment, now full of sludge, and make a note on my visor to drop in on Ion for new filters. I hold my breath until I'm far enough from Lake Mongo not to smell its stench anymore.

The kilometre of road to Mundur takes me past the shells of hundreds of cars all in a line, an immobile exodus heading nowhere.

The entrance to the cemetery can be recognised as such because of the gargoyles acting as custodians on top of the columns covered in funerary graffiti. People prefer the expression provided by graffiti, rather than a banal epitaph. The boundaries of Mundur are marked by a perimeter of aerial signs.

The living with the living, and the dead with the dead. There's no need to repeat it because workmen, wearing jetpacks, are changing the panels that form the kilometre-high installations telling everyone who looks up about the mind-downloading services available after death. The messages are basically always the same.

Buy me and live on in another world

Inside, my footsteps echo on the paved floor, the cadence of the Podox bouncing off the walls. Below the vaulted ceiling, raised to unfathomable heights by the latest renovation, the hollow echo of the Podox makes a sombre sound. Behind the information desk, presided over by an old man called Tiris, a wall of elevators move up and down to the various floors. Walkways, as far as the eye can see, connect the cells of an immense but silent beehive.

The hardest thing isn't communicating with the dead, but talking to Cleo as if she were still alive while attempting to shake off the feeling of guilt, the suffocating remorse I feel for what happened.

Alba, then Cleo, both dead.

With Charlie in the middle of it all, spinning his sticky web.

Since I updated the functions of Cleo's tomb, I have visited a little more often, but still not that regularly. Lately, technology has given me back part of my relationship with my mother. It was worth the money, not only in terms of sentiment but—today—for its practicality, too. I can ask her questions and she can answer me.

"Hello, Mr Tiris, I'm here to see Mrs Payne."

Mundur is more of an archive than a cemetery. There are more chips and tags than candles and flowers and the departed have as many displays as memorial stones. It's a place where people's lives are filed away and preserved for posterity.

"You're the younger son, right? Your mother talks to me about you. She's a nice lady, but so sad."

"I know. We've had some... family problems."

"People who end up here should be able to rest in peace. We do our best, but some things just can't be erased. The past casts its shadow into the future... I'm sorry, I'm speaking out of turn. Please, identify yourself."

I can't tell whether Tiris is human or not. Mundur is the first step towards an eternity that remains trapped inside the graves, a level of sophistication that is far below that of nexhumans, who allow themselves the pleasures of a body equipped with more highly-developed sensorial interfaces than those of humans.

I have found out all about their synaesthetic devices. What they hear, smell, eat, and touch is perceived as if composed of more than one sensorial event that, in some way, coexist. All the senses converge in them; nexhumans lead a life that transcends carbon biology. In comparison, my prosthetic limbs are pale caricatures.

I run the back of my Tantalium hand under the RFID reader. Tiris checks that everything is as it should be by consulting the parrots flitting in and out of a towering aviary behind him.

"The system informs me your mother has been moved to the 229th floor. We are doing some maintenance work. Next time you come by, she'll be back in her usual place."

After chirping out its notification, the parrot flies away while other flocks converge on the aviary for the latest updates.

"Thank you, Tiris. Up to 229, it is. What number?"

"Number 1552. At the end of the corridor."

The loss of my mother hovers in this place like a nightmare. I have transferred all the audio/video material from her black box into a mortuary avatar that has taken Cleo's place. This is how I now interact with the digital existence of my mother. She is the first survivor in the Payne genetic line.

In front of display 1552, I switch on the grave, place the flowers in the vase, then sit down on the sofa opposite.

"Hello, Mum."

Cleo would have been eighty by now, but her holograph shows her in the flower of her forties.

"How nice to see you, Peter. How are you?"

"Fine. You won't believe it, but I'm on a diet."

This titbit surprises the avatar, and it takes a while for it to dig up a suitable answer.

"Really? Are you sure you're okay?"

The intermediary invents nothing, but I notice that she is improvising with greater facility this time. Emulation software is moving ahead; maybe it will even be able to reincarnate her, one day.

"Yes. I came to ask you something." The dead might not be able to see into the future, but they can certainly remember the past. I have questions that only my mother can answer. "I found some old jackets in the cellar, hanging in the wardrobe. Do you know anything about them? Whose are they?"

I show her one of the incriminating jackets I brought with me in the bag. The avatar scans it and after a few seconds projects a hologram memory.

Cleo is sitting on a sofa, cradling a crying baby. I recognise the baby blanket—the child is me. Behind her, I can make out the figure of a skinny man. There is a weary air about him. He is as faded as a ghost, his hair is slicked back and he is watching the scene with wide, bewildered eyes.

Has he been reduced to this piteous state by my screaming and crying, a cacophony it's impossible for a parent to ignore? My howls are so deafening, so strong, so desperate, that my hands begin to shake. It sounds like a failing compressor. The volume of the recording is approaching ninety decibels and my visor warns me that the noise is approaching the danger zone.

The neighbouring avatars are disturbed by the noise.

"Hey, you, Payne, keep it down!"

"We're trying to rest in here!"

"Hooligans, have some respect for the dead!"

After hours upon hours of this torment, my father must have been a wreck. From the grimace on his face, I'd say my screaming must have reached right into where the body is most fragile. He looks as though those frequencies reverberated in all his organs, making them all suffer at the same time. Is it this that made my father, without wanting to, without realising it, decide that he could no longer tolerate my presence? Is this why he left? Why, after surviving the strain of a first son, was the second fatal?

I can only suppose that it was me who pushed him away with all that crying. It might not be fair, but even the innocent can be guilty.

"Why are you doing this to me, Peter? This memory is as painful as it is loving. Can't you see what a state I'm in?" Cleo says.

"I didn't want to hurt you. It's just I want to be sure about something."

"What?"

If I try to hide my pain, Cleo might accuse me of not loving her anymore; if I don't keep my grief in check, I'll look weak. I'll be, once again, the kid who is incapable of self-control.

"I wanted to know my future."

"Your future? From your father's clothes?"

"Not from the jackets, from the fact that you kept them as a memento like I did with..."

I stop abruptly and mentally kick myself for my thoughtlessness. I see her eyebrows shoot up, even though it is an avatar pretending to be Cleo.

"...with you."

"Oh, Peter, you're so sweet. Yes, that is your father's jacket."

Even if my obsession is folly, I am no different from my mother, or countless others. If I really am mad, that's okay, too. My fixation is no different from that of anyone else who dedicates their life to something bigger. Like kamikaze pilots and Ion's firemen.

Cleo's avatar fishes out another family memory.

"Do you remember why I called you Peter?"

"Because I wanted you to stay with me forever."

It breaks my heart to see the hologram of Cleo, a sprinkling of data on the gravestone, shrug and tear up. She wanted me to be like Peter Pan, but with a surname like ours, a different fate was almost a certainty.

Then I hear footsteps coming down the corridor. I'd recognise the rhythm of that gait anywhere. I turn and watch as Charlie, in polished black shoes and an impeccably tailored suit, approaches. He has also come to pay his respects. At least on the first of November, at Halloween, the day for remembering the dead, he remembers he is part of the Payne family.

I'm grateful for the precautions I took: a knife in my jacket pocket and a thick stack of magazines strapped to my chest, under my jumper, for protection.

"It's been a long time, little brother."

"Hi, Charlie. How're things?"

The usual tension between us ionises the air. I bite my tongue and keep my eyes on my mother. Charlie leans over to the grave, removes my already-wilting flowers from the vase on the shelf and replaces them with his bunch of dewy white roses. He could afford Cleo's favourites.

"Fine, I just came in for a quick hello. Jo and the kids are waiting for me."

I wipe my clammy palms on my trousers.

"She's listening. You can say hello now if you want."

Charlie starts and takes a step backwards.

"What the fuck, Peter? Is this another of your crazy ideas?"

"No, I just updated the software. It's not just multimedia; it's interactive too. It learns from experience. It's basically an avatar pretending to be Cleo—so much so that it believes it is Cleo."

He is perplexed, and when our mother speaks to him, he is confused.

"Thank you, Charlie. You are so kind. You should thank your brother for this gift. Now we can talk together. Isn't that lovely?"

I can already imagine what is running through my brother's head. If Charlie thought of Alba as a disc with a voice recorded on it, Cleo must seem like a ghost summoned from the afterlife.

"Yeah, incredible."

He looks slightly scared. Surprise has withered his arrogance.

"Listen, Mum, this thing... Can you really hear me?"

He shoots me a surly look and in an instant, a series of almost shocking biometric values show that I am about to feel bad. The diagnosis comes from the sensors in the fabric of my coat and trousers. With no insurance, I don't even have a shred of online cover. I know that I am ill, but no one will come to save me.

"It's not another trick, is it, Peter? Another of your stupid schemes?"

"No, Charlie, don't say that. I can hear you perfectly.

Tell me about you now, about little Tommy and Lisa. And how is Jo?"

Charlie is at a loss. He keeps staring at me as if I have ruined the pleasure he gains by appeasing his conscience with a bunch of flowers. Now he has to waste time and words on a thing that must appear to him like a kind of static putrefaction.

"They're fine. The kids study at a school in Worrisham, the usual stuff. Jo had a little domestic accident, burned her hand. Nothing too serious. I've been promoted to the Trashware Department at Reverse. I analyse electronic scrap now. It's a big step up for me."

His stance is unnatural; he is holding his torso too far back as if scared that the holograph will launch itself at him and drag him into the dataverse.

"Have you really never heard of this funerary service?" Cleo asks.

There is a vein pulsing in his neck. His racing circulation is a symptom of his rising resentment.

"Yes, of course, but I thought it was just video and recordings. I mean, like this, you don't even seem..."

"But I am, dear Charlie—I am dead, but don't be scared. This is me, too. I have learned to my cost that our worlds are divided by barriers that only really exist in our minds. I see it every time when I see the two of you. But now, you two have to get along, understand?"

I see Charlie try to swallow.

"All right, Mum. I have to go now. Y'know, the kids won't wait, and Jo asked me to be quick."

He is already turning, ready to make his getaway.

"Why didn't you bring them up here? I'd like to see them; you never bring them."

"Well, I'm not sure, this thing..."

Is it just the surprise or is Charlie actually scared of Cleo's avatar? Like he used to be scared of Alba's head?

Alba's ghost has returned. It's here between me and everything I do. I can't let these spectres from the past come back to haunt me now. If my future is destined to be what it was always going to be, I have to take as much advantage as possible of this meeting with Charlie. Even if he hasn't kept the pieces, he must know where they are.

"Mum, I'm going, too. I'll be back soon; Christmas is just around the corner."

"All right then, boys, you have things to do, I understand. I'll get back to my rest. Come and see me soon. Let me hug you as best as I can."

Cleo opens her arms wide and draws us into her holographic space. With a little imagination, I can almost believe it is true.

It is the first time that Charlie and I have left the cemetery together. Every other time, I have stayed behind with Cleo while Charlie hurries away, using his family as an excuse.

His face hardens as soon as we move away from the protective aura of our mother. He looks disgusted.

"You did it on purpose, didn't you?!"

"Did what?" I find it difficult to keep up with him. It's not a question of legs, but rather a question of weight.

"That virtual agent shit."

"Mortuary agent."

"Whatever... I don't like it. It smells of trickery."

Charlie wasn't always like this. I remember when we used to fly model aeroplanes from the roof of our home, or when we played with plastic yachts on the banks of the Akeren. We used to invent nicknames for people; we would whisper to each other in code to keep our secrets to ourselves. Charlie liked telling stories and had a weakness for embellishing the truth. To him, even lies were a form of entertainment. Now, though, he has that air of a person who has had all the imagination sucked out of him.

"Look, I didn't do it for you."

"So, what's it for? So we could cry over the past? Sigh over the fact that she is no longer with us? Pretending that we're talking to her is like pretending she's still alive."

"I did it for us. So we could carry on being a family."

The simulacrum of Cleo could be a comfort to both me and Charlie. She is our heritage, our link with the past. This is how I have come to terms with the fact that she is no longer with us.

"Have you forgotten what you did to this family?"

"Listen, I'm sorry. I know I did a bad thing, and I served nine months in Lobony for it. I'm trying to fix it. What d'ya say to meeting up one of these days?"

"I don't think that's a good idea."

"All right, fine. I'll come by Trashware to see you. I haven't been to head office in ages."

We step into the next elevator. It's as if Charlie doesn't believe I have any sanity left in me.

"What do you want, Peter? Why all of this interest in me, all of a sudden? What's going on?"

I'm trying to put our history behind us, but it's like trying to move a mountain single-handed. If I could work out why I have never stopped loving Alba, despite her never having done anything to requite my passion, perhaps I would be able to understand why I don't love Kiko, who, in her own way, does her best to make me like her.

But there's no point in trying to explain all this to Charlie. Feelings mean nothing to him. He cleans his shoes with feelings. It would be futile to try to convince him that love can be found in the dump.

"What's going on is that you still have the pieces."

"What pieces?"

"Don't try to pretend you don't know. I'm talking about Alba."

"I don't know anything about it."

This dialogue, worthy of adolescents, is starting to annoy me.

"Pity. I was going to suggest a trade."

When the lift doors open, Charlie doesn't rush off like he did before. If I'm lucky, he might tell me something, and if I'm even luckier, he might reveal a clue to the truth.

"But if you didn't get the pieces, it doesn't matter."

I'm going to have to use the crystal as leverage. I know he hates me because he still can't understand how this life-long coward managed to summon the courage to nearly fracture his neck. I struck when his back was turned, and he still hasn't forgiven me.

We say goodbye to Tiris and walk through the entrance bordered by columns.

"I knew you were going to ask me sooner or later, but ten years, Peter? You've made me wait so long..."

He thinks he's got me where he wants me, but I just had to see how tight he wanted to pull the noose around my neck.

In front of us, a saloon car crammed full of people is waiting with the engine running. Not only Jo and the kids but a gaggle of Charlie's acquired family, none of whom I have never met.

Jo is the eldest child of the Azevedos, a family of immigrants who came to the megalopolis to seek their fortune. They produced children, partly to pass the time and partly to have as many hands as possible at work on the Durenico dump.

Charlie met her during one of the 'missions' that took the Dead Bones outside their usual stomping ground.

Durenico is known as a disgusting place, even when compared to the rest of the megapolis: full of abandoned factories and industrial archaeology from past centuries. Even so, Charlie loved it; he told me as much when we still lived together. He even went to live near there, later on.

"Let's talk about it then." I stop in the hope that he'll follow suit.

"Not now. They're waiting for me."

"I'll call you tomorrow, then. We can arrange something."

He rubs his hands together briskly. The clouds descending on the Varmaq skyline have covered most of the sky, trapping the cold air close to the ground.

'No, it's not that simple. I'll call you when I think of something.'

I detect a whiff of deception. Am I getting any closer to Alba or am I simply once again putting myself at the mercy of my brother?

Chapter 17
Alcova

Days go by waiting for a call from Charlie, and while my hands are constantly stuck in rubbish, my head is wandering elsewhere. The paths of Kathal Hill, paved with computer motherboards, car chassis and industrial metals, crunch under my feet. It's like walking in the ossuary of an information technology market.

Rasha drops the motherboards into a big, blue oil drum full of boiling acid. The barrel is as tall as he is and he has to stand on the tips of his toes to reach the rim. Those boards have to stay in there for hours before the acid removes the thin layer of copper.

Today, I found a Gameboy console, a portable snack dispenser, a hedge trimmer, two toasters and four vacuum cleaners; I also found some unopened DVDs, which will be recycled without ever having been either seen or sold.

The most interesting find is a packet of saffron. I sniff it and it makes my nose tingle. I look for some information about it on the Net and find out that it used to be one of the most expensive spices available, its thread-like stamens harvested by hand at enormous cost because it was a sterile mutant, unknown in nature.

I don't want to get to the point of hating people, I don't want to see them as a kind of pollution, but for me, those who throw away certain types of things are marked by environmental sin. Every time I have to throw something away, I am gripped by a kind of phobia.

One of the things I have learned about the dump is that it is in a state of continual change. It expands and grows, absorbs and engulfs the health of the land with everybody's and any-body's leftovers.

I get so irritated today that I lose my patience.

My anger rises and I pick up a pair of spray cans and chuck them in Rasha's oil drum. The flash of their explosion makes him jump back.

"Oi! What's wrong with you? Be careful with those!"

"I'm in a bad mood, sorry. What a waste of a day."

"Well, warn me next time."

My plan, first conceived fifteen years ago, has regained some of its verve since seeing Charlie at the cemetery. I had given up, and perhaps, deep down inside, I had wanted to for-get about Alba. I was wrong, and the other day, Ion provided me with a further sign. When I dropped in on him for some new AquaSan filters, he gave me a present. It was a metal trin-ket box decorated with marine swirls someone found in Wor-risham, and inside was a fragment of a poem by Edgar Allan Poe. It's called 'To One in Paradise' and it goes like this:

Ah, dream too bright to last!
Ah, starry Hope! that didst arise
But to be overcast!
A voice from out the Future cries,
'On! on!'—but o'er the Past
(Dim gulf!) my spirit hovering lies
Mute, motionless, aghast!

And all my days are trances,
And all my nightly dreams
Are where thy grey eye glances,
And where thy footstep gleams—
In what ethereal dances,
By what eternal streams.

All the signs are starting to come together. The omens are no longer mute and I can interpret them now. Even though Alba's memory acted as an opiate, living with Kiko has turned out to be a traumatising experience. Putting happiness on hold, suspending my life like this, has worn me out.

So, now I sift through the unending piles of crap on the Kathal Hill dump without rest. I find antique wristwatches, silicon and limestone encrusted mobile phones, the carcasses of tablets, piles of DVD players, cash registers, and a monster of a multi-function fax machine. Nothing, nothing is right.

"Rasha, I'm under the weather today... Have you got any kind of pick me up?"

"Sure, take a look. I went to the Genshoij market yesterday."

He empties his pockets on the ground; a random pile including two small hedgehog skins to counter rheumatism, a dog's kidney to excite the libido, two newts for stomach aches, and scales of dried snakeskin to dip in milk as a kind of tonic.

"Swap you the newt for a vacuum cleaner?"

"The newt is worth all four of your vacuum cleaners."

"Yeah, but does it work?"

"My mum chops and fries them. Then again, she fries everything."

I nod to the rest of the team and make my way wearily home, a place that now belongs more to Kiko than to me. Too much running away has left me with nowhere to call home. I don't want to ask for asylum in the Kathal Hill trenches. I would rather be like Ion and live amongst the bins. Not least because your average street bin receives at least a pair of reusable objects a day. This means that, in the roughly 450,000 bins of the megalopolis, there are at least nine hundred thousand things in good—if not excellent—condition. Over the course of a year, that makes 330 million.

Without a doubt, enough to make a living.

In the end, all this effort gives me hope—the hope of being able to get out of this stagnant relationship I've thrown myself into. A relationship that started off as a stopgap, but that soon became a trap. The love that was torn apart on the streets fifteen years ago is more alive than the one I sleep next to every night.

With the bits Charlie has of Alba—if I can get them off him—I only need her legs and she will be complete. To get the legs, I need to get closer to Jimmy the Loins, and I'm afraid I will need Kiko to help me in my search. I can't go to the Loins's shoe store alone. I need a cover.

"How do you fancy going into town today?" I ask her.

Kiko's forehead wrinkles below her helmet of electric black hair.

"I don't know, Peter. I have urgent business to get on with. My mother wants to come visit us and I have to tidy the house. Can't you go on your own?"

"Yeah, but... It's just that I wanted your advice. I'm going to see Charlie again soon and it's almost Christmas. I wanted to get him a special present, but I'm not as good as you at that kind of thing."

"Why not from the dump? If you bring me some things, I'll help you choose."

How am I going to hide from her that I need a cover story? How am I going to convince her to come with me to a 'certain' shop, so that I don't stick out?

"He's my brother, Kiko. It's years since we were in touch. I'd like to make an effort."

She mutters in disapproval. I'm going to have to do better than this to get her out of the house.

The fake window, where a moment ago there were swimming sharks, changes view. Kiko's friends have started watching a programme they think is one of her favourites. It took me six months of digging to put together the nine screens that make up the wall.

Kiko is a fundamental part of the plan: Jimmy the Loins might have something unique, not as a present for Charlie, but for me. Going by what Mickey told me years ago, the Loins cleaned up his act and opened a shoe shop in the Green Towers area.

The time has come to discover if he did the same as the rest of the Dead Bones. The time has come to find Alba's legs. Judging by the looks of his sales staff, I just might be in luck. The Alcova website only shows nexhumans working there. An encouraging sign.

"Not that I want to buy anything, course not... I'd just like to find him something good. I want to go to Green Towers to copy a tag."

Kiko doesn't mask her reaction. The bait makes her open her mouth and turn off the TV, turning the wall of screens into an aquarium again.

"Green Towers? Where were you thinking?"

For her, human interactions in flesh and blood are superfluous events and avoidable, events that happen independently of whether we want them to or not. She is satisfied with her visor, the gamesphere, the wikimirror, and the TV window.

Once I had fun seeing whether her emails were more important to her than I was. I called out to her just as the visor beeped. I kept calling with an annoying frequency, but Kiko ignored me. In the end, I had to pretend to be ill to get her attention.

Another time, during one of the gamesphere's frequent black-outs, there was no mistaking her withdrawal symptoms: she cried desperately until the connection came back online. All these details have convinced me that Kiko has an almost filial relationship with her visor and her kitschery and chippery in general. Every time she has to get something repaired, every time an appliance shows signs of malfunctioning or it doesn't respond to her commands instantly, she acts like the object is in physical danger and that she might never see it again.

"I don't know exactly where, yet. We could stroll along Piccalorda Way. I have the address of a shop all the shoe forums are talking about. If the weather's nice, it'll be fun."

I have no proof, but I reckon that at night, while she is sleeping, a part of Kiko misses the visor on her eyes. I'm surprised she hasn't yet suggested I buy Charlie's present on the Earthsalvage site.

For Kiko, leaving the house is a kind of holiday to exotic lands. It doesn't matter how hard I try to see her as a human being. I can't see anything in her except circuits that open and close and programs that run and rerun in terror of what could happen if, perish the thought, something crashed.

"I'll just finish cleaning the bathroom, then I'll get ready. I hope I'm not going to regret this."

I suppose the vacuum in her gaze might indicate that there is nothing inside her, that she is a vacuous girl, not even malignant, merely devoid of passion and enterprise. In a way, I admire her coldness, her way of being distant from things. She always appears lucid, not livid and susceptible like me.

Around Green Towers, I don't feel like a complete nonentity. Everyone else here shares something in common, something the nexhumans don't share.

Between us, it is not only the clothes that are different—we with our leftover fashions—even our facial features are innumerable in variety, whereas they have refined the aesthetic repertoire, leaving us behind—an inferior and primitive level of humanity.

For most of the megalopolis, the seasons are simulated and sponsored. This year, the Spring Lot, which is already following the winter one, has been assigned to a food company and the blooms of advertising anticipating the change of season are budding in the shape of 'Spring McBucks' on every street corner.

Here in Green Towers, though, things are the other way around. In other neighbourhoods, nature appears only on billboards for 'Pastoral Lots' that can be enjoyed through the surrealism of visors. But in Green Towers, nature has reappeared with biological areas, mini botanical reserves and environmental decoration. A scattering of artificially cultivated punctuation marks, designed by computers, but still real—nothing like the 'Spring, Summer, Autumn, and Winter' lots available as a sensorial experience elsewhere.

The facades of the buildings along Piccalorda Way are explosions of chlorophyll and carotene pigments. Every building is covered in green, swathed in climbing plants and carpeted with grass and a profusion of vegetables and herbs.

In the background, low-maintenance hanging gardens flow over the tops of the Green Towers themselves. The roofs are cloaked in plants, a solution which helps reduce the flow of rain water, capturing the pollutants and protecting the apartments below, as well as acting as soundproofing and air-conditioning and filtering.

It takes two full minutes for my visor to download the building data and Kiko, impatient, pulls me aside. I'm going to have to put up with numerous detours into just as many shops, endure forced marches chasing mirages displayed in the windows, practise patience and stay calm.

Anything to make her, as far as possible, relax and lower her guard.

I let her wander through the various stores, ready to lose herself in a forest of discounts and promotions, a jungle of instantaneous wishes where she, the new savage, moves fluidly and untiringly with visor and fingertouch at the ready to capture and copy every tag. It takes an hour for Kiko to investigate every object for sale, every live demonstration of the goods on offer, and the displays of the trendiest models.

In Sasboro, her favourite perfumery, her anaemic face brightens in a way it rarely does.

"Look! These are what I've been asking you for, for months."

She is pointing at a display of lipsticks and it comes to life. The video proclaims they should smell of honeysuckle, but to me, they reek of common carbolic acid, used to detoxify the sewers. Detecting Kiko's interest, each chromed capsule lines up and points towards her lips. I feel lost.

My trashformer instincts have let me down. These objects are all equally captivating. I don't know how she can like one more than another.

Her maniacal attention is disturbing. Kiko lives with me: not for money, not for safety, and certainly not for love, but simply to flaunt the signs of a bond of affection. I feel like I'm her cover story.

"Look at this, it would look great in black."

Anyone could see that it would look great on her. This means I'll have to sift through the rubbish twice as carefully for twice as long.

"It has to be this one, got it? Don't come back with an imitation, as usual, or a different colour."

I make a note of the RFID code and tell her what she wants to hear, 'Okay, you'll get it when I find it.' It's a small price to pay for convincing her to carry on to Alcova, which is where I really want to go.

I have never seen so many nexhumans all in one place. I can see at least twelve beauties, eternally twenty-something, but they are very different from the Alba I remember: their hair is tall and voluminous, their lips bee-stung, their eyes made up with purple and coal-black streaks, a vampire look that leaves me numb.

I stare at one with marvellous blue eyes. I daren't look down at her cleavage, nor let my gaze climb those long legs. I don't remember ever having been this desperate in the last fifteen years.

In the gamesphere, I can cut off images at the push of a button, but here I'm powerless to turn off the apparition of the nexhumans and their movements even if I wanted to.

All this beauty reminds me of my pain. I have Alba's whole body map illustrated in front of me, her evolution in the flesh.

I don't know whether to shout with joy or beg for mercy.

Full of doubt, I grit my teeth. They do not belong to the same species as us. Nexhumans are like the sarcophagi and totems of the past; in carrying our souls into the future like those ancient vehicles carried our spirits into the afterlife, I see in them a similar attempt to imprint ourselves on the continuum of eternity, a mark of our desire to last forever.

I fall into a trance, captivated by this intimidating vision.

I have to do something. I must make up an excuse and get away from Kiko. I need time to explore the area.

"What do you say to seeing the hourly show?"

"Good idea. Trisha and Lynne will die of envy when they see the codes..."

Alcova is divided into departments, each teeming with people who never tire of renewing themselves, though they always remain themselves. The holographs suspended just below the ceiling advertise the fact that, at this exact moment, the store is home of hundred types of women's shoes available and 360 types of men's shoes.

We line up for the amphitheatre, where the fashion show is about to begin.

Once we take our places, the lights dim and the stage darkens. A roll of drums puts me on my guard.

We are about to witness Jimmy's latest gimmick: shoes with a special plaque that emits your company logo or personal brand so it is recognisable throughout the megalopolis.

I half expect to see the Loins jump out, dressed up as a hungry wolf, ready to grab his workout/workshop nymphs. Instead, the curtain rises on a round man with an air comprised of equal parts elegance and arrogance.

I do a search on him online, with half a K connection credit, and discover that Jimmy has neither a wife nor children: he lives on his own with his shoes. He made his fortune six years ago when he patented a shoe capable of generating energy from every step taken by means of a piezoelectric generator in the heel.

The Loins is wearing an absurd get-up, a lizard-skin kaftan with bone buttons down the front and shoes with toes curled like those of a maharaja.

The scar on his face is still there: a yellowish ridge crossing from his left cheekbone to the temple. He got it one day while he and Charlie were playing their usual violent games. They used to prey on crows that flew too low or the notorious seagulls that nested around Kathal Hill.

Flying things made their bile rise.

It didn't take the poor beasts long to realise they couldn't fly tied together like that. They all did the same thing, even the birds they tied together using a longer piece of line: after some clumsy attempts to lift off, after the usual distressed cries, they always fought each other in the end.

Even if one bird managed to overpower the other, it still hadn't resolved anything. The line that at first forced it to deal with an enemy now bound it to a carcass. Some of them would peck at the other bird's leg until they managed to sever it, others became so exhausted that the rats came to claim the corpses of both. Some—very few—freed themselves by pecking through the fishing line. One of them, a raven that had been flying over and around the area for months without anyone managing to bring it down, pecked Jimmy in the face with its beak a number of times before Jimmy got hold of it and dispensed swift justice. He killed it with his teeth like a savage, roasted it, and devoured it.

From Jimmy's sides, from a belt of leather, hang the traditional tools of his new trade: an awl for making holes, an eyelet puncher, and a nail gun. He resembles a cobbler more than a shoe designer.

I find it hard to believe that this is the same Jimmy: he of the bloody bites and the tendency to salivate uncontrollably after legs of all kinds: human legs, nexhuman legs, table legs.

I set my visor to 'tag-grab'. I run through all of the devices emitting an electronic call sign until I find the frequency I'm interested in: Jimmy's personal chip.

Every boss likes to be in control. In Jimmy's case, I'm sure he'll have arranged it so that his personal chip can access everything without limitations throughout Alcova.

"Listen, Kiko, I've got to find a bathroom. I'll be back straight away."

Absorbed by the show, Kiko doesn't even glance in my direction.

I get as close to the Loins as I can to capture his code. It takes a few seconds: easy and unnoticed. With this sequence in my hands, I can clone his chip and 'become' him, without him knowing anything about it.

I can get into any place he can.

I can do anything he does.

I just need a few days for a cryptographic analysis and to crack the reading key. At this point, I will have the consultation table. Before I had my visor, this would have been a tedious job. What would have taken weeks is now only a matter of days, thanks to the power of the visor, effortlessly calculating and recalculating thousands of lines of code.

Wandering around looking for the toilets, I bump into more nexhumans—customers this time. I can't think straight anymore.

They look like they have been poured into their body hugging sheaths of lace, which barely conceal the forms they are supposed to cover. Strategically placed pockets obscure the most private areas. Some of them are strolling around completely at ease with their breasts visible under light layers of fluorescent netting.

I am getting increasingly agitated and have to force myself not to look at them, to keep the situation under control. I dodge each feminine curve, shifting my gaze anywhere else to avoid falling victim to their magnetic auras.

I set the search function to look for Alba's legs—code 8–952–395–78–08–05—and open every RFID channel. The response is disappointing.

If I'm wrong, if Jimmy hasn't kept the legs, I'll be left with nothing but absurd solutions, like assembling her on a wheelchair or stealing the limbs from one of these girls milling around the store.

I wonder whether their limbs can be substituted. I wonder if nexhumans are affected by the same problems of rejection as human bodies.

No. The more I think about this, the more I realise that would be an abomination. Alba's head wouldn't be right on anything but her own parts.

I walk through the men's department, determined to find Alba's legs.

In the distance, an assistant who has noticed my peculiar behaviour points me out to a colleague. Gripped by panic, I dive into the changing rooms.

I embarrass some women trying on thigh-high boots and girls posing in half-naked selfies.

I make a complete circle of the area but can't shake the attention of the assistants as they start coming after me, alarmed by my suspicious behaviour.

Their footsteps—the clicking of their high heels—excite me, but I can't allow myself to be seduced by my imagination. I have so many weak points that the only way to avoid trouble is to close every access point to my perception. If I were to look behind me, if I were to let my gaze rest for too long on their ankles and taut thighs, I would use up all the time I have left before Kiko becomes suspicious, and then all hope would truly be lost.

I have no choice. The sales girls, taking full advantage of the speed of their interconnected brains, have driven me into a dead end corridor. The insistent signal of an RFID distracted me and now I'm trapped.

"Wait, sir! You can't go in there."

The noises in my stomach make me twist my face. Despite my weakened body, I don't let myself be taken in by their breasts, straining against skintight shirts.

At the end of the corridor, there is a door with a sign saying:

STOCKROOM—NO ENTRY

I am not put off by the warning. I charge the Podox and make a run for it.

I speed up and my overfed size makes me knock over the displays. I trip and fall to the ground. As I get up, I can hear the click of heels behind me. I gasp for oxygen, close my eyes and carry on until I hit the door sharply with the Tantalium.

When my hunters catch up with me, they are perplexed.

I have tumbled to the bottom of what seemed like an endless staircase and am on the verge of losing control of my bowels.

"I'm s-s-s-sorry, I c-c-couldn't find the b-b-b-bathroom. I p-p-panicked."

I am stuttering because I'm staring up from below at their unending thighs. Then I give in to a snort of liberating laughter and simultaneously let off an embarrassing fart, which calms them. In the midst of my humiliation by my ragged body, my inner demon roars with happiness.

"You should have told us you were in difficulty. We would have happily shown you to the nearest toilets."

"You're too kind. It's just I was embarrassed to let... you... see me like this."

Their mischievous smiles cut right through me. Whether for good or bad, it doesn't matter anymore. Those synthetic curves washing against my eyeballs are now ineffectual, harmless: my ecstasy lies elsewhere: there is one bar flashing in the surreal environment of my visor.

8–952–395–78–08–05

Alba's legs are here, in Alcova's basement. Over time, the batteries powering the RFIDs must have run down. The signal can't be detected from more than a few metres away.

I could hug Jimmy and his sales girls.

I could party for a week to celebrate.

I now know that the Loins has changed his look without losing his vices.

I sincerely apologise to the nexhumans as they grip my

arms and legs and lift me up. My carcass is carried through the shop amidst the disdainful laughter of the customers. Then, with gentle delicacy, I am deposited, raving, at the door to the toilets.

"Thank you! Thank you! You're all truly wonderful. You've saved me."

The image of Alba's legs, even aged by years, paralyses my senses and floods me with joy. As much as the new thighs of the nexhumans were driving me mad, Alba's beloved old legs help me find myself, my own identity, again.

The toilet paper in Alcova is so soft that it seems a pity to wipe my arse with it. Even more incredible than this softness are the reams of risquhe ream printed on the paper, which I read before it ends up sullied. I swipe a whole roll to give to Rasha.

I walk back triumphantly to get Kiko. I find her sitting immobilised with devotion. She looks almost embalmed, but elegant nonetheless, moving only to applaud the clothes that have just passed.

When I touch her arm, she appears to wake up.

"Everything okay?"

"Wonderful. I've recorded everything."

After another two minutes, the lights come back on and she entwines her fingers in mine.

"I've found what I was looking for, too. An incredible tag in the menswear department. In a month, at the most, I'm sure I'll find it round our way. Shall we go?"

Jimmy waves to the public and retires from the stage. I'm planning to pay him a visit over the next few days. To face him, though, I'm going to need reinforcements.

I'm planning the perfect disaster and all I need is two people. When I reach Ion's cubicle, he and Rasha are discussing something in undertones. I can't hear what they are saying. All I can see is that they have lined up a series of objects on an old trunk.

The problem I gave them to solve was this: how to create panic in Alcova, get into the stockroom, snatch Alba's legs, and escape free and clear.

Rasha is an expert in chemical matters—explosions and combustive phenomena—and Ion's experience is essential if we are to avoid the rescue landing us in Lobony, or worse, the whole thing turning into a fuck-up suicide mission.

"I reckon we should use nitrogen triiodide. It'll make a bang so loud that no one will come bother us."

Very carefully Rasha opens a bottle of ammonia and pours ten millilitres in a plastic food tub. Then he draws a syringe of dark amber liquid from a bottle with no label.

The care he is taking over his movements fills me with trepidation.

"Now watch. We inject the tincture of iodine into the container and let it settle."

After a few seconds, tiny little black stones form before our eye. Explosive marbles, if I've got the gist of it right.

"Here, this is ready. Once the ammoniac has been removed, even just the weight of a feather resting on it will make everything explode."

Ion's grin is pure satisfaction. It is easy to see how excited they both are. They need a bit of danger to liven up their lethargic existences.

"I don't know; my idea is dangerous and the solution is unstable, so we will have to prepare it there, but it'll buy us some time before everyone realises it's only smoke."

As an alternative to Rasha's potion, Ion opens a bottle of Rici-Cola and empties half of it onto the ground. Then he fetches a sheet of aluminium foil, a funnel and a small flask marked with a skull and crossbones. He tops up the larger bottle to the three-quarter mark with hydrochloric acid.

"You just have to roll up the foil and put it in the neck of the bottle, like this."

He closes the bottle and seals it with duct tape. He doesn't even give us time to take shelter before he throws the bomb about thirty metres away. The deafening explosion claws at our eardrums and the shockwave ruffles our hair. When we open our eyes, there is a two-metre crater in the garbage, already falling in on itself.

"If you throw this at the target, let's say the shop's electric switchboard, you'll short-circuit the whole place. Not only will the cables start frying, but the fire alarm will go off and the sirens will clear everyone out. We'll be able to grab the legs and be out of there with time to spare."

"Okay, Ion, but won't the fumes possibly harm someone? Mine makes a cloud of purple smoke that'll set the fire alarm off. Apart from that, the triiodide only smells of ammonia. It irritates your nose and eyes, but it isn't toxic at all."

I look at them proudly.

"Great. That will work as a diversion; now we just need the details. For example, do you think during the day or night would be best?"

"At night, we'd be quicker but more visible. A webcam in the wrong place and we'll end up like kipple on the wind."

"Rasha is right. A rainy day would be best, as even a web-cam would have a hard time identifying us."

"I've got that covered. All thanks to the Loins."

So here we are, a normal rainy day: Ion, Rasha, and me, in the Green Towers territory. Rasha and I are wearing the discarded uniforms of MegaElectric labourers. Ion didn't want anything to do with such symbols. Reverse or not, he's dressed up in his best coat.

We haven't just dressed for the part, we have also disguised ourselves: each of us has had fun changing our features with fake noses, long beards, padded shoulders and fake teeth. In our business, finding material is never a problem if you have enough time and patience.

It isn't dusk that is falling at the end of the day, but a hazy gleam just above the horizon. As usual, a tempest of hostile material is rising from Cochilde, a storm that divides and agglomerates into clouds and tongues of flame dancing to the wind.

Rasha is at the doors, hands stuffed deep in the pockets of his jacket, ready to dive into Alcova on my signal.

I am crouched on the roof of Jinsu, a three-storey delicatessen. As soon as Ion and Rasha have played their part, it will be my turn for the grand finale.

On the other side of the crowded Rotterquay Road, lashed by the howling Nubrea and pouring rain, I can see Ion concentrating on readjusting his hair and flapping waterproof coat. Dressed like this, in someone else's Sunday best, he looks like a respectable old man.

Above his head, a barrage of lightning is cranking up its charge in rushing, whirling air. The claps of thunder roar twelve seconds after the lightning flashes, telling me the storm is a little less than four kilometres away. The dense waters of the Selam River will already be boiling.

Down our way, some days are so dark that the incoming weather makes my good hand tingle. It might get even better: it might snow. That would really make it difficult for the webcams; it could even stop them working altogether.

Even if the snow doesn't come, I've managed to reconfigure the ones trained on Alcova's entrance and those inside the shop. It's amazing what you can get done if you know how to use the web. And if you know someone like Rasha's uncle—Smiling Baasim, a badass hacker with a thing for sharing his knowledge—the whole thing becomes a lot of fun. Baasim taught me the 'buffer overflow' trick, which launches a wave of tags against the webcam receptors large enough to overload the buffer capacity of their memories.

The overloaded system cut out, and when it restarted, I fed it a worm program, setting new target coordinates to replace the old ones. This operation has created a number of 'blind corridors' for me and my accomplices to enter, reach the stockroom, and make our getaway without being seen.

We will be phantoms. The only record on the server of our presence will be the inexplicable presence of the Loins in the stockroom.

Malevolence doesn't come easily to me, but invoking my demon and drawing on its unknown strength has become easier of late. Whatever it costs, those legs are coming back to me.

All around us, electrical cracks split the sky this way and that, ionising the air. A discharge of lightning hits the ground near us; I choose to see it as auspicious and it spurs me on.

I motion to Ion to come in. This is one of those moments when things could head in any direction. There is a whistling in my ears. I have left behind many opportunities at the crossroads that litter my life: when I was a child, out of weakness; when I was an adolescent, out of ignorance; and as a man, out of indecision.

It is time for me to act the part of a man, now.

Exactly on schedule, Ion has attracted the attention of the Loins by the shop window and is keeping him there with a footwear demonstration, providing cover for Rasha, who is already in the shop's toilets.

"Dear Mr Corrigan, look at your models carefully... You don't really mean to say that you consider them more contemporary than this sumptuous Aguillon. Even though you run a modestly successful shoe shop in Green Towers, you are still, and I say this with no disrespect, a cobbler... At best, a trader on Piccalorda Way."

My visor reads their lips, providing me with access to their conversation even though I can't hear them. The timer superimposed over the scene tells me that at this precise moment, Rasha is tinkering with his magical compounds.

"You must allow me to disagree. A simple Aguillon is nothing compared to our shoes."

Ion raises an eyebrow and switches to manipulative mode.

"Come on, Jimmy—can I call you Jimmy? Please, don't be impertinent. Are you really saying you think your shoes are at the same level as nexhuman shoes? Sure, you have nexhuman staff in here, but that's not enough to raise your goods to their level; they remain human products with limitations that anyone can see."

Rasha comes out of the bathroom and trots towards the exit. A short distance away, the Loins draws back sharply, insulted. He looks around him as if to dismiss Ion's insult, but he has stiffened, and with a raised voice, reveals his plans for the future.

"Human? I just need a few more years. Not long now, and I'll be able to afford the mortgage for an upload. Cobbler indeed! Trader! I'll live forever! I'll use champagne as mouthwash!"

The countdown has started, and not just for Jimmy. Ten seconds.

I shimmy down the drainpipe, running down from the edge of the roof, and cross the road, walking briskly towards Alcova.

"You are fooling yourself, dear Jimmy. It's not that easy to become one of the nexhumans."

The doors scan me from a distance and open on their own. Even though security now has the right and the means to get under customers' clothes, to check for possible threats or danger, consumer data privacy regulations mean they still can't access my identity.

Five seconds.

I follow the route indicated on my visor. I keep my eyes down, dodging the sales staff. To the customers, I am no one. To the webcams, I don't even exist.

"Do you really believe that gaining residence in Rizoma is just a matter of Ks? If you think that, well, you haven't understood a thing. In fact, you've missed the main point, my friend. You lack altruism."

The colour drains from Jimmy's face. As I walk past him, I see his legs give way. If not for the sales girl, who catches him just inches from the floor, he would be lying there, flat on his back, out cold. Then the floor shakes.

A roar rumbles through the air. A cloud of purple smoke closes in on the customers. The acrid stench of ammonia creates consternation. People begin to shout in panic. Water rains down from the fire sprinklers and the alarm sirens start wailing wildly.

Ion grabs hold of Jimmy, more to keep him there than to help him stay on his feet. Rasha attends to the exit, taking up a watchful position and pretending to call for help as I, with a confident step, turn into the corridor that leads to my bounty.

The door hasn't been fixed since last week's adventure and it's easy enough to open. Salty tears slide down my face, tasting faintly of ammonia. My heart stops as I step into the storeroom. Under a set of shelves, a box calls to me intermittently.

Even at a distance of only two metres, the signal is weak.

8–952–395–78–08–05

I pull it out and open it. Alba's ankles are so slim, I can circle them with thumb and forefinger. These are the stems from which her form and her unnatural grace flower. I wrap tinfoil around her legs to keep the tag from showing up on sensors as we escape.

The storeroom's motion-activated webcam snaps a photo as I shift the box, but it's pointing at the window. I retrace my steps, and by the checkout, I pose for a webcam photo to immortalise the baseball cap of Mr No One.

As I step out of Alcova's front door, my eyes meet Jimmy's horrified gaze.

A few metres ahead of me, Rasha and Ion motion me to run. Instead, I walk calmly, even though I know I have Jimmy's eyes on me. Who knows what thoughts are running through his head, now he has seen the box I am carrying under my arm? Who knows if he has realised how deeply he has been deceived in just a few seconds?

"You, you in the hat... Where do you think you're going?"

His voice reaches my ears just after I pass him. The Podox gives force to my leap but I'm still restricted by the limitations of my biological body.

If good luck were something that was shared, some of it should surely come to me once in a while. But it never does, so I toss the package to Rasha and we split up. Not only can he count on both his legs, he is also as lithe and agile as a greyhound.

The Loins is chasing me, but he, too, has seen better days. The role of the hunter, once again on the tracks of his prey, doesn't fit well with the flashy clothes or his neo-dandy look. You can see a mile off that the Loins's days as a predator are over.

When I turn to check on him, he is sweating as much from shame as anything else. After two hundred metres of vociferous swearing, he is forced to slow down, double over to control his panting, dull the stitch in his side. I'm sure he's not going to give up this easily so I follow Ion across Piccalorda Way towards the centre of the megalopolis. I don't know exactly where we're going. All I know is that it's all I can do to keep up.

The main roads are monitored by webcams and gadgets that post constant updates to the web. Plus, there are the passers-by who turn wikitube reporter at the first opportunity. The rain protects us, blurring the air around us, reducing visibility to a few metres.

We left Jimmy behind hundreds of metres ago. Other presences run by my side, loyal and discreet like a team of huskies; the directional agent reconnoitering our surroundings and the privacy function monitoring the presence of webcams and recalibrating every step in response.

We are heading to Rizoma, the nexhuman residential area, where the buildings look cleaner and seem to last longer than anywhere else. I slow down and make an attempt to take in as many segments of the spectrum as possible.

The immense avenue that leads to Saphira Square is lined with yellow trees, their luminescent foliage creating a covered archway a hundred metres above our heads. At their base and on their trunks, I can just make out the movement of small animals. In my head, they are wild creatures: squirrels and lynxes, macaques and lemmings.

Are they uploads too?

Their cheeks are rotund and their claws shine with health.

I want to stop and look at them, but Ion urges me on, pointing his finger at our destination a few kilometres in front of us.

Chapter 19
The Moore Temple

Ion leads me towards Saphira Square. In the background, I can see the chalice-like profile of the Ramada Inn, an immense tent-like structure mounted on six ancient motorway overpass pilings with round arches. The Rizoma artists come here in search of inspiration, or rather, a mystic narcosis with which to bolster their creative powers. It resounds with synaesthetic melodies flowing from the incorporeal minds of nexhuman musicians: the Children of Prodigy, the Synaptic Brothers, the Rolling Stars and the Evergreen Days have all had themselves uploaded and continue to deliver musical frequencies from beyond time, for the centuries to come.

How can we blame them for having swapped their bodies, organic containers that go on collecting imperfections until they no longer work, for new, fully functional models?

The nexhumans have fixed their present and future, and in music, they have found a place that weathers the erosion of time even better.

At the tip of the revolving spire of the Ramada Inn, a selection of aphorisms from the prophet Mick Noxtrum run continuously.

Human nature is inconstant; nexhuman nature is not

When Ion points out the crouching figure of Rasha to me, half hidden in a corner, I run towards him and hug him. He immediately hands me the box.

"Here. We couldn't tell you anything about our destination until we were sure."

"We did it! Did you see Jimmy's face?"

I unpack the legs, removing the sheets of tinfoil, and show them to my companions.

Ion rests a hand on my shoulder.

"A fine job."

He removes his disguise and slips it into his shoulder bag.

Our feet are in Rizoma and the adrenalin rush shows no sign of abating. I look around me.

"Why here?"

"Because we had an idea. There are people here who might be able to help you with Alba."

"Who? What do you mean?"

I've hardly had a chance to process this information when a beam of light shines down from the other side of the piazza, lighting us up and blinding us.

The laser is part of a tracer device on the arabesque-decorated facade of Moore Temple.

"Don't worry, Peter, we came here for them, anyway."

My visor floods me with data: the building was erected in 2032 and designed by the founder of nexhumanism, Duggan Moore. It is based on the golden rectangle: the ratio between its base and height is absolutely perfect and the perimeter domes taper towards the sky, spiralling upwards, an echo of the shapes present throughout nature, in nautilus shells, whirlpools of water, fingerprints, human DNA, and galaxies.

The temple is a mixture of the architectural styles of the world's main religious doctrines, a choice made by Moore himself. He was the man responsible for the dramatic mutation created in the evolution of humankind, for the arrival of the nexhumans.

Rumour says that he was part of the circle of free-thinkers, who, since the previous millennium, had defended the sacredness of life. During his biological lifetime, he was vigorously opposed to abortion and resisted the temptation, which spread like wildfire through the less wealthy, of assisted suicide.

Many people joined him when he offered humanity a way to escape old age, giving them the chance to take a step towards immortality.

I exchange a hesitant look with Ion and Rasha, to see what they think. Then a voice speaks to us.

"Come closer. Do not be afraid."

Even though it's not unusual to run into nexhumans, it is not an ordinary event to be spoken to by a temple. I suddenly want to throw myself down at the base of its steps and plead for mercy from the beings destined to replace us.

"Our calculations show that you are Peter Payne."

This recognition comes as a shock. Despite our disguises—ample cover for wandering around Rizoma—we can't pass close scrutiny; we are seen for the trashformers and re-consumers, tramps and swindlers, that we are.

But the voice holds no undertones of accusation, so we feel safe enough to move closer to the Temple.

"We believe you have something that belongs to us."

These words stop me in my tracks. I don't want to find out that they, too, are usurping ownership rights over Alba.

"I haven't stolen anything. I'm just putting the pieces of a friend back together ... someone who was turned off a long time ago."

A flash of blue light erupts from the door of the Temple, blinding us to the contours of whatever is inside. My visor is immediately inundated with clouds of RFID numbers.

"We confirm what you have said. Enter, then; enter the Moore Temple with serenity."

Intimidated, Rasha rubs his eyes. Ion has the confident look of someone who knows more than he has let on. We are accompanied by a hypnotic voice with no hint of the sinister about it. The stairs announce our arrival by playing a sequence of notes as we step onto them.

We enter the temple, the perimeter of which is adorned with arcane effigies and symbols. In the centre of the space, the data emitted by the walls comes together, coagulating into a cloud-like avatar with pseudo-human features, changing appearance like a shapeshifter every few seconds.

"Welcome. We are Brother Biddulf."

I find it hard to believe that this vapour is a priest. His tunic is inlaid with texts written in forgotten and indecipherable languages—even the visor cannot identify where they come from. In compensation, the device rattles off a steady stream of data about Nexhumanism, running in real time in the periphery of my vision.

The old religions never objected to technological advances that lead to lowering infant mortality or extending average lifespan. The Bible, its icon blinking on the right-hand side of my visor, is neutral on the argument: in the Holy Scriptures, there are references to extremely long-lived people, like Methuselah, who lived to be 969; Noah, who died at 950; and others like Abraham and Jonah, who lived to 175 and 180 respectively.

Old age, then, is not a condition imposed by God. Every good believer, the flow of data informs us, believes that the efforts made to alleviate the pain and suffering of illness, to improve the quality of life of the elderly and keep the body healthy, are dedicated to God and the prolongation of Faith.

Since the encyclical *Humani Generis,* written by Pope Pius XII in 1950, it has been the determination of the Church that there is no conflict between evolution and the Catholic doctrine. As Pope John Paul II said, "Today [...]

there are new discoveries that lead us to the recognition of evolution as something more than a mere theory."

In his message for the celebrations of Peace Day in 1970, Pope Paolo VI expressed a concept very close to nexhumanism: "Humanity is walking, or rather progressing, towards an ever-increasing dominion of the world: thought, study, and science guide the way; work, tools, and technique perform this wonderful conquest. And what is it all for? For living longer, for living more."

The length of the human lifespan depends more on free will than on some divine law that no one knows about. Where humanity has to rely on the slowness of genetic evolution, the nexhumans can assess the best characteristics of a generation and include them in the next round of uploads. When they discover a useful feature, they deliver it to everyone without having to wait centuries like biological beings do.

Two eyes gleam in the darkness.

"The definition you used earlier, a friend who 'turned off', is inexact. Alba Vicente isn't dead, nor has she disappeared. She merely took on another form."

My jaw drops. Mouth hanging open, I start stroking the box. Ion holds me up with a hand on my shoulder and his theories about fuzzy logic come back to me.

"Is she alive?"

The cloud of Brother Biddulf quivers in a haze of divine information.

"Life and death are not such easily defined events. I can assure you that Alba is present within our data flows."

My stomach twists. A dusty shaft of light from above shines down on my agony.

"Can I talk to her? Can I see her?"

The religious symbols around us fill me with awe and a level of hope that, until today, I've never dared entertain. Suddenly,

Ion pulls me aside with wild eyes. He wants to say something.

"Remember what I told you... Brother Biddulf isn't talking about the Alba you knew. If you meet Alba now, it won't be the Alba you knew in the past. The idea is like that of flowing water; she won't be the same because what she consists of has changed."

"Why? What's changed?"

I'll be honest: real life without Alba has been so futile, so desolate, that I invented another. In doing so, I have lost contact with this plane of reality. These thoughts sound like an admission of guilt, a confession a priest like Brother Biddulf might be eager to hear.

The vaporous priest speaks, as though he has intercepted my thoughts. 'The original continues from the original, but each copy will always be different, individual. This is what Father Moore intended.'

All I want to do is be close to her. I open the box of desires and lift the tinfoil wrappings.

I want to re-experience what she used to give me, whatever form she might be in. I lift the box and hold out the legs to Brother Biddulf, whose eyes narrow to slits in a kind of mystical recollection. I want to give back to her what was taken from both of us, from her and me, in any way I can.

"Please, Brother Biddulf. I need Alba."

"So be it, Peter Payne. Your prayer will be answered. True love doesn't count costs, only value."

The gaseous exhalation dissolves grain by grain and re-forms into a configuration of female forms. I can make out sunken eyes, emaciated cheekbones, a row of rabbit teeth behind dry lips and the wrinkled face of someone heading towards senescence.

If she had real skin, it would be saggy. If she had real flesh, it would not be firm. The truth is worse than lies.

Only my deep respect for the decrepit holds back my disgust.

"It's you, Peter Payne!"

That voice makes my head spin. The Alba I knew was older than me, but this venerable old lady looks more like one of her ancestors. I take a step backwards.

"You're surprised, but let me reassure you. I am not your Alba. It is more like I am her mother. After my upload, I chose to have the body of a young woman. But I am not her, nor is she a copy of me, because as Brother Biddulf said, that is forbidden. We are bound by the same past, but our futures are divided. I only know of you because of the beam Alba sent to me before shutting down."

I am holding a part of my fixation in my hands, an obsession that I've never thought of as negative. At times, I even felt that it might bring me good fortune. Or maybe I was far too naïve to think that behind the biggest ideas—like bringing my Alba back from the dead—there could be a fixation just as big. Was I wrong to think that someone who lives for one single reason is more likely to leave a mark on his world?

"Peter, when uploading first became possible, a portion of the population transferred into artificial bodies to escape illness and old age. Some did this out of vanity, on a whim; others just wanted to live at least once. Fifty percent of uploads were elderly people; another thirty percent were terminally ill. When I was eighteen, I was diagnosed with a degenerative form of arteriosclerosis. Technically I was alive, but my body was hostage to a pharmacological hiatus which prevented all contact with reality for forty years. The Alba you knew was the incarnation of my desire to own a physical body capable of giving me tactile, emotional sensations."

The cyan outline of the elderly Alba expands until it is almost stroking my face. The crackling air makes my skin crawl. I step back from the cloud and look at the grainy face of Brother Biddulf.

"Can you bring that Alba back to life if I bring you the pieces?"

Ion nods. I have faith in his competence, but the tools at his disposal are not so reliable.

"Just because you have the pieces does not mean you own them. You know that, don't you?"

I lower my gaze, flushed with non-guilty palpitations.

"I found the head fifteen years ago. When you find something in the dump, it isn't stealing, it's salvaging something from becoming kipple. I don't want to keep the pieces. They are Alba's. They are Alba!"

"And suppose we could do as you ask? What would you do, then? Would you really give them back to us?"

"I've been keeping them for her because I was there that day…"

A lump is forming in my throat. My glands are secreting like mad.

As a pledge and a sign of my goodwill, I place the box on the ground and take a step back. For me, true poverty lies not in death, but in running away from what I consider to be my destiny.

"Well then, tell us where we can find the final pieces. We will help you."

My chin goes up. This is not what I meant. No one must know about Charlie. No one must interfere between me and him. It makes me sick to the pit of my stomach to imagine that Alba might be lost forever.

"I can't tell you. If you intervene, the person who has the pieces might destroy them. Ion and I had put nearly all the pieces together, and then… they were taken from me. It's a delicate situation, and at the slightest wrong move from us, they'll be lost forever. Thank you, but the only help I'm asking you for is to bring her back to life when I get all the pieces back."

"As you wish, Peter."

A delicate rustle marks the departure of Brother Biddulf and Alba.

Chapter 20
Mister Stinky

With a prophetic tone, Ion urges me to leave the Temple. 'You did the right thing.'

I nod pensively. 'All I can do now is wait for Charlie to call.'

We walk past the Ramada Inn. A little further, on the platform from where the giant spores of nexhumanity's future are launched, a ship called Govinda is vertical and ready for take-off. It looks like a flaming egg about to leave this world to implant others with life. We stop for a few minutes to look at it as it spirals up towards the unknown. The ship twirling through the sky gradually disappears leaving behind only a melancholy dotted line.

Beyond the launchpad, the luxurious roofs of Esperia look like a canopy of blooms visited by motorised insects.

The position of the moon reminds me that we left Kathal Hill about five hours ago. We hurry along, painfully aware of the fact that Ion's cubicle is undefended. As darkness falls, the risk of it being plundered increases by the minute. Things on our slice of rusted and wrinkled land may well have taken a turn for the worse.

I am sluggish, on the edge of collapse with the day's exertion. Rasha takes pity on me, and I lean on his arm to carry on. Without even the shadow of a K for the metro, we have to get back on foot.

The encounter with the nexhumans has shaken me. As I see it, they have regained their childhood without losing the memories or the knowledge they gained during their biological lives. It's as though they have regained the innocence of childhood without having to sacrifice the intellect of adulthood.

"Is it true that nexhumans are eternal, Ion?"

"Eternal? Not exactly; they are limited by some of the same things as us, like accidents, murder, wars."

"But if they can be reloaded..."

"They respect death, though in their case, death isn't necessarily an absolute. One day, they will cease to exist just like the rest of us. And, like the rest of us, they don't know when this will happen."

Something doesn't add up.

I was never a happy or carefree child. My childhood was spent in a limbo where it was never my turn. I was the mascot of the Dead Bones, the smallest in the house, the cripple of Kathal Hill. I always felt like I was on the naughty step, being punished for something I hadn't done.

When I was a child, Cleo used to fill me up with paracetamol. She was convinced my sighs were caused by the pain in the stubs of my arm and leg when in reality, I was sad about how I was treated—not just by her, but the whole megalopolis. Throughout my childhood, Charlie was always the dispenser of every kind of evil. Nothing has changed.

Surely it can't be regaining this infantile state—a sense of amazed innocence lasting for all eternity—that makes nexhumans happier? Perhaps they just have less strife and don't worry about certain things anymore, things that are a consequence of human frailty and the limits of our knowledge. Maybe they solve problems more quickly with their processing power that's infinitely greater than ours. Or perhaps they take longer over these matters because for them time is a different concept.

"Ion, this upload business is bugging me. If there is an original Alba matrix, then that should mean that there is no limit to possible uploads. If I can't get all of Alba's pieces, can I load a copy of Alba into a different body?"

"Peter, don't think about that. You're tired; your mind is wandering. The problem isn't memory. If memories can be forgotten, altered, or even constructed, what do you need them for? How many parts of yourself can you forget and still be you?"

"What do you mean? Do you mean that each copy becomes an original because nexhumans survive at the price of one life at a time? Like we do? But that they get to live longer?"

"That's it; you've got it. Even though it has taken thousands of years to reach this point."

As we get nearer to Kroonval Station, I darken my visor against the blinding light reflected by the fresh snow on the ground. Here, everything is opalescent. Ion and Rasha also benefit from this nocturnal effect, but I can't shake my unassailable gloom.

I can see the Cirei Fields, the last nexhuman outpost before the Genshoij Hills to the right and Raon to the left.

When I was a child, wandering around this area with Charlie, we used to empty our intestines in the clean, disinfected public toilets installed in the park. Now, though, specimens of germs and bacteria not only infest my mind and the memories of my childhood but have also ravished the remaining vegetation.

Rasha offers me his arm again.

I am beginning to believe that the broken recording Charlie was talking about is inside us. A recording that reminds us to suffer for the past and for everything else it seems impossible to change or fix. What would happen if someone made a copy of me without my knowing? What would happen if the original was killed while I slept and the copy was put into my bed, its consciousness set to start from when I fell into slumber? Would I wake up and suspect anything?

Perhaps the trick of an upload is to have it done without your knowledge.

When we reach Rabaul Street, leaving behind the swampy maze of cardboard and sheet-metal buildings of Raon, I drop to my knees, unable to go any further. Ion does the same next to me.

We are surrounded by crumbling brick shacks and hovels made of nailed-together planks and bedraggled panels, and we catch glimpses of the poor, haggard, time-worn souls who live here.

Rasha leans against the frame of an erstwhile lorry, now a chicken roost. Dusty birds brood meditatively on the seats. Waste gas rises from cracks in the ground, almost as though the inert materials above are the waste products of the kipple processes below.

Not far ahead, we can see the advancing LED lights of a UCU. It moves through piles of kipple like a predator stalking across the savannah, showing the same attitude as the big cats I've seen on the National Geographic channel in the gamesphere.

It gobbles up rubbish in great bites, drawing in strips of fabric, boxes, bottles, rubble, furniture, plastic and cosmetics. We wait in silence for its next bite: plastic sheeting, polystyrene packaging, leftover food, and crunching bones. This devourer of value is untiring.

The LEDs never go out. It pauses, sensing prey that will be more difficult than usual: a kitchen appliance that should be in the dump, not here. So we hang about, posing as curious bystanders.

We press on, aware that time is not on our side.

"Are you scared, Ion?"

He rolls his eyes. His breath condenses in little clouds shooting out of his mouth, and his lips are damp with spittle.

"What's going to change? Mister Stinky can't get up to much harm on his own."

Rasha starts rocking on his heels. Not weighed down by the years like Ion, or extra weight like me, he offers to run ahead of us.

"I can do it. Maybe it's not too late."

He repositions his cap, and while we try to catch our breath, we see his silhouette disappear into the banks of fog, fading into a moon grey shadow.

"Come on, Peter. You're still young. Just another few kilometres."

"You might not have noticed, but all this flesh weighs more than your years."

We head off, unworried by the excessive silence of our footsteps. We make no echo, no sound. The pavements of Rabaul Street have been overtaken by a layer of rubbish that mutes everything.

In the middle of the road, cars perform a dangerous rally, sliding on the ice. We risk being flattened the moment we step down onto the patched tarmac.

Ignoring these obstacles, speeding vehicles rush over our heads without having to touch the ground. Vehicles and cargo transporters wait to dock in Rizoma amidst a confusion of air traffic. Further off, the vapour trails of spaceships lead to remote points in the abyss of space.

The last few kilometres before we reach the derelict Visconia are harder on my mind than on my body.

It's strange: in the past, no one has ever wanted to create garbage or throw away rubbish. Even the thought of holding something in your hand, or keeping it in a bin to then take out to the dumpsters, was a kind of taboo, a hidden ritual like that of visiting the lavatory. Then everything changed. People wanted more and more stuff and found themselves with rubbish as a consequence. They accepted it and threw out their shame.

Now the rubbish grows, mutates and reorganises with the help of a dangerous ally—electronic waste. Some believe the millions of low frequency processors that find themselves thrown together in the dump have combined their processing power to create an intelligent organism: primitive, but structured like a community of bees or ants. Over the last sixty years, more than 150 million PCs have been scrapped annually. That's nine billion chips—close to the number of humans on earth—a number that makes me fear the theory could have some truth to it.

Rasha's bony hand waves from higher up, urging us to run. As we lean into the ascent, everything under our feet crumbles, flakes, and decomposes. A whiff of death strong enough to wring our guts brutally fills our nostrils.

Ion is hypnotised, his gaze nailed to the top of the hill where his cubicle is.

Disasters are often preceded by a fortuitous event, an event that is taken as a harbinger of doom. Round our way, there's no need for a warning to expect the worst.

The temperature has dropped to below-freezing. The dragging sound of our feet is muted by the eroded crumbling matter and the now ankle-deep snow. Even the flies have stopped buzzing.

Lying in a hole full of soot is a lump of flesh over which the worms are beginning to take the first steps of their macabre dance. As straight as corroded poles, four threadbare limbs and a knotted stump stick out desolately. Mister Stinky's bristles are burned along with the fleas that lived on him.

"I found him like this," Rasha says.

Ion goes to the body mournfully and lifts a flap of skin. He kneels before the skinned carcass, its innards seems to be still gurgling. The death mask is set in a paralysed growl.

"My poor hog. What have they done to you?"

Something has boiled Mister Stinky's brains until his skull exploded, littering the ground with blobs of soft matter.

"What have they done to you?"

It hurts to hear Ion's pain; the distress in his voice is plain to hear.

"The bastards... It was them."

"Which them?"

Ion's agony is clear to see. The curls of skin and bristle are all that is left of Mister Stinky, Ion's pride and joy, his companion who wandered around the dumps with him, seeking out value.

"Those Reverse bastards. Who else? It's all my fault, I should have kept him in the bunker. Pieces of shit... It's their revenge because they didn't want me to have my memory back. They must have found out somehow about you copying my memory files from the archives."

I don't want to contradict him, but I doubt Reverse harbours any rancour towards Ion. It couldn't care less whether he is of sound mind or not.

Mister Stinky's snout is covered in a greenish mess of gloop, and this makes me think something more serious has happened. Something I can't mention in front of Ion for fear he will be overwhelmed by his worst obsession.

This is the work of kipple.

Ion heads towards his cubicle and unlocks the padlocks before entering. "You see, what did I tell you? Look here: nothing's missing. Those creeps haven't taken anything. They just wanted him. A punitive expedition. They killed him to get at me."

The towers of objects in the cubicle tumble noisily to the ground. An avalanche of junk spills across the floor.

"What are you doing?"

Sifting through his bits and pieces, he pulls out a metal pole, the one I saw him carrying years ago.

"You'll see. Those shits have no idea who they're dealing with. I'm not the empty-headed amnesiac I used to be."

He sticks the rod in the trash, standing up like a flagpole. Then he disappears, bustling around inside some more. Rasha and I wait outside like two dilapidated effigies. We can hear him wheezing and puffing. We light a fire and roll a cigarette to share.

"Hey, Ion, d'you need a hand in there?"

Rasha strikes a match. First, he savours the smell of sulphur, then the warmth released by striking it, and then he plays with the flame.

Match in hand, Rasha pulls a bag of sawdust from his pocket, puts the match to it and then quickly throws it up in the air.

"Thanks, lads, but I've almost finished. You'll see what I'll do to them, now I remember what this stuff is."

My heart is in my throat at the idea that Ion wants to take revenge on Reverse, but who am I to criticise an absurd and impossible plan?

When he appears in the doorway, Ion is holding a box full of mirrors, scraps of metal and other odds and ends. He sits down next to us and starts picking out pieces about the size of pack of cards.

"Solar panels. I've been collecting these for ten years."

The box also yields dozens of chrome sticks that he inserts into holes along the length of the pole at various heights. At the end of each stick, he attaches a photocell.

"Are you going to explain? Or do we have to guess for ourselves?"

"Just a minute. This is the good part. This is the plan I spoke to you about years ago…"

He fetches an old laptop from his lair, boots it up and connects it to a socket at the base of the pole. He types a few commands and the pole starts to vibrate. We can feel the matter on the ground begin to tremble. Something is moving, burrowing down below the surface kipple, sliding through with ease.

"This a heliotropic tree, or—if you prefer—a solar tree. This is what made them throw me out. It was a threat to Reverse."

I read the instructions for its assembly years ago, but seeing this skeletal tree first hand is quite impressive.

"The branches with their panels serve as solar collectors and provide energy for the roots. And down there, in the roots, the structure creates a system of nanotubes that burrow into the kipple."

The tree vibrates and the branches start swaying. The soles of our shoes begin to heat up. Rasha and I lift our feet off the ground and he grimaces to play down his discomfort.

"That's just an exothermic reaction. Decomposition always generates heat."

"Is that it? It's a solar stove?"

Ion whirls his hands in wide circles. 'It's so much more. The roots decompose and transform the waste into fertile soil, they change the molecules structure infected by kipple and, using the solar energy, they make it a useful composition.

Then he magnifies the gestures and descends into a rant.

"The roots are conduits for nano-assemblers that I have collected together over years and years of searching through laboratory bins and private storage. With the computer, I can manage what materials to assemble and which molecules to produce."

"And what has Reverse got to do with all of this?"

Ion is scaring me. He's wearing the same wild expression as fifteen years ago when he followed Alba and me waving a torch.

"Oh, it concerns them all right. Planting the tree in the middle of kipple converts the substances it is made up of. If you plant it in a marsh or a sewer, it purifies the water leaving it drinkable... Reverse would have no reason to exist."

We could laugh spitefully at the thought of taking our revenge on Reverse, but we don't. We sit in silence passing the cigarette from hand to cold hand.

Then Rasha stands up and starts digging a hole. I help him while Ion, with a mournful face, winds down from his explosion of enthusiasm. We start to dig and the more kipple we remove, the more our hands warm up.

When the grave is ready, we grab hold of Mister Stinky's carcass by the trotters and lay him gently on the bottom. Then we form a tumulus over his grave with the same kipple that killed him.

Ion doesn't look satisfied. He shakes his head and spits on the ground in disgust.

"Bloody cowards. They'll pay for this."

Wet with sweat and with aching backs, Rasha and I say goodbye to the older man and head home. I walk towards the Akeren; Rasha heads north, to Lazar.

When I turn to look back, the solar tree rooted next to Mister Stinky's grave resembles a crooked cross.

When I reach home, I find Lily, one of the crows, roosting on the window ledge, scrutinising every movement. I must remember to delete its memory log and reprogram the observation points so Kiko doesn't get suspicious.

I did the right thing by leaving Alba's legs at the Temple, otherwise, I would have to head down into the basement now.

With the stench of decomposition clinging to my clothes, hair, and skin, I can't enter the flat. Kiko has been very clear about this: I have to get undressed outside, stuff my clothes into a bag, empty it into the washing machine and hop straight into the shower.

One of the Dragon Ladies—as I call the three women next door—have left a bathrobe hanging from the clothes rail outside their apartment, full of clothes ready to be shipped off to Genshoij for sale. I borrow it and head into our flat.

A quick look around confirms Kiko is not here. It's Tuesday, so she'll be at Trisha's. Nara comes and pecks me on the neck, enough to amuse her and annoy me. Kiko is probably behind the animatronic crow's behaviour. I throw my socks at it and Nara returns to her perch in the kitchen.

"Pick those socks up and put them in the washing machine," it says.

I'm never quite sure if Kiko leaves me these messages or if Nara has picked up the household routines.

In the shower, I check my body for hog bristles and suspicious stains. There is no hot water left; the neighbours have had the pleasure of using it all and I pay the price of being late. I wash vigorously and rapidly. Shivering with cold, I rub myself almost hard enough to chafe the skin.

In bed at last, teeth chattering, I fall asleep.

Chapter 21
Papillon

I wake up groggy, with the feeling that only a few hours have passed. Turning over, I see the notches on the calendar tell another story: it's the twelfth of December.

All I can remember of the last two weeks is an insubstantial feeling of anxiety and the sense that Charlie, by keeping me on tenterhooks, is torturing me.

If I call him, I reveal my weakness: my chronic and incurable addiction to Alba. If I press him, he will probably react badly and go out of his way to destroy any chance of rebuilding her. But simply waiting for the moment of the exchange is unbearable and leaves me completely at his mercy.

I'm tempted to go to the dump, to let off some steam. Kipple drives out kipple, as Charlie would say. If I can laugh about it, maybe I'll be able to survive.

I get out of bed with all my usual movements. Not even the household objects have the energy to moan and argue with me. I thank whoever it was who threw out these expert home automation systems that make me happy with rare moments of solitude and silence.

In the kitchen, Kiko is beating eggs with a metal whisk. She doesn't even lift her eyes from the table.

"Morning... Are you hungry?"

"Very. What is there?"

The smell of oil and eggs, as the mixture hits the hot pan, seems like an atrocious omen. The semi-congealed mass frying in the pan makes my stomach turn. I hope something goes wrong with the infallibility of my predictions.

"I'm making an omelette."

"I can smell that."

"Take some, if you want."

"Reckon I'll go for cereal today."

I make myself a bowl of cereal. I swallow a mouthful, but the milk makes me feel ill. Kiko's high voice is making stilted conversation.

"My mother's coming to visit us tomorrow."

This means that I'm supposed to clean myself up and offer to do the housework.

"How long's she staying for?"

I put the cereal away and spear a forkful of cooked apple.

"A couple of days. She gets lonely at home."

"That's hardly surprising, I can understand that."

Kiko ignores my allusion and changes tack.

"While she's here, would you be so kind as to turn up in a less rough state than this? Just for a change."

I open my mouth in a wide yawn, hoping to make her change topic. She carries on, twittering away.

"Have you heard from Jo?"

"No. Jo who?"

The apple tastes good. I take another out of the fridge.

"Jo. You know, Charlie's wife."

I leave off with the apple and start picking at the cereal again. Kiko doesn't look at me and takes the apple away.

"What's happened to her?"

"We spoke over the mirror the other day. She says she's been really bad."

I pour myself a cup of coffee and top it up to the brim with a drop of gin, just to wake me up.

"Why? What's the matter with her?"

Kiko emanates mock candour even as she tries to express healthy contempt.

"It's Charlie's fault."

This sounds familiar. Even though I don't know Jo, I know what my brother is capable of.

"Apparently, he fell ill a few days ago and Jo is at her wits' end. He won't go to the doctor and just keeps saying everything will be all right."

Typical Charlie, acting the tough guy.

"So what's the matter with Jo?"

"She has the kids to look after and has to look after him too. Charlie in the house is a nightmare, so she says, even worse than two brats like Tommy and Lisa."

That's easy to believe.

"She called just to tell you about this?"

"What's wrong with that?"

From what Cleo has told me, Jo only talks about concrete facts and actual experiences. Her world revolves around food, around enchiladas, tortillas, and burritos, around satisfying her children's need for food and Charlie's need for sex.

"Nothing. It's just I was wondering if she told you anything else."

"Oh, yes, she wanted to know if I knew of a good hospital."

"You mean she asked you to call your mother?"

"Exactly."

"And what did she say?"

"She said the Papillon is the best. It's where she had her insemination treatment. She knows people there."

She goes on to explain that only on the fourth day of suffering had Charlie given in—he could no longer stand the virulent disease that had hit him in the groin and was hospitalised with a relative sense of urgency, thanks to the intervention of Eiko and the savings of the Azevedo clan.

"All sorted, then," I say.

"No. Now the problem is, Charlie won't let the doctor near him, he's behaving like an idiot. It's a difficult situation."

I think I know why Charlie is too embarrassed to go to the doctor. The day has definitely taken a turn for the better. As things are, it's worth digging deeper into the matter.

"If he's really so ill, maybe I should go visit him."

"Are you sure that's a good idea? Won't you come back feeling worse than you do now?"

Kiko might be right: spending time with Charlie often ends up in fraternal antagonism.

"Nah, I'll go, look stupid, and come home."

The highland looking over where the rivers Akeren and Selam meet is, as usual, surrounded by beggars. They stand right up against the fence around the hospital, imploring with their hands for a chance for survival, a mass of tramps and beggars, all desperate to get into the Papillon clinic.

They are usually quite docile, camping out on the sides of the hill, stirring pans of soup. They fight and make peace without bothering the vehicles heading into the clinic. There are times, however, when they organise protest pickets and curse the world, chanting 'Amendments for Everyone', a slogan that has become popular amongst the shiftless and destitute against what is considered to be the unfair death sentence reserved for us by our biological bodies.

There must be around three thousand demonstrators, maybe even more. Half of them are in wheelchairs, people with no legs, cancer, stroke and Parkinson's disease, sufferers of polio whose shrunken legs look like pairs of withered stalks, victims of sclerosis and who knows what else. Poor bastards with juddering heads and drool on their chins.

When they see a white lab coat coming down the tarmac driveway, they get stirred up, caught in a strange kind of euphoria. They hurry towards it en masse, crushing themselves against the fence, risking getting hurt and trapped by the impetus of their happiness.

This whole situation appears as a paradox to me, with the prisoners on the outside and the others closed in.

Over recent months, a rumour has been going around that the hospital's board will choose some miserable sufferer at random for a free upload as part of the Moore Temple's new policy for widening the circle of its acolytes. They openly cultivate the hope that it could happen to them.

To push my way through this mass of hopefuls, I wait for bad weather and go out just as a snow storm is in the offing.

Whipped by icy gusts of wind, the highland appears nearly deserted, though even in this weather, there are some idiots out here, hoping to achieve their goal. They sift through the piles of the hospital's rubbish and break the thin layers of ice that have formed over the puddles with rakes and sieves.

Then, from above, lumps of ice begin to fall, hailstones and shards of ice as big as bullets. The drunkest tramps fall to the ground like straws, the others run for cover under metal roofs. It isn't that unusual for 'bodies' to be taken there in the early stages of hypothermia. Many may wake up on gurneys in the Lazar morgue and I can imagine Georgie Boy's horror at the sight of a cadaver waking up and swearing ...

As a relative of a patient, I have the right to go in during visiting times. Along the driveway to the front entrance, in between trees with icy leaves hanging like tears, there are still some working animated gigalographics. Amidst a swarm of exhortations to upload, to board the fleet of Govindas, and offers for family holidays in space, I can see the precepts applicable to the human condition.

Precept 1: We do not accept the tyranny of illness and death. The upload of synthetic organs will give us a long life, pushing back our expiry date. Each of us will decide for ourselves how long to live.

I look for the second billboard. The precepts derive from Mick Noxtrum's letter to Mother Nature, a prayer to the creator of the world summarising nexhumanist philosophy.

Precept 2: We will expand the human perceptive spectrum with biotechnology and computers. This will enable us to increase our knowledge of the world and our appreciation of it.

A couple of ambulances whizz past me, their sirens silent.

My progress is getting slower and slower.

The Papillon hospital not only uses almost miraculous cures on the ailing patients but is also one of the places where uploads can be performed.

The third billboard is rocking in the strong wind, it marks the difference between us and them.

Precept 3: Though recognising your genius in using carbon compounds for human evolution, we will not limit our physical, mental, and emotional capabilities to those of biological organisms. We are committed to dominating our biochemistry, but we will also proceed with integrating advanced technology into our beings.

By the side of the landing area, I see the final installation, right over the car park.

Precept 4: We reserve the right to add new items to this list whether collectively or independently. We do not aspire to perfection, but we pursue forms of excellence in accordance with technological values and development.

These messages are more than the projection of myths for the masses, they are declarations about the use of evolution and the precautions followers will take against the onset of humanity's dusk.

Some politicians are thinking about giving nexhumans the right to vote. They must assume that the nexhumans are interested in the sad practice of voting, which is only used by a minimal percentage of the population of the megalopolis anyway.

At first, only objects were upgraded; now people are too. Even at the cost of seeing their brains and bodies rendered redundant by the upload process. Here, the organic dissolves and makes way for the inorganic. They would prefer to attempt to realise themselves, rather than just existing.

Who wants to be stuck in the chrysalis when you can be free to fly like a butterfly?

The hospital is laid out like a sideways figure eight and the Papillon sign is decorated with thousands of mechanical butterflies, which make it tremble and flutter in the air.

To get into the hospital, I have to prove I am Peter Payne. I let the entrance scanner do its job and then I am free to pretend to be who I want.

The truth is, I don't want anyone to recognise me. With my silver-bordered orange overalls, I pass myself off as a road maintenance labourer. The tag sewn into the jacket tells me the uniform belonged to a Genshoij theatre company before it wound up on the Kathal Hill dump.

Hiding behind my disguise, I follow the hospital agent's directions to find my brother's room. There is none of the usual hospital stench around here.

At the end of the twelfth floor corridor, in Infectious Diseases, I catch a glimpse of Jo and a crowd of people I imagine are part of the Azevedo clan.

I linger in the background and attempt to hear what they are saying.

Jo is standing beside three ladies. One of them, judging by her features, appears to be Jo's mother. A couple of elderly, white-haired men are playing with Tommy and Lisa. Leaning against the wall by the window are two thickset young men, chatting with their girlfriends.

"Well? Where is he then? The nurses said—I heard them with these very ears— that the doctor would be here by now. But he's not here..."

"Calm down, Jo. Have they said when they're going to discharge him?"

"I don't know. They've been keeping him in bed for two days, now, and still don't know what's wrong with him."

"It must be serious. Did he come here too late?"

"Too late? You know what that pig-headed husband of mine is like."

"Yes, but... Jo, you should have been more insistent. Men have to be convinced. How many times do I have to tell you? Men reckon an aspirin will cure everything and anything."

"Don't start, Mum. Look, he's coming; let me talk to the doctor."

Behind me, I hear the swish of a lab coat, so I flatten myself against the wall and read the necrologies pinned there. Next to them, in a glass notice board, are notes of thanks from discharged patients alongside the promises they made to appeal to the fates for mercy and beg for recovery.

The doctor takes Jo to one side, bringing her closer to me. Keeping my back to them, I can gather more choice titbits of information.

"Mrs Payne. I'm sorry to have kept you waiting. The results of the histological tests have only just come back to us. We have many patients at the moment, but your husband's situation has been classified as an emergency."

Jo clasps her hands together in her lap. The doctor lowers his voice until he is whispering. I raise the microphones on my visor and manage catch a few useful snatches of their conversation.

"...he has caught... rare disease... aggressive virus... through a mutagenic bacteria."

"A mutagenic bacteria? What bacteria?"

Jo is worried for herself and even more for her kids.

"Starting organism... common bacteria... floating around. In the rubbish... putrescent ... possible... through faeces. The nucleus... modified. It is very interesting to analyse."

"In faeces? How did he get that?"

Jo covers her mouth with a hand. The doctor says nothing, embarrassed. Out of the corner of my eye, I can see he is blushing.

"Well, could be... anus or vagina."

"Vagina? Anus? Whose anus?!"

There is a contemplative silence, then Jo goes white. She lets her hand drop to her side.

"We'll have to keep him under observation for a few more days, so we can study his case. We may have found a new form of infection and your husband can help us synthesise a new vaccine."

Jo turns and leaves the doctor to his duties. She looks like she is frowning, probably doubtful about the wisdom of revealing this secret to the rest of the Azevedo clan. A look of vengefulness crosses her furrowed brow, her mind's eye fixed on a despicable thought. This vanishes and a new thought comes.

Juicy Jo knows she didn't infect Charlie. Juicy Jo is not infected, so Charlie must have found other orifices elsewhere.

With icy calm, she grabs Tommy and Lisa by their collars and drags them towards the lift. Then she turns to the circle of relatives.

"I need to talk to Charlie alone for a moment. Can you all wait downstairs?"

The elders are offended but comply. The men don't even notice Jo's resentful tone and walk quickly down the corridor.

I can't hear what happens next, but I watch the reflections in the window opposite the doorway. I like finding out other people's secrets; it's a way of lightening the pressure of my own.

Jo, at Charlie's bedside, is pointing a finger at him. He lies back, arms crossed behind his head.

Mouth flapping, Jo is railing against him, her stiff index finger jabbing the air. I even see her prodding him in the ribs. Then she waves it in the air again before going back to jabbing him. He opens his eyes wide and shakes his head, lifting arms and knees to defend himself.

If I'm reading their lips right, and if I know my brother, Charlie's defence is accompanied by vague recriminations about Jo not allowing him near her as much as she used to, since the kids were born anyhow, an attempt to convince her that any other man in his position would have done the same thing.

And there I was thinking Alba was enough for him.

As distraught as she is, Jo must be the type of woman who, without complaint, would do everything for her man and do it with pleasure, for the greater good.

She would be hard on herself so as not to be hard on him. She would be sweet to him and tough with the rest of the world. But by the way she is laying into Charlie, I can tell that she is also a woman who, while happy to share in his endless corruptions, can only stand so much of the lord and master that Charlie attempts to be.

I imagine that during their years of marriage, Jo has learned patience, has learned to wait for him to come home from Cali Nova or Vermillion after a night out with the pimps and his junky friends and rubbish dealers who tip him off about where to find the juiciest goods.

She must in some way have forgiven him the lascivious leers he saves for the Kroonval hookers. Maybe she even resigned herself to him bringing delinquents like Rafail Ciconi or Todd Morkum home with him. As far as I remember, they were in no way averse to taking advantage of a girl, even under-age girls, and then bragging about their exploits.

These are all suppositions, but I bet the only thing Jo can't accept is the lowness of the lie, the presumption of the lie used to cover the truth.

For as long as Charlie made her a part of his vices and weaknesses, including thieving and shady business, she must have gone along with him, however much she didn't like it. But as soon as he was ashamed of what he had done and hid the truth from her, he started sowing doubt in her mind. Doubt breeds suspicion, and suspicion is the beginning of the end for any relationship.

It is clear from the food plates Jo is hurling at him now that she's repudiating her mission to stay by his side. It is obvious from her attempt to stab him with the plastic cutlery that she can't stand it any longer.

Charlie weathers Jo's fury, but he's not getting off lightly. He opens his mouth, tries a verbal defence, though even he doesn't believe anything he can say will help. Once the spell has been broken, there is no enchantment left that can fix it.

When Jo withdraws from the room with a last jab of her finger and an air of defeat, I reckon it's a good time for me make my entrance. I'm convinced that true discoveries are made by taking wrong turns, sometimes going against the flow, some others taking the silliest of the available options.

Weakened by the virus and his fight with Jo, Charlie doesn't even look surprised to see me; if anything, he seems almost pleased to see someone over who he has always kept the upper hand.

He quickly gets a grip on himself, straightens his shirt and smooths the sheets.

"Peter. Little brother. Did you see Jo when you came in?"

"Jo? No, I didn't see anyone in the hallway."

"That's good, she was out of her mind."

"How come? Because of your illness?"

"Eh... Yes. This virus is taking its time. Nothing to worry about, though; I'll be home in a few days."

This invincible man act convinces no one but him.

"Come here. Pull me up a bit; my back's a wreck."

As I help him, I can see the evidence of their fight. "You've got some bruises."

"It's nothing... I tripped. That bloody bathroom door. It's impossible to piss in peace with all these tubes."

My brother is a phenomenon. He can invent so many ways of lying that he covers the entire spectrum of deceit, from omission to sidestepping to prevarication to simulation.

"Have they said when you can leave?"

"No, they're keeping me in observation. These doctors, shit... I've never liked them. Right now, too, I've got contracts to close." He looks at me sideways. He must be plotting something. "Y'know... Now you're here, I can see why Jo was behaving so strangely."

I am hanging on his every word. Maybe he wants to confess and get the weight of his shitty actions off his chest. Maybe he's finally in the mood to open up to me, his brother.

"It's that fucking head. You have to admit it, Peter, it really does bring bad luck."

Despite everything I've seen, Charlie can still surprise me. Even now, stunned and just about unscathed by his wife's anger, he is thinking like an idiot. From his point of view, he's not in the wrong at all.

"You don't have to keep it. Remember the exchange?"

"Exactly, with all this going on, I haven't had a chance to think about it." I forgive him. He almost seems to want to get rid of it without a fight. "This whole thing has got to stop."

What for him is the end is the beginning for me.

"Listen to this, then try telling me I don't love you. I'll give you a present. That head has to leave my life. I should be out in a few days. If you want, you can come to us for New Year's Eve. As soon as I'm feeling better, Jo will calm down. That's how women are; without a man in the house, they go mad."

He grins and then grimaces and holds his nether regions, whimpering in pain.

"That sounds like an excellent idea. I'll bring Kiko, too, if that's okay?"

"Of course, of course... Oh, shit, this hurts!"

He rings the bell to summon the nurse.

"The Azevedos are very welcoming, you'll see."

After a few seconds, a nurse comes running into the room. She is young, too young to be human. I'm sure she's gone through the upload process. Nexhumans don't have to wait until they are adults before being productive, they start in their eternal youth where they left off, merely interrupted by old age.

When she lifts Charlie's shirt to check on him, he doesn't even notice the difference.

For the last three hundred metres, since we exited Durenico Station, my ears have been hurting. I turn down the sound in my visor, which has been amplifying the music of casual vibrations, syrupy rhythms, and joyous yelling. It's worse than a flatulent discharge, and a measure of the fact that even sound is coming to resemble kipple.

We are heading to the third of fifteen identical buildings. They say it is senseless to set up green spaces or squares in the most deprived areas because no one would appreciate them anyway, and over the last few decades, this has been the urban planning policy behind the construction of the outskirts of the megalopolis.

Number 1448 Doloth Street is covered with an enormous Halloween decoration. The people who live here must have put it up in October and it's been there ever since. Tongues of fake fire flutter from the windows and two eyes have been painted between the eighth and ninth floors. The windows of the first two floors have been blacked out to look like rotten teeth.

Inside the jaws of this terrifying pumpkin head, the ceiling copiously adorned with colourful streamers and paper chains, I feel that perhaps my luck is changing. Perhaps, for once, fate is on my side. Is it possible that my demon has come back to hover over my head? I can't see or hear it, but I can feel it.

I can't explain this series of favourable coincidences in any other way. Had Charlie not contracted a mutated form of gonorrhoea, he wouldn't have been taken to hospital. If I hadn't gotten hold of him then and there, dazed and sedated, he would never have agreed to the exchange. I wouldn't now be at this Azevedo family gathering with the opportunity of getting my Alba back.

For the occasion, Kiko has straightened her hair with a purple-red colour and has squeezed herself into a tight yellow dress, elegant in its own way, with a green sash around her waist and shoes that have been newly polished and re-soled. I can imagine the busy hands of the Dragon Ladies constructing her outfit.

I tend to pass unnoticed in anonymous clothes like their previous owners probably did before me. A worn overcoat, lined with chips and sensors, waterproof trousers, and a pair of boots whose tips illuminate my path. It's almost as if the clothes are capable of finding the kind of people who, recycle after recycle, are most suitable for them.

The Azevedos are no strangers to recycling. Their clan deals in the business of death. For seven generations, they have been burying and disposing of the dead. Only the poor have no choice but to end up in the ground to become worm-food. Worms may recycle their flesh, but it is humans who fight over their objects.

The movement of K is minimal. The Azevedo fortune comes more than anything from extortion and theft; leveraging the sadness of grieving relations and taking everything they find in the pockets of the departed.

They have taken over a housing estate at the point where Rotterquay Road, at the end of a big curve, becomes Grange Bridge and crosses the Selam.

It is a residential complex designed for evacuees, a building born and raised on Durenico's garbage. It was like an abandoned beehive until the Azevedo clan repopulated the place and made it liveable. In fact, as is customary with them, they have transformed it into a thriving and noisy entity.

The air smells of burned popcorn, onions and peppers. I recognise the perfume of roast chicken, sweet fritters, and oily pies. With no breeze on the stairs, every smell ends up ingrained in the walls. It is like standing with your nose stuck in a busy cook's armpit.

On every floor, we pass people carrying plates of food, meat threaded onto skewers, jugs overflowing with stews, aluminium trays spread with fruit—not the freshest, but not rotten either.

They are all heading up the stairs. We slip in behind three domes of yellow jelly and a tray covered with banana leaves, raisins, hazelnuts, peanuts and a mosaic of praline.

Hardly knowing even my own neighbours, the reserved Dragon Ladies, I am left perplexed by the combined efficiency of the Azevedos. Sinister sounds from the sewerage pipes accompany us on the way upstairs to the tenth floor of the building.

"You must be Peter. And you are Kiko, right?"

A young girl with dummies in her hair and a stick of candy hanging from her lips leads us to the rooftop terrace. She is wearing a visor like mine and identified us right away.

"Yes, and who are you?"

Kiko chirps and leans forward to see her better with her receptor earrings. I can see her now, dissecting and discussing the party with her friends later. New Year's Eve: I can imagine what they will say and force myself not to think about it.

"I'm Nadia. Tommy and Lisa are my cousins because my mum, Patty, is Jo's younger sister."

We pass a man ambling around the corridors on his own business. He lifts a bottle of alcohol by way of a greeting, then drinks our health. Already drunk at nine in the evening; for him, the New Year has already arrived.

The dogs—also decked out in party clothes, hats, and gift bows—whine, unaware of the reason for all this confusion.

"Come with me, the party's this way."

Under a large veranda, lit and warmed by flaming oil drums, Charlie is sitting at the head of the table, or rather in the centre of a horseshoe, the branches of the family hierarchy descending from him along both arms.

Next to him sits the elderly Ramiro, Jo's father and the Azevedo patriarch, who straightens his old-fashioned pinstripe suit as he whispers something to his wife, Sunny. Having married their daughter, Charlie sits on Ramiro's right. The respect he has earned in the field has taken him high up the family pyramid in less than ten years of marriage.

All around, a chattering crowd is sitting squashed up against the walls. Hordes of kids crawl and run around, enjoying themselves around the table.

In the midst of all the chattering, the coarse laughter of the young, the grumbling of the old, the toasts and the inevitable good luck rituals, Charlie stands and with solemn gestures quietens the mob.

Silence falls as he lifts two shining blades over his head. He sharpens them with four or five quick strokes. Two fat cooks carry a whole roast pig into the dining room and lay it in front of Charlie. He pulls it towards him and asks everyone to come together for a moment.

From the backside of the caramelised pig, all bows and greetings rosettes, he pulls the two-metre-long spit, sniffing the inebriating fragrance of pinkish barbecued meat.

He slices into the animal and makes Jo, sitting opposite him, serve the salad.

As the only representatives of the Payne family, besides Charlie, our place is at the very end of the table, on the left-hand corner. The starters don't reach us until everyone else has begun their second course. It might matter to Kiko and those beings made hungry by biology, but it doesn't to me. I didn't come here to enjoy the delicacies the Azevedos had to offer.

I stare at Charlie, studying him in the context of his new family.

I wonder where he has hidden Alba. It's hard to imagine she is in this building, considering all the people who wander around in it.

He sees me and makes a gesture of greeting with his hand. Everyone knows that there is little time to dedicate to individual relatives at these events, and I'm not at all sorry about it.

Faced with such an abundance of food, I'm only going to be able to make a show of eating a couple of squids so as not to offend anyone.

On the contrary, Kiko seems strangely hungry. She washes down every dish with a gulp of brownish wine poured from tall, vintage jugs by girls conscripted to service from an early age.

At one point, I notice she has started chatting with Milandro, who is kind of Jo's uncle. He is part of Sunny's family (Jo's mother's real name is Asuncion, but everyone calls her Sunny) and it looks like he and Kiko have found something in common. There are whole areas of Kiko's character I still know nothing about, and many I am sure I will never even get an inkling of.

For the first time in my life, in the middle of all of these strangers who are technically my family, I start worrying about who will succeed me. Not that Kiko has any intention of becoming a mother, or even of adopting—the hassle of nursing and weaning is best avoided, in her opinion. Though the maternal instinct survived somewhat in her mother, even she eliminated all male presences from the procreation and raising of her daughter. I should imagine that the desire has completely withered in Kiko.

I feel in need of a cigarette. These thoughts are like the meandering coils of smoke: they swirl for a bit and then vanish without a trace.

Who will I leave my bag of things to when I die?

I take a plate out onto the veranda. I pick at it and inhale the smoke of my sticky tobacco. From here, I can enjoy the party and its louder protagonists without being in the thick of it.

Everyone in the Azevedo clan flaunts their vices and vanities: showy watches with no tags, prised from the wrists of the dead; do-it-yourself perfumes cobbled together from the dregs of many salvaged bottles; shoes so new and shiny they could only have been bought for the recently deceased and stolen off their corpses; an abundance of luminous chippery, web pendants, and proximity rings.

I turn off my visor to concentrate on Charlie, on what he might be hiding behind his haughty air. I'm waiting for the right moment to bring up the exchange.

When Kiko's head tilts back just enough for me to realise she is drunk, I throw away the cigarette butt and move towards my brother.

"Stealing from a UCU is hard. You have to remember that it only stays in one place for a hundred and twenty seconds. Just long enough to open its jaws swallow kipple. Then it starts moving again at thirty clicks."

"Did you do it?" a small boy holding a sweet fritter with sugar coating his chin questions my brother.

"Of course. When I was young—I must have been more or less your age—I was as agile as a cat and as strong as an ox."

Fritter lowers his gaze guiltily. He wipes his chin clean and puts the uneaten portion on a chair, keeping a watchful eye on it to make sure no one steals it. The small Azevedos are hanging on every word Charlie says, a sea of snotty, up-turned noses, in awe of his courage.

"Lots of kids end up dead trying to steal from UCUs. It's a matter of seconds—fractions of a second—as the blades slice and chop and snap."

He pronounces the verbs clearly and dramatically, imbuing them with terror.

"And when they snap shut, the hatches bang down and break up everything. Just the stench is enough to make you feel ill and the sound is enough to freeze the blood in your veins. I remember seeing pistons this big inside it."

Charlie mimes the scene for them and obviously exaggerates.

"I saw metal walls impossible to drill through. I felt those jagged blades right here on my own skin."

He demonstrates with sharp pats on his arms and shoulders.

"There's only one way out of a UCU: the same way you get in. It takes timing and cunning and speed: you have to be faster than the beast's mechanisms."

I join the gang but stay in the shadows. Fritter is whining because he was distracted for a minute and someone took his dessert.

"The hunger and greed of a UCU are only equalled by its efficiency. The more it gobbles up, the longer the megalopolis resists the kipple. And we hate kipple, right?"

"Yeeesss!" the kids answer in chorus and raise their hands

in the air. Charlie, the inveterate bragger, bathes in the glory of their adulation.

"Kipple is our enemy. Kipple steals our food, our clothes, and our future. Remember, though, the UCUs are not bad, they belong to Reverse, too."

"Yeeesss, the UCUs belong to Reverse."

"Kipple is our evil enemy and the UCUs are our only saviours from death and extinction. The UCUs recycle, the UCUs help us reconsume, so remember, it is forbidden to steal from a UCU."

I feel like I'm taking part in a training course for new recruits.

Then Charlie turns and we find ourselves face to face. I am not quick enough to say anything before he throws out a denigrating barb.

"Look here, boys. Let me introduce you to someone who wasn't good enough."

He points first at my Tantalium and then at the Podox.

"You see? This is what happens if you are not quick enough."

Astonished eyes, pitying and deprecating looks. They have already made their judgements, have classed me as a loser, someone not to emulate, someone not to be relied on. It's like there is a huge, flashing sign above my head saying:

defectivedefectivedefective

"You know that's not how it was."

"Wasn't it? What was it like, then? Did you just happen to grow those prosthetic limbs?"

Someone laughs but I don't care. I wish I thought it was funny, too.

The kids are horrified and I can see the residual traces of my humanity vanish from their eyes.

"Listen, Charlie, have you got a moment for that thing?"

"Let me introduce my brother, Peter. He ran the risk and it went wrong. Remember him next time you see a UCU."

The Azevedo cubs blink their eyes in silence. I wonder if they will ever feel brave enough to doing anything after this speech. I wonder if they will dare live their lives without worrying about being compared to others. This is the best example Charlie can come up with: you're either like him or different from him.

Kiko is no longer at the end of the table, nor is Milandro. I pull Charlie aside by his shirt and he throws me a dark look.

"I'm talking to my family. Be patient. These are our youngest elements."

I let him go and turn to look for traces of Kiko, her avatar, any signal of her presence in the midst of all this hubbub. What might look like jealousy is actually fear of being spotted confronting my brother? It is the irritation of having to explain this whole scenario to her.

Charlie is taking his time with each of the kids: he caresses, hugs, and pats each of them in turn. Eventually, I grow tired of this pantomime, so I plant myself in front of him and wave the crystal and the gift box under his nose.

If Juicy Jo was furious about the gonorrhoea, how would she react to seeing her husband screwing the pelvis of a nexhuman?

He hurriedly takes his leave of the circle of kids and motions for me to follow him.

"Fucking hell, Peter. Are you mad? You really thought we were going to do it here? On New Year's Eve? In front of everyone?"

Boiling anger turns my flesh to liquid steel. He has taken the piss yet again. He always has done it and always will.

"But... You said..."

Every word that comes out of Charlie's mouth is a lie. Any proposal he makes is a trick full of insidious toxins.

My fuse is so short, I could easily explode or shatter at any moment.

"I said, I said... I'm better now and we can meet up soon, all right? No funny business, though, I'm warning you, Peter. If Jo gets wind of anything, then nothing doing. The pieces will be gone... do you follow me?"

I am following attentively; he's the one who doesn't care.

"Now, put that away and enjoy the party. It's nearly time!"

He says nothing more and leaves me alone. I stand there, motionless, stewing in my own impotence. I stuff the box of shoes I wanted to give him back in my bag. A wave of nausea overwhelms me. A barrage of cramps in my skull almost make me cry.

I would choose to die if that would make me different. I know it won't happen. I should have exposed him; I should have disgraced him in public, but it would only have been another disaster like the night Cleo died.

My thoughts go to the Moore Temple: maybe I should have accepted the nexhumans' help. How much longer will I have to wait? The love inside me, reawakened by Alba's legs, can't be muted.

My stomach roils and the squid I just ate come back up. The chewed bits spurt out of my mouth. Despite my attempts to stop the flow with my hands, it gushes through my fingers and spatters over the floor tiles.

This time, the stench in the air is mine.

I don't even know any more if what I feel is true love.

Is this love?

How can fifteen years of torment be called love? What if love exists in a variety of flavours and essences? What if my type of love is valid because it hurts? Could that possibly be it?

Perhaps love is a disease, an infection that we call affection. It's just a different kind of illness, mysterious and undecipherable. It is impossible to stop something you can't understand.

All these ravings leave me bent over on a chair, dazed.

Lifting my eyes, I see thunderclouds hanging over the megalopolis. Meteorological explosions rip through the night.

The kids are getting ready, mounting ramps to racks of fireworks, lined up like soldiers at attention. On the other side, beyond the nearest loop of the Selam, something denser than the night is moving towards us. It is rising majestically and is higher even than us. It is everywhere, oily and smelly. All around us, a low mass of cloud is spreading, thin and lumpy. As soon as it comes into contact with the pools of water, it sparks and bangs like the kids' fireworks.

Charlie is shining the barrel of a gun; he's going to use it to shoot the New Year as it arrives. I swear, if he were to die now, if he were to get caught by 'friendly fireworks' or a rogue splinter of something, I would get drunk enough to embarrass his lovely new family. That wouldn't be my way of mourning; oh, it would be a real fucking party in his honour. A liberation with bells on.

It is only one minute to midnight. An icon flashes in my visor. Reception level five out of five. Thirty metres away, I can just make out Kiko letting uncle Milandro fondle her arse. The Azevedo is sticking his furry tongue into Kiko's ear.

The truth is never hidden. It is just difficult to accept, so we pretend not to see it.

Dodging between the tables, little Nadia comes to find me, clutching an embroidered handkerchief.

"I don't like fish either. With all the grease my aunt puts on it... It won't stay down or come up, it ends up hanging around all day."

She makes me smile. My face might be haggard, but I am still me. It's quite amazing, really. I'm embarrassed to open my mouth and laughter almost overwhelms me. I wipe my mouth with the handkerchief and give it back to Nadia.

"Thanks. Do you like the fireworks?"

I just have to discover who I have always been without knowing it. I just have to reach the nucleus of myself. Then I can die.

"No. Those things scare me."

We look up, shielding our eyes with our hands.

"Me too."

The children, urged on by their mothers, massacre Oh Happy Day and play saucepan lids like drums with plastic and wooden spoons. The adults sing in the New Year, waving their forks in the air as though they want to stab the sky and pull it down bleeding.

Some of the bigger lads lurk around the edges of the party, getting high. They're sipping Tsai Chin, a dense chocolate-like infusion made with spices, honey, and a hallucinogenic mushroom that proliferates in kipple.

Just before the stroke of midnight, everyone holds up their palmtops, greetings flexopaper, their visors emitting a subdued light. Charlie loads three shots.

Five.

The sky lights up with thousands of sparkling night time acts of pollution.

Four.

Flaming darts sear the vault in a chaos of scars and roaring bruises.

Three.

My contribution to the festivities goes into the spittoon on the floor in the shape of a bilious filament. I stand and help Nadia up onto a stool.

Charlie points the gun at the sky.

"Happy New Year, Nadia."

I start to move away.

"Are you going already?" She has guessed my intentions.

Two.

"This year has ended badly."

"I'll come down with you if you like."

One.

Charlie shoots away happily. I wonder where those bullets will fall after carrying his merriment up so high.

I take Nadia by the hand. She jumps down and I let her lead me through the tables and down the stairs to the main entrance.

I say goodbye to the New Year's show: laughing masked half-wits, dancing shadows kissing each one another, others entwined in embraces.

Kiko has found in an hour what I have been seeking for fifteen years. It's not the same thing, and I hope she is not just flirting to get back at me in some way. What would be the point of that?

"Here, this will help your stomach. I use it to help my digestion."

Nadia pulls a can from the pocket of her coat and holds it out to me.

I thank her and give her a hug. I take a sip of the lemonade, hoping it will ease my walk home.

"Could you give this box to Charlie for me please?"

She nods and turns back into the jaws of the building.

Snow is falling and gradually covers my footprints as if to conceal that I had ever come here.

CHAPTER 23

UCU

Charlie decided that our meeting should take place on Kathal Hill, familiar ground for us both, though the grotesque pyramid has grown taller, halfway between a tumulus out of a science fiction story and a cathedral devoted to waste.

The time he has decided on is the worst: dawn.

Sometimes, to move on, you have to shake off your fears and take a leap of faith.

But why here? Why this time in the morning?

I'm cold but I put up with Charlie's choice without argument.

With me, bleary-eyed from the early wake-up call, are Ion, Rasha, and the lads from the dump: Duggan, Norbert, and Pongo. Smiling Baasim has also come along; he wants to lend me his support on behalf of the trenches.

I don't know why Charlie comes alone. Maybe he doesn't need anybody else's help. Judging by the weight of the bag he is carrying, he has brought my reward.

It is as though all these years of disputes and arguments will finally reach a conclusion through this exchange, a transaction which could leave us both satisfied and thereby close a circle.

"Are you ready, little brother?"

As soon as I take a step forward, I hear that sound, the strident whine that precedes the arrival of a UCU. I have always avoided being in the dump when they pass through. They bring back terrible memories. I curse Charlie for making me think about it. But perhaps his choice of time and place weren't a coincidence?

"Open the bag. I want to see."

"What's the hurry, Peter? Calm down. How do I know you're not the one trying to pass me a dud? Have you made a copy of the crystal?"

"You're going to have to trust me for once. No copies. Cleo's fingerprints are still on the crystal."

"That's fine, then." He's here, so at least a part of him wants to close the deal.

I take a step forward and Charlie stops me by raising his hand and hiding the bag behind him.

"Wait... This is how kids do stuff. You and me aren't kids any more, right? This is our chance to see which of us is right."

"Right about what?"

From a corner of the clear area we are standing in, I see soot spurting out of the top of a UCU, and I suddenly realise just how far Charlie is willing to go to humiliate me. I feel so stupid; I didn't believe he could be so evil.

I am stupid because I didn't believe him to be capable of getting so much pleasure from seeing other people dragged through the dirt. At this point, I am no longer prepared to let him think of me as the kid whose life he ruined.

It should have been obvious he would want payback for that blow to the neck. It should have been obvious that he would do everything he could to keep me from Alba.

I should have realised Charlie would never change.

It's a showdown and Charlie just can't wait to put the boot in, even though there really is no longer any need for him to do so.

My hand shakes a little, almost as if to warn me that, even in the very moment that I manage to fool myself that the exchange will take place smoothly, an invisible, vengeful force is setting itself against me.

Twenty-two years ago. Same time. Same place.

Charlie and I were here, bent double for two whole hours, hunting for value. We saw a UCU, the first ever sent to sift through the rubbish in our neighbourhood. It was a surprise move on the part of the megalopolis—or Reverse, to be more accurate—trying to curtail our foraging.

We looked at each other incredulously, not understanding its mission, and hid ourselves in the vanishing shadows, ready to run.

Now, the shadows lengthening over us are almost the same, except I'm no longer a boy of eight.

"What are you going to do? Are you up for it or are you going to back out? Aren't you a man yet? Or are you a big doll made of bits and pieces, first stumps and now prosthetics? You still live surrounded by the same old wrecks. You still collect the same old rubbish. There is no hope for the likes of you... even kipple proliferates, but not you, you haven't even managed to reproduce. At least garbage multiplies, its mass grows, but you... shit, Peter, you haven't even done that. No children; you're going to get old and die, that's all. Even if you manage—and I don't see how you expect to do it—to reanimate this Alba, she'll stay young and one day will see you for what you are; she'll realise that you're the real wreck. When that day comes, she will dump you for someone else."

"And just who are you to judge me, Charlie? Do you really think you know what love is? You... you of all people... you have nothing to teach me. Especially where love is concerned. And my prosthetics? We both know what really happened. You can show off in front of the Azevedos, but you can't twist the truth. I know."

The UCUs coming round the corner are agile creatures with infallible olfactory sensors and a discouraging concentration of power mounted in a bulletproof shell. They can destroy everything in their path and transform it, atom by atom, into anonymous molecular matter. Back at the Reverse base, an intelligent polymer 3D printer turns this matter back into reconsumerism goods.

I remember Charlie pushing me towards that first UCU. He pointed out I was skinnier than him, managed to convince me that I wouldn't have any difficulty getting into the opening, into the inner chamber where all kinds of value had been collected. He said he would come in after me and we would hunt in there together.

I was young. I knew nothing about Charlie then. These are the things he loves: atrocities exposed for the world to see, torment, public exhibition. Thieving wasn't enough anymore, and neither was all the screwing. Charlie is part of the human race, heart and soul, the most pestiferous species in nature. He gets wound up over anything; it turns nasty over nothing.

"Are you ready, then?"

No one else here has realised the bloodshed that is about to begin. Because no one else knows what happened here twenty-two years ago.

"Believe it or not, I am. Are you sure you remember how to get into one of these things?"

His silence alarms me. The suspicion that he is trying to lure me into a trap is confirmed by his arrogance.

He rests the bag on the ground and rubs his hands together.

"I won't disappoint you, Skinnyribs."

Someone behind me mutters something. They might be sniggering.

"Stop trying to wind me up. Let's get on with it."

"Oh, you're a hard man, are you? Good. When the UCUs reach us, you throw the crystal into the first, and I'll throw the bag into the second. The first one to retrieve his prize wins."

"Peter," says Ion. "Don't do it. It's a trick. Getting a crystal out of a UCU is not the same as dragging out that bag."

He's right. But my prize is worth so much more than his. I saw Alba's death; I was there at Cleo's death. Despite knowing that they are dead, I have never stopped believing that I can hear them, reach them.

I've been screwed with enough. I have no intention of letting Charlie have it easy.

"I have to try, Ion. It's dangerous, but at this point, my demon demands it."

I stretch and ready my prosthetics. If I can't step up to this challenge, if I can't stand up to Charlie this time, well, then I don't deserve anything more than being chewed up and reduced to kipple.

He looks like he has nothing to lose, so sure that he can beat the UCU, so confident that Jo will forgive him and that the Azevedos will make him their next leader. I have everything to gain. I have only loved once in my whole life. That love has never vanished. Surely that counts for something.

"All right, Peter. I understand. We are here for you if you need help."

I reassure the mad, wise old man by resting my hand on his shoulder, and then another memory surfaces to haunt me.

Swarms of midges attracted by the halogen lamps in the dark formed dense clouds around the headlights of that old UCU. The badly lit surface of the field of kipple vibrated with shuddering shadows, the noise a terrifying mixture of chewing and ripping. We should have run.

Soft rubber fangs hung from the UCU's mouth, not the sharp blades they now have. Getting in was easy. The problem was staying in there and getting out again in one piece.

Charlie had wanted to get in there so badly. It was a mobile treasure chest in his mind, just waiting to be ambushed and pillaged.

Once I was in, my heart was beating so fiercely, it felt like it would burst out of my chest. A sickening stench made my oesophagus clench. The sharp objects, jagged shards of glass and metal, cut into my clothes, sliced my skin and scraped my face. I didn't care; I was a warrior doing what warriors do.

Then Charlie followed me in, brandishing an axle shaft, which he wedged between the base of the rubbish-ruminant's mouth and its palate. For a few seconds, we managed to make it spit out value.

Snow glasses.

A pair of military binoculars.

A statue of the goddess Kali.

A whole water dispenser.

I scrabbled around like a maniac and Charlie gave his expert tradesman's opinion on everything I found. I dug around, my hands deep in the rubbish and he flung out the good or passable things I found.

Antique picture frames.

Rusted but still functional toys.

Wedding clothes.

Then, after two huge hiccups, the UCU bent the axle shaft. The crack of the third hiccup snapped it like a toothpick. Charlie leaped out like a shot. As soon as he turned to help me climb out, he saw a gleam in the middle of the junk. He caught my attention and pointed it out to me.

Fate has frequently presented me with unthinkable absurdities. The closer I move towards the truth, the more complicated things get.

I hurl the crystal into the maw of the UCU. The machine locks onto it and draws it in greedily. Charlie does the same with the second UCU. The jaws open wide and gobble up the bag containing Alba's remains. The purity of the nexhuman is violated yet again, but her splendour only shines on in my crazy folly.

Charlie starts running, yelling, 'It's time to move! Run!'

We both spring forward: two idiots fighting a senseless duel, facing each other for a pipe-dream prize. As we advance, our eyes meet and there is no hatred in the exchange this time.

We both insist on the rectitude of our respective illusions. Mine is love, Charlie's is power. What is the point of all this?

Five metres from our goal, the warning sirens sound. A brief whistle is followed by a longer one. We ignore both of them. The eye on the UCU turret picks up the invasion of its perimeter.

The UCU-9 is designed to defend its kipple. That's not all, though. Knowing how many divers risk and lose their lives every day trying to grab some value, they can call on reinforcements.

Just like twenty-two years ago, I launch myself. This time the Podox gives me the benefit of its enormous power and I dive between the descending blades, protecting myself with the Tantalium. Out of the corner of my eye, I see Charlie slow down. A metre from his UCU, he stops dead.

My brother, the bastard.

My brother, the swindler.

I lose it and I am caught in its teeth. The impact of the blades is violent. I manage to get the Podox and the Tantalium between myself and the blades. The pressure is cushioned by my artificial limbs. The jaws snap shut on emptiness and I slide in unharmed, now just the same as then.

Ion was both right and wrong. Charlie never had any intention of grabbing the crystal. His guilt will come to an end in the stomach of the UCU, anyway. From the beginning, the only one risking anything was me.

The bag is about to be swallowed in a stream of rubbish. I jump on a shelf tilted at a forty-five-degree angle and grab it by the handles just in time.

Back then, Charlie wanted me to get him a ring. Something to make him look good with his new flame, Juicy Jo. To give him what he wanted, I left a foot behind in the kipple. My shoelace got caught on the carbonised shell of a car, and soon I felt my knee joint pop, giving no resistance at all. Then the muscle and cartilage holding it all together went. I scrabbled for a handhold with my other hand, and the a rusty blade of a ceiling fan cut right through my forearm.

That wasn't the end of it. It was just the beginning of the nightmare.

First, my leg was crushed. My arm followed almost immediately afterwards, leaving me with two artificial limbs bolted to my real flesh. I found out later that he hadn't sold the ring at Junkland at all. He'd all but given it away.

As incredible and ridiculous as it may seem, it is all happening again, right now. Far from protecting my face from the heaving corners and jagged edges of the UCU's contents, that same damaged arm is now out of order. The Tantalium creaks; it's not broken, but the power's gone—it won't move.

This UCU is indomitable. Even my prosthetic limbs give me no hope of overcoming its ravenous fury.

I clutch the bag tight to my chest and look out just as the UCU's jaws open up to better chew me. Just like twenty-two years ago, Charlie is standing there watching me. He is bewitched; I must look like I'm done for, like an innocuous fish in some hellish aquarium. When we were kids, we used to scrape together a few Ks selling half-stunned fish to the sushi restaurants in Genshoij. First, we would daze them with bottles of cyanide, then we'd fish them out with a net from the banks of the Arkeren, and rinse off the residue of the poison before running with them to Isou, the head cook of the Karia.

This situation is more or less the same.

Something hard presses against my leg. Then a sudden, violent movement bends it in the wrong direction and a stream of blood joins the corrupt, noxious liquid all around me.

I stay upright, standing on the Podox, even when something hits me in the face. An exhaust pipe and a cabinet leave their prints on my body. My visor's LED is flashing manically: the pain equaliser tells me I've been run through. This news isn't followed by any sense of suffering or shaking, not even the need to react.

No sweat, no tears, no more flushing.

My ears are bleeding. One of my teeth comes out and another two wiggle loosely in my gums.

My vision starts fading. The visor shows quivering patches of data. As I stumble through the UCU, I realise that it wants to swallow me. It doesn't care if I am still, if only temporarily, alive. It knows the fate of organic matter.

Regaining control of my body, I steady myself by grabbing at the controls of a washing machine. Behind Charlie, the outlines of my friends run towards me to help. They throw stones at the UCU's sensory tower. They hurl insults at it. They do their best to distract it.

Is it because I am finished? Is it because I don't understand what they're trying to do?

The UCU judders to a stop and I lose my balance. From the floor, I slip the Podox between its jaws. The other leg is gone. Metal is my only hope. Scraping along the reinforced surface, the blade slides up the prosthetic leg. As soon as it goes beyond the Podox, it encounters my flesh, then the femur. A bubble of blood bursts, spraying everywhere. I press against the kipple and manage to get to my knees. Sobbing and trembling, I am on the verge of falling apart—not just metaphorically.

The scent of defeat smells bad.

I turn around, lift the arm holding the bag and manage to stick my head and shoulders out. If I were as skinny as twenty-two years ago, I would already be out by now. Now my paunch causes me to get stuck and I yell and curse Kiko.

No one dares come closer. Their fear and disgust at my imminent fate make them step back. They don't make a sound, shocked by what is about to happen to me.

I'm so close and yet so far away. The world I'd like to be a part of is always just a step, or a light year, away from where I am.

The fingers of the Tantalium lift two millimetres of blade from my left shoulder but thirty kilos of steel beam fall on my remaining knee. I don't think anymore. I just draw in my breath when the joist rolls to one side and pull myself away from the biting jaws.

Alba is in my remaining hand. Even the Tantalium has been sacrificed to the UCU.

The lads take the bag, six of them protecting it.

Charlie licks his lips and spits out his laconic, twisted judgement.

"Well done. Now I'm not so ashamed to call you brother."

I don't know whether he set the whole thing up for revenge, or to teach me something. In either case, as soon as I taste the happiness of having salvaged Alba's missing pieces, it all fades away.

Charlie yawns and ambles away empty-handed towards Rabaul Street. The last thing I hear is a stentorian voice from above.

"Let us take the bag. And Peter Payne, too."

I hang on for a moment longer before losing consciousness in Ion's arms. Ion, as ugly as an ogre and as welcoming as a demon.

This existence of mine is like a roulette wheel. It's a pity someone else is spinning it. It's a pity the game is so often rigged. The more I play, the more I lose.

The only way to win is to end it all.

PART FOUR
EPILOGUE

"Peter, can you hear me?"

I stretch out a hand and it bumps into something transparent. I can't feel my other hand and everything I do feel is foreign.

"You've been sedated. You can't get up."

It's Ion's husky voice. The rest of the world is out of focus, a haze of confused images.

"Where am I... Is she alive?"

Ion turns as if looking for the answer somewhere else.

"We have her parts. She's... safe."

The demon with long wings that brought me to this point through perseverance, fixation and unwavering madness now seems to me like a succubus, an energyvore capable of giving me equal measures of happiness and pain ever since it took a hold of me.

My stomach gurgles gently.

"Not long, now, and you'll feel better, too." Something about Ion makes me think that he is my personal demon—or its terrestrial representation.

"The nexhumans, did they put her together?"

Once again, he turns in the other direction to find the answer. He pats me on the shoulder, and the pain it causes reassures me.

"They're doing it now. I think they're nearly done."

I try to lift my head, but it connects with something hard and cold—a glass bell floats above me. Then I see my body, all mutilated flesh and metal. My stumps are marked by clotted rivulets of blood, with ragged metal edges alternating between the white and purple of my bruised flesh.

Every fibre of my being strains towards the source of Ion's answers. If I screw up my eyes tightly, I can almost make out elusive figures that meld and take on hazy outlines. They are clear, yet incorporeal, and fluctuate above the bed where Alba rests. From the centre of their wispy mass, they discharge cauterising flashes to various parts of her body, joining and soldering.

It's strange: despite being dismembered and maimed, I feel together, complete.

"Ion, take me closer; I want to see her."

"They said it's the first time they've done this. It's a very interesting exercise for them."

"I don't care. Do you have any idea how long I've been waiting for this?"

My bed is pushed closer to the other, and now I'm only three metres away.

"I'm sorry, Peter... I was just telling you how much they appreciate what you've done."

"I didn't do it for them."

Falling silent, Ion lets me concentrate on Alba: an inanimate woman, a being considered dead, to whose head I gave fifteen years of my life. In the end, finally, the dead lady is going to return my love. I hope.

What if she doesn't love me?

What if, even worse, she only loves me out of gratitude?

What if Alba's complete body, after each of her parts has satisfied the members of the Dead Bones, isn't enough for me? What if what I'm looking for isn't even in the body renewed by the nexhumans?

I'm waiting for a sign that's been missing for too long.

"You know, Ion... while the dream was still unattainable,

while I was still chasing a ghost, I counted the days and every day was a necessary agony. I had a reason to go on and a task to fulfil, and even if I lost my path many times, trusted the wrong people and all the rest... now, now that she is nearly fixed, I'm almost scared of her."

"Shit, Peter... This isn't the time to have doubts! Look at what you've managed to achieve instead of how much you have left to do. You've helped recreate life from death. Anyone else with a pinch of common sense would have given up on such a plan... I'm sorry if that sounds absurd."

He lifts the palms of his hands on the other side of the glass.

"Look up."

He points up to the temple's dome, where an animated inscription shines out.

The serenity prayer
Give us the grace to accept the things that cannot be changed, the courage to change what should be changed, and the wisdom to be able to distinguish one from the other.

—Reinhold Neibuhr

In the darkness of the Moore Temple, a place I have fantasised about for years, I finally give in to tears.

When I was a kid, I cried nearly every day, often in silence when there was no one around to notice. When I grew a little older, those tears took longer to deposit behind my eyelids and then, as my anxiety dropped into my stomach, the tears would come out in a spurt as if I had been hit on the head.

These are the tears of a snivelling kid and they disgust me. I wipe them off my face with the back of my hand and stare at the spectacle of a body beginning to quiver with life again.

Alba's fingers begin to move as they used to do while caressing my head. I shiver down my spine.

Beyond the nexhumans, there is a status display:
mind downloading—95%

The Alba who is about to wake up is the Alba of Boreal Skies. The Alba who is twenty-three, while I am now thirty. Who knows if she will remember me? If she will recognise me? That skinny kid, nothing more than skin and bone, who spied on her from the top of Kathal Hill is now a ruin of a man who can hardly lose a few grams without being threatened by some electrical device, the fridge, the crows and all the rest.

When it comes down to it, I detest reality. It would be better if I only existed in a fantasy world. If I had the certainty that this were only a game, I'd take more risk—one life is not enough to discover who we really are. My mind is wandering again, away from the fear that this long-lasting dream will come true at last.

Ion looks on as Alba is brought back to life. It must be every engineer's wish to play at being god. As if though he's reading my mind, he starts telling me how his mission is going.

"I haven't told you yet... Rasha and I have made great progress. I have written a program to teach other people how to build my solar trees. We've made copies and Rasha has distributed them to the other dumps. Anyone with a visor and a network connection has sent it on to everyone they could."

"Mr Stinky would be pleased."

Ion lowers his eyes and represses his anger.

"This is not revenge... My motives haven't changed."

"You have a demon to assuage too."

He scowls at me. His is the only companionship I have managed to accept over the years. I don't want to hurt him or tell him what I know about his time in the madhouse. If he doesn't already know, he will remember in his own time.

"Reverse won't be happy with your little present."

"They'll have to rethink a lot of things."

The claws of my malaise are retracting, chased away by the twitching of Alba's hand as she reanimates.

I have never doubted that a dawn would eventually rise for me.

Her spirit, even when it was dormant, plotted and schemed, calculated and expressed itself through me. I have the proof. As her eyes open, mine light up.

"Peter, can you hear me?"

I open my eyes and don't know where I am, but the voice is familiar.

"Where am I?"

"Where you've always wanted to be."

I am surrounded by bamboo canes. A ceiling fan stirs the warm air and it feels good on my skin. From the window, less than a metre from my feet, the ocean is reflected on the wall. Below it, vases of ferns decorate a room I don't recognise.

Am I dreaming? Am I dead? Am I in the gamesphere?

"We have to hurry up... The excursion to the cave leaves in forty minutes."

"What excursion? What cave?"

Kiko. I am assailed by the doubt that Kiko has won some or other trip and wants to drag me who knows where. The voice though doesn't have that threatening undertone that normally hides behind Kiko's gentle words.

"The Barton Creek cave. We're going in special canoes with night vision lamps. The guides think the Mayans used it for ancient burial rites."

I lift myself up on my elbows and a smile spreads over my face.

Alba.

I can see the uplifted corners of Alba's lips below her elegant cheekbones; I can see my reflection in her bright eyes.

I reach out to her. Goose bumps run across my skin. Her face is the colour of caramel; her flesh is firm. Alba shines with exotic brilliance from every angle.

"How long have we been here?"

A hairy head peeps in through the window. Alba peels a banana and throws it to the hand hanging over the windowsill.

"Nearly three months."

The monkey screeches its thanks and disappears.

"Are you sure? I can't remember anything."

"That's normal; it happens sometimes."

"What do you mean? What happens?"

I sit up on the bed as she pulls on a fluorescent thong. My eyes brim over with joy. Her breasts inflame my muscles. I moisten my lips and grab a glass from the bedside table, drinking, pretending to be thirsty.

"Sometimes data goes missing. Weeks can go missing, months, even years sometimes... but it doesn't matter."

"Has it ever happened to you?"

"Of course, it happens to everyone. Once I lost fifteen years, but then I found you again, in the end."

She winks at me and, as if on queue, a bulge forms under the sheets.

"There's nothing to worry about then..."

"No, the only thing we have to worry about is the trip to Barton Creek. You've been planning it for months. It's what we're here for."

I move to get up, but Alba moves first, throwing herself on the bed.

She tickles me. She teases and tantalises me, pressing her breasts against my face.

"Oh, wait, now I remember. The trip starts in forty minutes—but tomorrow!"

I smile and grab her by the leg, pulling her to me. She kicks, resisting even when I lick her neck. Then we kiss.

Maybe I'm lying, maybe I'm not, but she falls for it, or

perhaps she is playing along. She becomes docile, flutters her eyelashes at me and goes quiet.

We wind our fingers together. We mingle our thoughts. Then we melt into each other.

I am surprised at how love has made real what was no more than an illusion when I first saw Alba, a desire beyond all imagination.

Everything that was compressed and segregated inside her—pain, regrets, nostalgia, and hopes—liquefies and runs down her face in a watery solution. I kiss it off her cheeks.

I adore seeing her so close.

Storm clouds hang over the dilapidated vestiges of Mundur Cemetery. Swollen growths full of toxic agents waver, ready to discharge their venomous loads over the megalopolis.

Two hooded figures walk up to a doorway and ask to be allowed inside.

The decrepit face of Mr Tiris gives the hint of a smile. His parrots are all at home in the aviary.

"Welcome. How can I help you?"

The taller of the pair opens his raincoat and pulls out a raggedy bunch of flowers: a bouquet of mistletoe, honeysuckle, gladioli, and a few red chrysanthemums.

"We're here to visit someone."

"Do you know where to go?"

"Yes, we've been before."

Touching his hand to his hat brim Mr Tiris takes his leave as the two figures head towards the lift. The skinnier of the two seems to be in a hurry.

"We have to be quick and get back within two hours. The other dumps have confirmed the schedule."

"We won't be late... it's partly thanks to him that we've got this far. Without his help, I wouldn't even know who I am."

"I know, I just wanted to remind you about the appointment. How many more copies do we need to make?"

"As many as we can. There is only one megalopolis, but this kipple is everywhere."

When they get to the twenty-fifth floor, the two figures pick up speed until they reach halfway down the corridor. They place the bunch of flowers in the vase next to a display showing an image of Alba Vicente and Peter Payne, side by side. The dates of their deaths are recorded as 9th August 2040 and 22nd January 2056. There is a red light beside both icons.

"They aren't available. Pity. I would have liked to have been able to tell Peter the good news."

"He'll find out about it sooner or later, Ion. It might not be a revolution, but it's a start."

"You're right. When one moon fades, another grows. Every end contains the seeds of a new beginning."

"Peter, can you hear me?"

"Yes, it's incredible!"

My body is scanned at the entrance to the ship. No alarms go off; this is good. It is forbidden to bring flesh on board.

"It's not exactly the journey I had in mind. This is beyond…"

I hesitate briefly before stepping on to the gangplank leading into the Govinda. Alba gives me a hand until we are on board.

Knowing her—or rather, getting to know her again after so many years—has been my salvation and relief. Salvation, because the Ks from her nexhuman insurance policy paid for her downloading and my uploading; relief, because the anxiety and worries of my entire life have proved to be unfounded.

Now that I know everything about her, I'm a little embarrassed.

When I was younger than her, Alba had a feeling of pure affection for me, a sort of non-sexual empathy, given my age at the time. A sincere feeling, long buried beneath fifteen years of detachment, which has now had the opportunity to take root and grow.

I've not said anything for fear of looking like an idiot, but I'm sure Alba's brain, even when she was catatonic and without a body, was functional.

When the right moment comes, I will get to the bottom of that too.

Perhaps I was the last human being to be nice to her. Perhaps I am the only man who ever cared about her. The fact remains that the memory of me stayed with her, in a heart that Alba, in nexhuman terms, no longer possessed. Sometimes you don't need a heart.

Now that she is younger than me, things haven't changed. Perhaps they never will.

"Mr and Mrs Payne, welcome to the Govinda. I am first officer Pat Mooregate, and on behalf of the whole crew, I would like to wish you a pleasant journey."

This is the first time I've left the megalopolis and I'm heading towards the stars. At last, I can enjoy an observation point higher than Kathal Hill.

Alba holds my hand tight and the touch of her hand electrifies me. Her other hand slides over my flat abdomen and comes to rest on my hip. She is trembling too.

She kisses me on the lips, her mouth resting against mine longer than the hostess expects.

At twenty-three, there are few things you can do without embarrassment. I know her real age and I'm not shocked like the members of the crew.

On the main deck, we program our suitcases to wait for fifteen minutes. I turn on the security agent out of habit when Alba urges me to follow her.

"Guess where I'm taking you?"

She smiles mischievously and leads the way, the ship's blueprint already in her head.

"I know; you have to go to the bathroom."

We slip into the men's room. To Alba, *this* is our bridal suite. I don't know why she likes it so much. Maybe it reminds her of all those years spent in my wardrobe, of the intimacy that was such a risk for both of us. The cheeky look on her face arouses me, convinces me.

It's impossible to suppress desire this strong.

She undoes her shirt. I lift her skirt and undo my trousers.

Alba lets her hair down and her flaming mane tickles my chest. We do everything in silence, under the watchful eyes of the security officer, who is no doubt getting off spying on us through the CCTV security system.

She lowers her panties and turns around so we can both look at ourselves in the mirror. Her pupils dilate and she parts her legs.

I am nothing but a photonic impulse with a sexual charge.

"Alba, what does being semi-immortal mean?"

"It means men forget about you, and you about them. But I didn't manage it."

She scratches her fingers across my abdomen and I like it.

Mutual penetration used to be a fantasy, a mirage dispelled by obstacle after obstacle. Now that the oscillating flux binds us and connects us in a bidirectional way, I can't stop smiling. A smile that is gormless, pleased, and quintessentially male.

I have unlimited access to the only person who has always been beyond my reach, the being who was dearer to me than any other. The being I shared the oxygen in my room with for so many years.

My transformation was not a spontaneous event like the collapse of a star. It was a direct consequence of living with Alba.

What we are experiencing is a kind of empathetic saturation, a sensorial transcendence.

A rush of power shakes our bodies. The floor starts to tremble and the Govinda begins the vertical ascent.

We hold each other tight.

From the porthole, we can see the ragged edge of the sun plunging into the kipple-covered suburbs of Cali Nova and Lazar. The immense mound that is Kathal Hill is just a thicker scab than the others, a ziggurat born of human refuse and raised by consumerism.

Kiko and Eiko are probably lost in contemplation of the sacred wikimirror, the crows circling the flat in search of their missing target.

I'm a little sad at leaving Ion and Rasha behind. They are the only people I will miss.

In the sky, pinpoints of light spread out like an unending curtain. This universe is beyond all comprehension. Its intentions remain unknown, its dynamics inscrutable.

Something attracts my attention. It is not Alba, who is still assisting our connection with murmurs and whispers. At dusk, from various points in the ravines of the megalopolis, small neon shapes unfurl. Looking more closely through the shadows, I can make out burning pinpricks lighting up along the long stems, dozens and dozens of points of light which burn and give light back to the night. Inside me, the build-up reaches its peak.

The bumpy progress fills me with extraordinary warmth. My lips find Alba's neck and the sweet vibrations pass from her to me.

Even now, in this new form, hope exceeds reason. Then the overload dissipates; the flow retracts. Our breathing slows and stabilises.

We have no hearts, but we're more than machines.

This afterword is not intended to be a conclusive statement about this remarkable novel, but to serve as a springboard for discussion about the ever-elusive definition of what it means to be human, this time from transhumanist and literary perspectives. Transhumanism is an international philosophical and cultural movement, whose main tenet is the belief in the positive outcomes of enhancement and augmentation of all human faculties: organs, sentiments using reason, science and technology. The improvements go beyond simply alleviating pain or bettering one's eyesight. They involve using prostheses, implants, nanotechnology, exoskeletons, and much more, to augment human abilities beyond their natural limitations (for example, adding gills, making night vision possible, etc.). Transhumanism values reason, progress and optimism through self-determined, self-directed evolution. According to this movement, death is not inevitable: negligible senescence is conceivable and likely, through life extension, cryonics, or mind uploading. If science fiction can be defined as works of literature that are contingent upon some as yet unfulfilled scientific advancement, transhumanist science fiction refers to those works of literature which deal with self-directed evolution; therefore not with cyborgs created by others, but with subjects whose enhancement is directly willed by themselves.

Francesco Verso's Nexhuman can be considered a transhumanist trailblazer in the more and more verdant forest of Italian science fiction. Although the novel does not focus specifically on self-directed evolution, the narration proceeds towards one of the crucial aspects of transhumanism—that of mind uploading. Nexhuman paints a dystopian picture of the future, where the complexities of a consumerist, profit-driven, technology-obsessed, trash-filled world, populated by humans and nexhumans, seemingly obliterate those aspects of humanity which matter most: love, identity, family, friendship, and aspirations, to name just a few. However, these themes and many others find a common thread in the question of the Self: not just the basic 'Who am I?' but other probing queries, such as 'Who is the Other?' 'How do I interact with the Other?' 'Where do I fit in?' or 'What should I do with my life?'

Nexhuman offers a most noteworthy possibility regarding the relationship between the Self and the Other. For millennia, humans have acknowledged the fact that there exists a chasm between the Self and the Other: a binary, exclusionary relationship that separates the two fragments into clearly delineated compartments. It is true that anthropological triangulation, or double-consciousness, offers a tripartite view, but still of the same compartments: self, other and other-self. The novel describes, in stark and nasty detail, the results of the antagonistic stance: quasi-fratricide, possible matricide, 'nexhuman-cide', exclusion (Ion) and separation (humans vs nexhumans; male vs female). Peter Payne attempts to avoid falling into the trap of hate even when he is bent on vendetta. He falls in love with a being who he does not know is a nexhuman, and he keeps loving her even after finding out that she is a copy of a sixty-year old woman's consciousness that has been mind-uploaded. His search for Alba's severed pieces symbolises his quest to find himself—but not at the cost of exclusion of others. And here is the point at which transhumanism's mind-uploading technology shows yet another possibility, clearly illustrated in the novel: to live as Self within the Other(s). The Self can be uploaded into any form (human or not), at any age, and this can be done many times over—just as Alba's example shows. The Self can live within other people's memories: Peter Payne uploads his memories into his mother's hologram program and therefore he will live within those. However, the most inclusive sense of the Self within the Other is Peter's feeling that Alba lives within him. Of course, these serious aspects of the 'payneful' experience receive good doses of irony (specifically: love growing out of a trash-filled environment; trash-forming and recycling of garbage, but also of mind; Peter's willingness to upload his mind, not because of his mutilated, bruised body, but on account of love; etc.). Therefore, the Self and the Other(s) are categories that are not exclusive but are subsumed within each other: the new consciousness of both Peter and Alba are not simply imagined, but embodied, not dreamt but uploaded. There is no antagonism between the Self and the Other(s), nor are there blurred, indistinct outlines. They are enclosed, experienced, practised, familiar and deeply felt. They are not fluid but embraced and readily received.

Frederick Pohl, the American science fiction writer, claimed that 'A good science fiction story should be able to predict not the automobile but the traffic jam.' Nexhuman's traffic jams include the usual problems encountered not only in science fiction—extreme environmental degradation, unscrupulous employers, failure to stop aggressive and violent behaviour—but also those created by new transhumanist technologies, such as self-constructed bodies, mind uploading, which requires stepping into the 'Temple of Moore', misuse of mind-transforming technologies, inability to educate the young, wide gaps between humans and nexhumans, 'become' others—Lombo, etc.) The novel does much more than this, since it redefines the relationships between the Self and the Other(s), offering a new way of being human: that of embracing one Self within the Other(s).

Jana Vizmuller-Zocco
Associate Professor Emerita
Italian Studies, York University
Toronto, Ontario, Canada

*Some of the ideas elaborated on here were first presented at the Graduate Students' Conference entitled "(Un)human relations/ Relazioni (dis)umane", held at the University of Toronto, Toronto, Canada, 6 May 2015.

ACKNOWLEDGMENTS

The word "kipple" was created by Philip K. Dick in *Do Androids Dream of Electric Sheep*. I borrowed that striking term and used in a wider sense, a kind of "kippleization" of the world we live in.

The original novel, *Livido*, was written in Italian with the help and good advice of many friends, readers and editors: Giammarco Raponi, Giuseppe Panella, Francesco Mantovani, Nazareno Barra, Sandro Battisti, Diego Blanda, Paolo Grassi, Emmanuele J. Pilia, Miriam Mastrovito, Pia Barletta, Jana Vizmuller-Zocco, Francesco Lato and Salvatore Proietti. I truly thank you guys because you've helped the novel when there was no novel yet. I also owe a lot to Sally McCorry, who worked side by side with me to translate the book into English. It was a long way and a very hard bet: in 2011, we had no idea of who might be interested in *Livido*, given the tiny percentage of foreign novels being sold to English-speaking markets. But then my agent, Anna Mioni from AC2 Literary Agency, came along, and she opened a path: one morning in November 2013, she called me to say she's managed to sell *Livido* to Australian Publisher Xoum. The editor of Xoum, David M. Henley, made a wonderful work to revise the text and I must thank him and the whole team for their dedication and care. Now this new edition by Apex Books will hopefully spread the Nexhuman concepts to a wider range of readers across the world. Enjoy the ride!

Some of the ideas in the story were inspired:

'Augmented Reality Through Wearable Computing', Thad Starner et alii, The Media Laboratory, MIT, 1997.

'Diamond Trees (Tropostats): A Molecular Manufacturing Based System for Compositional Atmospheric Homeostasis', Robert A. Freitas Jr., IMM Report 43, 2010.

About the Author

Francesco Verso (Bologna, 1973) is one of the most relevant voices of Italian Science Fiction and editor of Future Fiction. Over the last 15 years he has won many SF awards (including 2 Urania Awards and 3 Europe Awards for Best Publisher, Best Author and Best Work of Written Fiction by the European SF Society) and since 10 years he's the editor of the multicultural project Future Fiction. His books include: *Antidoti umani, e-Doll* (Urania Award 2009), *Nexhuman* (Odissea and Italia Award 2013), *Bloodbusters* (Urania Award 2015) and *I camminatori* (made of *The Pulldogs* and *No/Mad/Land*). His novels *Nexhuman* and *Bloodbusters* – translated in English by Sally McCorry – have been published in the US, UK and in China with the translation of Zhang Fan and Shaoyan Hu for the publisher Bofeng Cultures. He's latest novel *I camminatori* has been published in English as *The Roamers* by Flame Tree Press in May 2023. His short stories appeared in magazines like Robot, MAMUT, International Speculative Fiction #5, Chicago Quarterly Review #20, Words Without Borders, Future Affairs Administration and international anthologies such as *Sunspot Jungle* (Rosarium Publishing, USA), *A Dying Earth* (Flame Tree Press, UK) and *The Best of World SF* (Head of Zeus, UK), *What's the Future Like?* (Guangzhou Blue Ocean Press, China). Together with Bill Campbell he has co-edited Future Fiction: *New Dimensions in International Science Fiction* (Rosarium Publishing, 2018). He has also edited a SF anthology called *What's the Future Like?* for Guangzhou Blue Ocean Press that has been distributed to Chinese high schools and universities in 2019. He's a public speaker and panelist to many SF Cons across the world, including World-

Cons, EuroCons, and Chinese SF Conventions. In 2020 he has organized the FutureCon an online SF convention with 67 panelists coming from more than 25 countries.

From 2014 he works as editor of Future Fiction, a multicultural project, scouting and publishing the best SF in translation from 13 languages and more than 35 countries with authors like James P. Kelly, Ian McDonald, Ken Liu, Xia Jia, Liu Cixin, Chen Qiufan, Pat Cadigan, Olivier Paquet, Vandana Singh, Lavie Tidhar Sedia and others.

He may be found online at www.futurefiction.org.

ABOUT THE TRANSLATOR

Sally McCorry was born in London in 1970 and grew up in the fantasy land of reading, devouring science fiction and fantasy from an early age. This love of words meant not learning Italian well when she moved to Italy in 1990 was not an option. She has been translating from Italian to English for quite a while, and jumped at the opportunity to translate science fiction offered by Francesco Verso, also a while ago. She was especially chuffed with this comment from Ian Watson in his review of Francesco Verso's *Bloodbusters*: "BloodBusters is plausible and powerfully written, a high- spirited page-turner thanks to a great translation by Sally McCorry."

Indice

Internal illustrations and cover image
by Federica Pernazza and Isabel Kay
Page layout by Alda Teodorani